THE LAST BEACH TOWN

DEB RICHARDSON-MOORE

The Last Beach Town
Red Adept Publishing, LLC
104 Bugenfield Court
Garner, NC 27529
https://RedAdeptPublishing.com/
Copyright © 2025 by Deb Richardson-Moore. All rights reserved.

---

1. http://StreetlightGraphics.com

To my first beach families—the Beardens, the Hintons, the Queens, the Reids, and the Williamses

To my newest beach clans—the McFaddens and the Daweses

Twenty-eight summers... and counting

Part One

Chapter 1

Monday
Sloane

The trees tell her she is home. Their Spanish-moss-laden limbs guard an ancient cemetery while their roots shove against a crumbling brick fence, forcing it into a precarious lean. These giant oaks and their gray shawls are cliches in this part of the Lowcountry, and with good reason: Their witchy aura of foreboding perfectly captures the old South.

She stares at the dripping trees for so long that her tire slips off the road, jerking the steering wheel from her grasp. But she learned to drive on this pitted lane and can hear her father's angry voice. "Dammit, Sloane, don't yank the wheel. You'll hit that truck head-on. Ease 'er back, girl. Ease 'er back." He spoke of their old Jeep like he did his shrimp boat. Too bad he never regarded her with the same affection.

With his growl in her head, she eases her aged Toyota RAV4 back toward the road, slowing and clutching the wheel. Gravel pings the underside. The vehicle returns to the asphalt with a bounce, jarring her teeth.

She passes the tiny Millicent post office, which is closed, and pictures postmistress Octavia next door, enjoying a midday nap on her four-poster bed. The azaleas are shaggy in front of the blue house, which is also shabbier than Sloane remembers. But Octavia must be over seventy by now, so maybe she's let her gardening slip. Sloane thinks about stopping, but Octavia will be at the service this afternoon. She is—was—her aunt's best friend.

The Toyota rattles for a few more miles along scarred SC 900, passing Bud's Boat Repair—where the turtle ladies are headquartered—Idelle Simpson's Gas 'N' Such, offering fuel along with sodas, Cheetos, and beer, and the AME church, the Methodist church, and the Baptist church. Millicent is nothing if not churched.

The Baptists, in fact, are the ones who have kept Millicent, alone among South Carolina beachfront towns, undeveloped. They owned a swath of beach frontage and used it as a camp. The summer Sloane was nine, she spent a week in one of the camp's rickety, un-air-conditioned cabins, enduring mosquitoes in the bath house and getting splinters on the amphitheater benches where campers gathered for bonfires. The trip was miserable enough that she never went back.

But then, she had no need to. Aunt Millicent owned the beachfront family home with its Casablanca-style fans, sweeping staircase, and grand verandah. The barrier island, the town, and even a road or two are named for her female ancestors. Sloane's school friends assured her that she had it made, that she would inherit the mantle of town queen. The thought was appalling at the time and still is, so much so that she hasn't set foot in her old homeplace for more than a decade.

She jounces into a pothole and inadvertently bites her tongue. The pain is sharp, and she's gripped by an unreasonable fury. She doesn't have time for this drive, for this entire trip.

The phone call that propelled her life into panic mode came as she was rushing from her creative writing seminar to her campus office at Warner College, silently reviewing her end-of-semester to-do list.

Attorney Raeford Carlisle's Lowcountry drawl stopped her abruptly, incongruous in the busy hum of an Atlanta afternoon. "I have some bad news, Millicent Sloane," he said, using the name she despised. "Your aunt died last night."

That's not possible. Not remotely possible. "But you said... you said she had a urinary tract infection. When you called earlier. There's no way she could've died, Raeford." Her voice rose stridently, and students turned to look at her.

"That *is* what we thought. But the infection must have been more severe than we realized, and it caused her heart to give out."

Memories of her aunt clamored to enter Sloane's mind, but she shoved them away. She would think about them later. She had no time for grief.

"We're holding her service Monday afternoon," Raeford continued. "I can have the sale papers ready for you to sign at the same time."

The information was coming at her too fast. Both Sloane and the old family lawyer had long known she would inherit Millicent House, but *not now*. That was to happen years—decades—down the road.

Sloane's to-do list rose before her, demanding, unequivocal. It might as well have been written in stone. "I don't see how... I can't do that."

"You're going to miss her funeral?"

"I... I..." She closed her eyes. "No, of course not." Final grades, a graduation speech, and overdue edits on her second novel flashed before her eyes and set her stomach churning. Every minute until the end of May was already accounted for, and she was going to have to shoehorn in a trip to her hometown.

The personal part, the guilt over her time away from her aunt, well, that would have to wait. The truth is she never thought Aunt Millicent would die.

Another pothole catches a tire, and her irritation spikes. At least the developer who has wrested the beachfront camp from the Baptists will strip and pave this road so that BMWs and Mercedes and Cadillacs can deliver swarms of tourists to the formerly undiscovered beach town. If the road is widened, these aged oaks will perish. A shame, but not her problem.

Salt air leaks through the vents, and she rolls down the window to let it flow over her. Red curls whip her face, and she lets them, despite the tangles she'll face later. The briny scent brings memories, unaccustomed, unwanted.

How have twelve years passed so quickly? She thinks of her mother, fleeing in the night. She thinks of her own flight three months later. She never meant for the move to be final, not really, at least not then. But somehow, a dozen years have come and gone.

On her right appears the entrance to Camp Resurrection, which never quite lived up to its name, unless the Baptists' view of heaven was a mosquito-ridden sandpit. Clearing has not started on the property, which surprises her.

On her left, she sees the Seafood Shack and cranes to look for any sign of Burle or Jesse. *Would I have heard if they passed away?*

Not for the first time, it occurs to her that her absence has carried a cost.

A half mile farther, a driveway snakes between brick columns. Each pillar is topped by an iron seabird in flight, and a rusted iron fence marches outward, all but buried in crossvine and jessamine, a blur of orange and yellow.

Unexpectedly, a lump rises in her throat.

She is home.

Chapter 2

Sloane climbs the steep wooden stairs that partially hide an elevated brick foundation—an architectural decision that has served the house well for more than a century of tropical storms. The stairs open to a wide porch, where more crossvine and jessamine, mixed with wild honeysuckle, blanket the railing. Raeford has left a key under a potted pink geranium blooming vigorously against the dazzling white of the wood siding. She unlocks the front door, which is painted coral and flanked by sidelights of original wavy glass. A familiar high ceiling and grand curving staircase greet her, along with the scent of lemon furniture polish. This house has always represented safety; now she recognizes its grandeur.

She passes through the foyer into the dining room, where Raeford has left a poster on the long table. "Mayberry by the Sea" reads the tagline beneath a photo of unspoiled beach bounded by sea oats. Similar publicity shots can be found for beaches all over the East Coast, but Sloane can tell this is Millicent by the J-shaped jut at the end of the island. Shorebirds love the broad expanse and waddle in flocks, unafraid of humans, shoving their needle-like beaks into the sand in search of crabs and sand fleas. She's walked that beach since she was two, toddling into the flock until they flew up past her face, delighting her with their flapping and shrieking.

The poster also features an artistic rendering of a beachy downtown with an upscale bookstore, an ice-cream shop—to be spelled "shoppe," no doubt—and, yep, a barber shop, complete with a red-and-white-striped pole. To be named "Floyd's," she supposes.

Mayberry by the Sea, huh? She is irrationally annoyed and stops long enough to ask herself why. She always hated the name Millicent, hated its old-lady sound and the attention it focused on her family, as if they owned the town.

To be fair, they did. Or some family members did, anyway, on her mother's side. Apparently, her mother couldn't take the scrutiny either because she left the day Sloane graduated from high school, and no one's heard from her since. Not even Sloane's older sister, Margaret Millicent Cheney Simpson, who stands to inherit the title of town queen now that Aunt Millicent is gone. Sloane wonders if Margaret is lobbying for a compromise on the developer's renaming. Say, *Millicent by the Sea.*

If so, she deserves it. She's hung in there, marrying Idelle Simpson's oldest son and helping him build a Gas 'N' Such empire all the way past Little River to the north and Savannah to the south. For all Sloane knows, her sister may answer to Millicent now rather than Margaret.

Sloane drops her black suit jacket and duffle bag and scrutinizes the dining room. Aunt Millicent has kept it imposing yet spare. It looks ready to seat twelve for a dinner of Burle's crab-stuffed flounder and Jesse's sweet corn, tomatoes, and hush puppies.

A swinging door leads into the beach-facing kitchen, and she raises the window over the sink, amazed that it slides so easily in the humid air. Immediately, the hiss of small waves hitting the shore takes her back to a day when Margaret was fourteen and she was eight. Margaret wore a black-and-white bikini and was trying to distance herself from Sloane and their mother. Sloane couldn't blame her; the dorky one-piece red suit Sloane wore did little to hide her chubby torso.

How benign that sounds, as if teenage angst was the extent of their family's dysfunction.

Aunt Millicent was sitting on the deep wraparound porch, sipping iced tea and watching the sun set along the coast, for their barrier island lies cockeyed and doesn't face due east. At least, Sloane thought that's what she was doing. Turned out, she was watching for something else: It was past time for shrimpers to be off the water, past time for Sloane's father to come looking for her mother, Aunt Millicent's much younger sister.

When he roared into the driveway, oversized truck tires spinning crushed oyster shells, Aunt Millicent flinched. Sloane's mother stood to face him as he careened around the corner of the house, red-faced and wild-eyed. He saw Millicent on the porch and stopped.

"We don't need a scene, Robert." Her aunt's steely voice carried to their spot on the beach.

"It's okay," her mother said, dusting sand off her bathing suit and pulling Sloane up by one arm. "Margaret," she called. "Time to go."

Her father hadn't uttered a word, but his face was a shade Sloane associated with danger.

"Annie, why don't you leave the girls with me?" Aunt Millicent walked down the porch steps and gripped Sloane's shoulders. Her aunt had been fifteen when Sloane's mother was born and pretty much raised her after their mother died of ovarian cancer.

Sloane's mother looked at her father, a question on her face.

His eyes flicked from Sloane to Margaret and back. "Fine," he barked and turned on his heel.

Their mother followed quickly, and his truck doors slammed in quick succession. Margaret looked worried, but Sloane was ecstatic. She loved sleeping in this house, loved the pale pink room with twin beds that Aunt Millicent kept for them. Sometimes-cook Jesse would serve hushpuppies, and Aunt Millicent always had ice cream.

It wasn't until three days later when their mother came to get them, walking gingerly, her left eye swollen beneath its makeup, that Sloane realized they shouldn't have stayed.

She spins from the sink, but the memories are everywhere. A breakfast nook protrudes into the side yard, where Aunt Millicent's climbing roses ascend a lattice screen. She and Margaret did their homework at this table.

She retraces her steps to the dining room and crosses the hall to the formal parlor, site of their tea lessons: how to offer milk, lemon, and sugar to guests; how to drink without slurping; how to take two small cookies—Aunt Millicent called them biscuits—and no more, even if she and Margaret were hungry.

"This is a training exercise," her aunt would point out. "You can have all the biscuits you want later."

"Training for what?" Sloane whined.

"Training to take your place in Millicent."

Her sister snorted. Back then, Margaret didn't think taking their place was a goal worth pursuing. She must have changed her mind.

After circling past the library and Aunt Millicent's study to arrive back at the ocean-facing verandah, Sloane lets the screen door slam behind her. From what she understands, the buyer wants to turn the house into a boutique hotel with rocking chairs lining this porch. Not a bad idea. She's stayed in historic beachfront hotels on Hilton Head, in St. Simon's in Georgia, even in the Florida Keys, but none has retained the simple Southern elegance of Aunt Millicent's house. The porch runs straight across and flares on both ends into rounded cupola-topped areas big enough for dining or game tables. A dozen wooden steps lead to a lush, grassy strip that gives way to sand.

The buyer will undoubtedly gut and renovate the interior, but if he's smart, he'll keep this verandah exactly as it is. To those without her emotional baggage, it must look like paradise.

Chapter 3

Sloane's cell phone rings as she mounts the steps to Raeford Carlisle's powder-blue Victorian on Millicent's Main Street. The caller is her department intern, and her stomach tightens.

"Yes, Sam?" she says, stopping on Raeford's spacious porch.

Her eyes wander to the street, and she notices people staring. Three hurriedly look away, but another two wave: Elsie, outside the diner that carries her name, and Kent, *not* on his shrimp boat. *Curious*. Word of her homecoming has spread. She waves half-heartedly.

"Sorry to bother you, Professor Cheney," Sam says, "but Dr. Avery is looking for you. He wants you to call."

Though Sloane is not a full professor, she's been unable to get Sam to call her by her first name. He's spot on with Dr. John Avery, though. The English department chairman wouldn't answer to anything *but* Dr. Avery.

"Do you know what he wants?" she asks.

"I think it's about your speech? At graduation?"

Obviously, Dr. Avery has rattled Sam. Not surprising. John Avery didn't want to hire Sloane. He told her to her face that he lobbied against the hire, not personally, she should understand, but because her terminal degree is a Master of Fine Arts. Unfortunately for the teaching purist, her first novel made quite a splash, and the Warner College trustees thought her presence would attract students. In her second year on the job, they'd suggested she give the commencement speech.

That unfinished speech is another reason she should be back in Atlanta and not here. Her heart flutters with the anxiety that comes from too many commitments and too few hours.

"I'm headed into a meeting then a memorial service," she says hurriedly. "Tell Dr. Avery I'll call the minute I get free."

"**M**illicent Sloane!" Raeford smiles broadly and comes around his desk to envelop her in a hug. "It's been too long, my dear."

"I don't go by that name," she says, pulling away from his white shirt striped by navy suspenders. "It's just Sloane. Please."

Her family has the weird custom of slapping the name Millicent on every female child as if to acknowledge that, even if some escape, there will always be another in the wings. She is Millicent Sloane. Her sister is Margaret Millicent. Her mother is Millicent Ann, and her late aunt was Millicent Rose, the only one who gloried in the name. Flannery O'Connor couldn't make this stuff up.

"Of course. Dear Sloane. How was your trip?" Raeford looks the same as always, with a full head of white hair swept from a patrician forehead. Perhaps his shoulders are slightly more stooped, his face more lined. But his rich drawl and effusive warmth are the same. Raeford was a young lawyer when her grandfather took him on as a partner, and he has continued as the family's attorney for decades.

"Rushed," she says, Sam's call taking up space in her head. "As I told you on the phone, I don't have time for this." She hears the petulance in her voice and pauses. This is not who she wants to be. She takes a deep breath and begins again. "I'm sorry. That sounds childish. Aunt Millicent didn't die to screw up my plans, did she?"

Raeford's smile is rueful. "I assure you, she did not."

"Well, I'm all yours until six o'clock tomorrow morning, then I need to hit the road. Where do I sign?"

Raeford looks as if he's going to say something but pivots mid-thought. "We're waiting for Robroy."

"Robroy?" Sloane is flummoxed by mention of her younger brother. "Why?"

"Did I not say that on the phone?"

"Say what?"

"Robroy is also Millicent's beneficiary."

She laughs with incredulity. "You most certainly did not."

"My mistake," he says. "At any rate, he's on his way. He shouldn't hold us up."

She flops into an upholstered wing chair, her face stretching into an involuntary smile. *Robroy.* Her brother is a musician, a good one, a guitarist and singer in a band that changes names as often as it changes song sets. Robroy and the Dirty, Rotten Scumbags. Robroy and the Pirates of Rock. Robroy and the Alleged Baby Stompers. That last one was a reference to a headline he saw during a gig on St. Croix when two mothers accused each other of stomping their babies. *Alleged*, since, apparently, no babies were harmed in the melee. Needless to say, her brother has a twisted sense of humor. When he plays more upright venues, his foursome is The Robroy Cheney Band.

Robroy was ten when Sloane left Millicent: a nut-brown, tow-headed island boy who could wrap their volatile dad around his finger. That's why she felt at least semi-safe leaving him. He got out of Millicent early, too, and has been on the road since he was seventeen. He checks in whenever the band plays near Atlanta. He sleeps in her guest room while his buddies scatter themselves and their equipment across her apartment.

Raeford clears his throat. "He and your aunt were close," he says. "Your brother dropped in whenever he was playing Charleston or Hilton Head or Beaufort."

"Did he?" *How did I not know that?* "Always looking for a free place to stay, I guess."

They hear a clatter on the front porch, and Robroy bursts in, his tall, lean frame filling the doorway and his face beaming.

"Sis!" he shouts. "Raeford! Good to see you, man." His blond hair falls unmanageably across his forehead, but he's got it buzzed on both sides in a new look. He yanks Sloane into a hug then reaches across the desk to shake Raeford's hand. "Let's get this party started!" he says, too loudly. Robroy is always loud, which Sloane suspects is the result of too many clubs and too many decibels.

"So, wait," she says. "Aunt Millicent left the house to me and Robroy, but not to Margaret?"

Raeford shrugs. "You've been in her will for years," he says. "As you know, she removed your mother on the seventh anniversary of her departure. I think she was hurt that Millicent Ann never got in touch. She told me you loved the house more than anyone in the family and that Margaret was well taken care of." He shoots a glance at Robroy. "She added Robroy this past Christmas."

Her brother falls into the chair next to her. "It was news to me," he says. "I had no idea until Raeford called this weekend. I figured if she ever booted you, she'd give the house to the turtle ladies."

Their aunt was a big supporter of the local sea turtle brigade that protects nests on the beach.

"But if you just found out, are you okay with selling?" she asks. "I mean, I've had years to think about it." Years to think about how she wants nothing to do with Millicent, no matter how chic it becomes. Years to ponder if the remaking of her homeplace will sever its hold over her. She bites her lip to stop the words. Lord knows she doesn't want to talk Robroy out of the sale.

"Sure," he says. "I mean, I loved visiting Aunt M, but without her, it's an empty house. I don't play the coast more than a few times a year. And the price Raeford mentioned..." He whistles. "Let's just say it's a little more than the House of Blues pays." He grins, his teeth white but slightly crooked. Braces would have been out of the question for their father. Sloane can't help but smile back. Unaffected, open, happy—her brother is the best thing to come out of their family.

Raeford indicates places for them to sign, in duplicate, triplicate. She signs and signs and signs. With each flourish of the pen, her heart lightens. She is nearly free of Millicent, South Carolina, nearly free of the clan of Millicents who, despite their money and silver services and tea biscuits, could not protect her mother.

Chapter 4

Aunt Millicent's memorial service is at St. James Episcopal Church, one of the many churches Sloane passed while driving in. She, Raeford, and Robroy take the attorney's gray Cadillac SUV, which handles the potholes better than her old Toyota did. Tucked away in the ancient oaks, St. James is not a large church, but its soaring roofline gives it a magisterial feel. It's been home to generations of Millicents, no matter their last names: the original Willinghams, the Roundtrees, the Cheneys, and with Margaret's marriage, the Simpsons. The husbands sometimes come, sometimes don't, but the Millicents have always been big churchgoers. And from the looks of this well-kept property, big supporters.

Sloane experiences a pang. She hasn't stepped inside a church since she left the island. Even weddings she's attended were held in outdoor venues with shade trees, slate patios, and open bars, not in churches. Through the vehicle's darkened windows, she sees Margaret and her brood across the parking lot, and her heart wrenches. This was a place they shared, she and her mom and Margaret, on Sunday mornings when her father took Robroy hunting or fishing or God knows what. Now Margaret is with her in-laws, Idelle and J.C., her husband, Joel, and their stairstep daughters, Emma Sue and Sarah. Seeing those girls with Margaret pierces Sloane with their mother's absence.

Her cell phone rings before she can open the car door, and John Avery's name flashes across the screen. *What a jerk!* He couldn't wait for her to get back to him. She glances at her watch—only five minutes until the service begins. She silences the phone, though her stomach squeezes in protest.

Just let me get through today. Then I'll deal with the graduation speech. And finals. And book edits. And John Dickhead Avery.

Pulling a jacket over her sleeveless jade tank, she steps onto the packed sand of the parking lot, where she and Robroy are greeted with hugs from Margaret's family.

"You came!" Margaret breathes into her ear, holding her close. "Sloane, I'm so glad you made it." She turns to Robroy. "And who is this handsome young man?" Margaret laughs as her seven- and eight-year-old girls grab their uncle's arms and squeal for his attention. Margaret shushes them with promises of a visit with Robroy after the service then ushers everyone inside.

The sanctuary's interior is cool and dim after the brightness of the day. Sloane notices that the stained-glass windows don't glow the way they did when she was a child. The live oaks and their Spanish moss have spread shade over St. James.

The organist, shoulders and legs pumping energetically, finishes the prelude as the family enters. Some people smile as the Cheneys make their way down the aisle, but more turn aside and whisper. Even the smiles, Sloane imagines, are for Margaret and Robroy. She is the ungrateful niece who hasn't set foot in town for years but shows up to grab the money.

They settle into the front pew, joining Octavia Hargrove, Aunt Millicent's closest friend. The old woman nods but doesn't smile, which surprises Sloane. Maybe she has offended her former neighbors more than she realized.

She glances down the row and doesn't see two faces she expected. Almost fearfully, she whispers to Raeford, "Burle and Jesse?"

"You'll see them later," he responds.

Well, they're alive then. That's good news.

A rector Sloane doesn't know rises and begins the liturgy. Her mind drifts to the phone call she needs to return to her department head and to her half-written graduation speech. Then the rector's tone changes. "As most of you know, we Episcopalians don't always share personal memories in our services, but Millicent and Octavia told me long ago that the surviving friend would speak at the other's memorial." He chuckles. "And as you also know, I dare not tell Millicent or Octavia 'no.'" Appreciative laughter from the congregation. "So, Octavia?"

Robroy helps Octavia stand, and she walks, back erect, white hair in a severe bun, up the steps to the chancel, grabbing tight to the handrail. She's wearing a belted black dress that hits her mid-calf and black lace-ups it's possible she's owned since the 1970s. She makes her way to the podium and pauses to put on the eyeglasses hanging from a pearl chain around her neck.

Octavia has gotten old since Sloane's been away, and it hits her what it must feel like to lose your best friend. She wouldn't know. She never had one.

Octavia looks over the congregation, her chin trembling. As the postmistress, she knows every person here, and her eyes sweep the filled pews. "This isn't what I planned to say." Her voice quavers. "I wanted to tell you what a great friend Millicent Roundtree was, what a great lady, the sort of person who made our little town such a lovely place to live. All the things she told me to say." Everyone laughs.

Octavia doesn't smile. "But I can't say any of that because there's something more important to say. I'm guessing it's the reason Dan Hartwell is here."

Heads swivel. Sloane looks at Raeford.

"Police chief," he whispers.

She glances at Robroy, who looks as puzzled as she feels.

Octavia takes a shuddering breath. "The truth is, Millicent didn't *die* last week—at least not in the way we were told." Octavia knows how to hold a crowd's attention. She pauses until she's a second shy of the cusp when murmurs will begin. Only then does she deliver her climactic line: "Millicent was murdered."

Chapter 5

At first, silence greets Octavia's bizarre announcement, but then whispers start like the hiss of a punctured tire. She retreats down the chancel steps, seemingly oblivious to the storm she's unleashed.

Raeford sits in shock on one side of Sloane, Robroy wide-eyed on the other. Next to him, Margaret turns to Joel so Sloane can't see her face. The whispers give way to raised voices then an angry buzz that grows louder, louder. Sloane lays her head back and the ceiling spins. She hasn't eaten today, and she's not sure she can stand. Her mind leaps from errant thought to errant thought, anything to keep from focusing on what Octavia has said. The rector signals the organist, who launches into a discordant postlude.

Aunt Millicent's service is over.

Bewildered, the family stumbles to the sandy parking lot and surrounds Octavia. Margaret motions for them to be quiet, and Sloane and Robroy fall into their childhood roles, obeying her. She nods at Raeford, who looks years older than when they arrived.

In a daze, Raeford beckons to a man in a khaki-colored uniform. "Dan," he says, "I believe you know Millicent's family, except for her niece Sloane and her nephew Robroy."

The police chief is slim and fit with a military bearing that doesn't jibe with the dark hair curling past his collar. His black eyes dart around the family's ragged circle.

"Octavia Hargrove reported her suspicions to us only this morning," he says. "She made a good enough case that we are having the

Beaufort County coroner look into it. I'd like for each of you to come into the station." He catches Sloane's stricken look. "This afternoon."

"But Octavia," says Margaret, directing her question to their aunt's friend. "What makes you think Aunt Millicent was murdered? I mean, she was what, seventy-three? Seventy-four?"

Octavia turns a cold gaze on Margaret. "She was sixty-eight. And you will soon learn that's not terribly old, my dear."

Margaret squirms. "Sorry. But you know what I mean. The doctor told me her heart gave out on the heels of that infection."

"I'm sure it did," says Octavia. "With a little help."

"But what... I mean why..." Robroy takes a breath to get his question out. "Octavia, why do you think that?"

"Do you mean 'How do I *know* that?'" She gives him a severe look over her glasses.

"Well, yeah, okay."

"I know because..." Octavia has really mastered the dramatic pause. "I know because... of something she told me. In the hospital. About fears that she'd be killed."

"*What?*" Margaret, Robroy, and Raeford chime in.

"Really, Octavia, whatever are you talking about?" Raeford asks.

"Chief Hartwell told me not to say anything. So that's really all I can tell you."

Sloane notes the police chief observing the circle of family and friends who have become little more than strangers to her. Margaret. Robroy. Raeford. Octavia. And beyond them, her brother-in-law, Joel. His folks, Idelle and J.C., who are trying to shield Margaret's girls. They all look genuinely puzzled. *Besides Octavia, does one of them know more than the rest of us?*

Raeford turns to her and Robroy, his face pale. "This changes everything," he says apologetically. "The will can't be executed. We'll have to put the sale on hold."

Everyone's eyes swing to Sloane, who can feel her face reddening. She's not thinking of Aunt Millicent but of her impossible schedule.

It's as if Chief Hartwell reads her mind. "I'll need everyone to stay put for a few days," he says, looking right at her.

"But I wasn't even here!" She blanches at the bleat in her voice and takes a moment to recalibrate. "What I mean is: Can I go back to Atlanta long enough to finish up my semester, then return? After that, I could stay all summer if you need me." She has no intention of spending the summer here, but she's desperate.

"Afraid not," the chief answers curtly. "A murder investigation trumps everything. I'm sure your college will understand."

Surely, he doesn't have the authority to enforce such a command, but Sloane is reluctant to get into a pissing match in front of everyone. Robroy puts an arm around her. "Screws up my schedule too," he says. "But what ya gonna do? At least we have a free place to crash."

Do we? She turns to Raeford and notices a little color has returned to his face. "Is it still okay to stay at Aunt Millicent's?"

"As far as I know. It's not a crime scene. She died in the island hospital." He smiles sadly. "You know how she felt about our little place."

Sloane does know. Aunt Millicent largely funded the hospital that sports eighteen beds for non-intensive stays. Heart attacks, strokes, and serious traumas are taken to Beaufort, forty miles away. But broken bones, domestic spills and run-of-the-mill illnesses can be treated at Mercy Hospital. Aunt Millicent got the naming rights and mercifully kept their name off it.

"Then how in the hell was she murdered?" Robroy asks the question before Sloane can.

Raeford shrugs. "Maybe Octavia is wrong," he says, glancing over as Joel helps their aunt's friend into her antiquated Buick. "I sure hope so."

Chapter 6

First things first. Sloane finds John Avery's name in her phone as she climbs into the back seat of Raeford's Cadillac. The department chair picks up immediately.

"Sloane, where are you?" he demands.

He knows good and well where I am, and why. "At my aunt's funeral in South Carolina. I left word."

He harrumphs. He actually makes that sound. *Har-rumph.* In spite of her clenched chest and stomach, she almost giggles. Then the moment passes, and she's in full-on stress mode again. "There's been an... um... unexpected development."

"What?" he snaps. "I'm calling about your speech. I need to see a copy."

The unfinished speech. "Of course, I will get it to you."

"So what's the 'development'? You'll be back in time for graduation." It's not a question, but a statement. Graduation is Saturday, five days from now.

"Yes, yes, no problem. But it turns out my aunt was..." *Oh my God, do I really want to tell him this?* She sees no way around it. "She was murdered. So the police are insisting I stay in town a few days."

Silence on the other end. Then Dr. Avery's voice comes through, rising in pitch and volume. "She was *murdered*?" He makes Aunt Millicent's demise sound like a personal affront. "My word." His tone suggests that having a relative murdered is exactly what he would expect of trash like Sloane. He hinted as much after reading her novel, a thinly veiled account of the hot mess that was life in her twenties.

"So," she says, thinking fast, "I'll post my final grades online from here. I have my laptop." She thinks of the exam pages in her briefcase, unexamined. The college didn't stock Blue Books anymore, so she'd handed out sheets of blank notebook paper and insisted that her students place their phones and laptops on her desk during the exam. She wasn't going to spend time figuring out if they'd used chatbots or AI or some other method of cheating. "And I'll get the speech to you. Tonight." She has no idea how she's going to accomplish this. "It's not polished, but you'll get the gist."

She breathes deeply, feeling a headache bloom at the base of her skull.

"Very well," he says briskly. "I'll expect your speech this evening." She hears the bang of his desk phone.

Maybe more like midnight. She's glad she didn't voice that thought. After their conversation, Sloane sits for a moment, worrying the lipstick off her lower lip and trying to calm down. Grades. Speech. Edits. Speaking to the police. *What first?*

She calls the department intern. When Sam picks up, she starts apologizing, but he stops her. "Professor Cheney, whatever you need. Name it."

It occurs to her that she must have been a nice person at some point to have Sam respond so warmly. She doesn't like this new Sloane, stressed and angry, a woman who elicits sidelong glances and snide whispers from her former neighbors. *This crisis will pass, but what will be their memories of me?* Ironically, she doesn't have time to dwell on it.

"This is a big favor." She explains about the murder investigation that will prevent her return to campus tomorrow. "My most immediate problem is the grades. I have to get this speech written, and I don't think I can do both. I know it's a lot to ask, but could you drive down here and grade these exams?"

Her students and their parents would not be pleased to know that an intern is grading their work. But they don't have to know. Besides, she already weighed in on their writing projects earlier this semester. Those were the important things. The final exam was a more objective exercise.

Sam jumps in eagerly, no doubt glad for a meaningful task rather than the grunt work Dr. Avery assigns him. "Yes! I mean, I'd be happy to. You're at the beach, right?"

"Yes, so bring your swim trunks." She tells him it's a five-hour drive and gives him Aunt Millicent's address.

"Okay, then," he says, sounding ebullient. "I'll see you around eight or nine tonight. Let me run home and… Oh, wait."

He's going to back out. "What?"

"My dog. I don't think I can get anyone to keep her on such short notice. Is it okay to bring her?"

Sloane exhales in relief. "Absolutely. It'll be just you, me, and my brother, and it's a big old house. Your dog will be fine."

Small bites, she thinks as they disconnect. She can accomplish everything as long as she takes small bites.

Next up, Chief Hartwell. Then the speech. The book edits—she can't even think about those now. They will take real concentration. *First things first.*

A knock on the window startles her. Margaret stands beside the car door. Raeford and Robroy are behind her, their heads bent toward each other.

"We need to talk," Margaret says.

Sloane exits the car and follows her sister to the shade of a giant oak. Sloane has spent a lifetime hiding her pale skin from the sun, and Margaret remembers. Margaret was white blond when they were growing up, but her skin tanned easily. A perfect beach girl. Sloane, on the other hand, inherited their mother's freckled skin and unruly strawberry blond hair with at least thirty shades of red and gold. After an unfortunate haircut that resulted in an Afro when she was seven, she learned to wear it long and finger-combed or piled messily on top of her head.

Margaret reaches out to push a curl off Sloane's face. "I've missed you, Leo." She's always teased Sloane that her hair resembles a lion's mane.

"Good to see you too." Sloane smiles and adds, "If you're there, God, is she still Margaret?"—a reference to their favorite Judy Blume book. "Or is she Millicent?"

Her sister laughs. "Margaret to my friends. Millicent when I speak to city councils up and down the coast."

"You sly thing. So, what's up?"

"You mean besides the fact that we're all under suspicion of murder?"

"Not me. I was five hours away."

"But you're the main beneficiary. Isn't that a motive?"

Sloane turns serious. "Actually, I feel bad about that. Why me and Robroy, but not you?"

"Raeford says Aunt Millicent thought I was set financially." She looks thoughtful. "Although why she didn't think the same about you and your book success, I'm not sure."

Sloane searches her sister's face. Maybe she's not quite as okay with Aunt Millicent's decision as everyone seems to think.

"Well, you might be surprised by how little authors make," Sloane says. "I certainly can't afford to quit teaching."

"Yeah, but it'll come. Your dissolute lifestyle will pay off. Eventually."

Sloane laughs uneasily, thinking about the episodes in her debut novel. "How do you know what was real and what wasn't?" She didn't see Margaret more than a handful of times during those years, and she was on her best behavior then.

"Oh, I have my ways." Before Sloane can pursue this conversation, Margaret switches tacks. "But that's not what we need to talk about. You do realize people are headed to Aunt Millicent's right now?"

"What? No! Why?"

"The funeral reception."

"Nobody told me that."

"I wouldn't think you needed to be told. Elsie is catering meat and vegetable trays from the diner, and a bunch of casseroles and desserts came to my house. My housekeeper was supposed to deliver them during the service, so I assume all the food is there."

Sloane's face reflects such dismay that Margaret bursts into laughter. "Come on, Sloane, it's not that bad."

"Yeah, it kinda is." The thought of making conversation with the people from the service unnerves her. "I thought we had to see Chief Hartwell."

Margaret shrugs. "Later, I guess. He understands Southern funerals."

Sloane closes her eyes. Robroy saunters over, with Raeford close behind. "I hear we got a shindig to put on," he drawls. "Raeford says Jesse's frying up hushpuppies."

Sloane's heart lifts. "Is Burle there, too? I didn't see them in the church."

"They sat in the back so they could slip out early," Raeford answers. "Elsie asked them to help."

They head to the car, Margaret hurrying to claim the front passenger seat beside Raeford. She spins and whispers into the backseat. "Shotgun!"

Robroy reaches over the seat to grab her in a mock headlock. "How old are you?" he demands. "Five?"

Sloane sighs and slides in next to her brother. She wants to join in their easy familiarity, but her body is rigid with dread. *Could Aunt Millicent really have been murdered?* For now, she clings to denial.

Chapter 7

Elsie and Jesse have outdone themselves, and the dining room is redolent with the fragrance of hot hushpuppies, fried chicken, and biscuits—real buttermilk biscuits, not Aunt Millicent's cookies. But even the food can't subdue the buzz surrounding Octavia's announcement in church.

"Murder? Miss Millicent? Is that possible?" Sloane hears the whispers before she enters the dining room. Neighbors stare openly, and she needs to speak to them, but instead, remembering her previous dizziness, she grabs a glass of sugary lemonade and a handful of hushpuppies. She catches Jesse replenishing the platter. Like Octavia, Jesse has aged. When Sloane reaches out to hug her, the old woman's bones feel fragile beneath her hands. Stepping back, Sloane sees wetness on her wrinkled ebony cheeks.

"Miss Sloane," Jesse says, but there is none of the warmth she exuded in Sloane's childhood.

Oh no, Jesse, please don't tell me you're mad at me too. "How are you? And Burle?"

"We're fine. I'm sorry for your loss." Jesse's words are polite, but her tone is wooden.

"Your loss too," Sloane murmurs. "You were with Aunt Millicent longer than any of us."

"Um hmm."

"Miss Sloane!" The deep voice almost melts her as she turns to Burle—massive, head shaved, navy-blue tattoos disappearing into his dark skin.

His bear hug envelops her, and for the first time since she's been home, she feels welcome, safe. She rests her head on Burle's chest and feels his chin on top of her head. She'd gladly stay there for the duration of the reception, but Robroy barrels toward them, yelling "Mister Burle!"

Chuckling, Burle extricates himself and greets the boy he helped to raise. Jesse's face lights up as well, and Sloane slips away, unnoticed.

She drinks the lemonade and gobbles a few hushpuppies, feeling better almost instantly.

She must look more approachable, too, because Elsie swoops in. "Sloane," she says, with a hug so heartfelt it brings an unexpected sting to her eyes. "I'm sorry about your aunt. But she was *murdered?* How can that be?" Elsie's kind face is broad and unlined, her brown eyes sympathetic.

"I honestly don't know. I'm hoping Octavia is wrong." She fingers the pink ruffle on Elsie's apron. "This looks familiar."

"It should. It's Millicent's. I forgot to bring mine from the diner." She waves a hand at the table. "We're using her china too. I thought we'd have one last hurrah before you kids clear out the house. But now..." Her eyes are asking if Sloane knows more, but Sloane's mind snags on something else she said.

Clear out the house? That wasn't part of the deal. Her mind boomerangs. Then logic kicks in. Clearing the house is the least of her worries. A murder investigation hangs over their heads, and from the ugly looks she's getting from Millicent's mourners, it's her fault.

Mack Sanderson stands behind Elsie, and as soon as the diner owner heads to the kitchen, he grabs Sloane's upper arm. Mack is in his midfifties, the third generation of Sandersons to run Island Financial Bank. None too gently, he forces her past the guests and into the empty hallway.

She yanks free of his rough grasp. "What are you doing?"

Mack retains the beefiness he sported as center for Beaufort High's football team. "I need to talk to you about your plans," he says then jerks his head to indicate Aunt Millicent's house. "For this place."

"It's no secret." She rubs her arm, which is turning pink. "I signed the papers to sell earlier, as you undoubtedly know. But Raeford says everything is on hold for now."

"Because of what happened to your aunt."

"You're making my point for me," she says. "I'm sure you know more than I do."

Mack leans against the wall, crossing one loafered foot over the other. "So how Miss Millicent died doesn't change anything, right? You're still going to sell?" His pushiness irritates Sloane, and her temper flares.

"What is the problem here, Mr. Sanderson? And how is it your business?"

His face darkens. "It's my business because my bank will be running point on financing for Mayberry by the Sea. I need to be sure you're on board."

"I have no desire to hang onto the family home, if that's what you're asking."

He smiles, and it strikes her as reptilian. "Well, then, good, Sloane. That's good." He glances around at the high ceiling and the gracefully curving staircase. "Your aunt, you know, couldn't see the value of turning this property into a boutique hotel so that a lot of people could enjoy our beach. She struck me as rather selfish." He pats the same arm that he wrenched before then strides the length of the hall and exits without saying goodbye.

Her childhood friend Kent Espey must have been watching the exchange because he appears at Sloane's side as soon as the front door closes.

"What an asshole," Sloane sputters.

"Did you get the banker's full-court press?" Kent murmurs, pulling her into a hug. Kent is a shrimper, like his dad. Their fathers operated a boat together for a while, until Sloane's father blew up the partnership. Like he blew up everything.

Kent is handsome in an outdoorsy way, his hair a tumble of blondish streaks from days on the water. He and Sloane were childhood friends and even dated a few times when they were sixteen—nothing serious because, even then, she was wary of getting tied to Millicent.

"Got it in spades," she answers.

"Well, it's good to see you, stranger," he continues. "You weren't kidding when you said you were leaving town."

"Guess not." She tries to switch her attention from Mack Sanderson's aggression, so unlike the mannered gentility she recalls from the past.

"But what the hell? Miss Millicent killed? What'd Chief Hartwell say?"

She shrugs helplessly. "Nothing really. That he's investigating."

Kent leans in. "It's got to be about the beachfront development. Nothing else makes sense. And I assume that's what Mack Sanderson was so eager to talk about."

"But the developer already got the Baptist camp, right? He's coming, no matter what."

"Yeah, but without Millicent House, there's not enough of a draw, as I understand it. The camp is big enough for rental villas and even a pool, but he needs a high-end hotel to anchor things. And there are plans to add more villas on your aunt's grounds." He flings his arm to indicate her extensive beachfront. "Mayberry by the Sea," he says with almost visible air quotes, "hinges on him getting this property too."

She looks around. So that's why clearing hasn't begun on Camp Resurrection. And that may explain the glares she's getting. She's the only thing standing between old-timey Millicent and new-fangled Mayberry by the Sea. Well, she and Robroy.

She peers into the parlor, where the neighbors are milling, and wonders where they are on the issue. Clearly Mack Sanderson favors the development—as attested by the welts on her arm. Elsie's Diner would benefit from an influx of tourists. As would other businesses. But what else may be at stake?

She returns her attention to Kent. "Where do you stand?"

He shrugs. "I've already got buyers up and down the coast driving over for my shrimp. And there's always the possibility of overfishing. We don't need to get bigger. There's nothing wrong with having one undeveloped beach on the whole damn coast."

"So you'd prefer us not to sell."

"Damn straight." He grins. "Since you asked." He grows serious and lowers his voice. "But Sloane, not everybody feels like I do. There's been some sentiment against Miss Millicent, that she was standing in the way of progress, of more money coming in." His eyes rake the room. "Strong sentiment. Like the Sandersons. They've taken a hit on loan defaults in the past few years. They're hoping to make it up with all this Mayberry by the Sea crap."

She frowns. "Are you saying you weren't surprised by what Octavia said?"

He wags his head to indicate indecision. "Well, yeah, surprised it went as far as murder. If it did. That's hard to believe. But I guess millions of dollars are at stake, so who knows?" He looks toward the dining room, where Elsie is replenishing cheese and crackers, boat repairman Bud Randolph is tugging at his unaccustomed tie, and Margaret's mother-in-law Idelle is deep in conversation with Mack Sanderson's father.

One couple is conspicuously missing. "Where are your folks?" she asks.

Kent looks embarrassed. "Um... not here."

"Are they sick?" Sloane can't imagine the Espeys skipping Aunt Millicent's funeral. According to Margaret, they and their younger son Scotty were champs about welcoming Robroy into their home. When Kent still doesn't speak, she asks, "Because of Dad?"

"Nah," he says. "Scotty and Robroy... had a falling out. Way after I'd moved out of the house, so I'm not sure what it was about." He's in a hurry to get away from her now. He nods toward the knot of people around the dining room table. "But as I say, sentiment is high, Sloane, concerning this development business. On both sides. You be careful."

Chapter 8

Sloane's sister, brother, and brother-in-law are effusive hosts, so she sneaks away from the reception to carry her duffle upstairs to her childhood bedroom. She tells herself she's simply getting it out of the way, but once she sees the beloved pink comforter on her twin bed, she can't resist. She collapses onto it, the murmur of voices below a gentle lull.

Why have I not been back here? All those years at Greenbrier College, all those Christmases with her college boyfriend's family, all the summers she worked at *The Greenbrier Herald.* She kept thinking she'd get back to visit her aunt, but time got away from her.

Her aunt wrote her letters, and she responded with emails. Her aunt asked when she was coming home, and she made excuses. Then she went off the rails.

She's still not totally sure what the cause was. In her novel, *Girl, Lost,* the narrator Murphy speculates that her wild experiments with sex and drugs stemmed from guilt over dismissing her family. *Subtle, huh?* She wrote it that way because it allowed her to ignore the preceding step—the mother-sized hole in Murphy. In her.

She didn't write about Murphy's mother. How could she? Her feelings about her own mother were too conflicted to put into words. Besides, Annie Cheney was two different people. With Aunt Millicent and Margaret and Sloane, she was lively and fun, a woman who rode the carousel and the Tilt-a-Whirl and the Ferris wheel at traveling fairs, giggling like a teenager. With Sloane's dad, she was tentative and reticent, even more so after Robroy was born. His birth seemed to suck the last remaining life out of her.

Sloane wondered at that, wondered why the loving, energetic boy so sapped her. It was years before she put it together, and her mother was already gone by then, deserting Robroy at a far younger age than she'd deserted Sloane. That summer after Sloane graduated from high school, she counted the days her mom had been gone, counted the days until she'd leave for Greenbrier College far away in the Carolina foothills, sure that her mother would return to see her off. But she didn't.

And in her relentless counting, she counted something else. It'd been exactly nine months before Robroy's birth that her mother had left Margaret and Sloane with Aunt Millicent that day at the beach. *Was our brother conceived during those violent three days? It's possible.*

When she whispered her suspicion to Margaret, her sister looked at her with scorn. "Had you not figured that out?" she scoffed. "The way Mom treated him?"

No, she hadn't. After all, there had been so many black eyes, so many sprained shoulders, so many stays with Aunt Millicent. And if Mom was distant with Robroy, she was also distant with her and Margaret after his arrival. He'd never known any other kind of mother. But they had. And they missed her.

That's why she feels guilty complaining, if only in her head. At least she had a mother, if a diminished one, for eighteen years. The night she graduated from Beaufort High—after they paraded through the auditorium in their cheap, shiny gowns—her mother hugged her, a hug that, in retrospect, was a little longer, a little tighter, than usual. Then the town kids joined the island kids for a traditional all-night bonfire on the beach. When she got home the next morning, Robroy was eating cereal and watching cartoons. "Mom's gone on a trip," he said, pointing to a note on the kitchen table.

Sloane was scared as she read it, scared of what their father would do when her mother returned.

Turns out, she needn't have worried.

Sloane struggles out of the doze that has overtaken her, struggles to shake away groggy dreams of her mother. The house is silent. Everyone has gone.

Margaret appears in the doorway of their shared childhood room, barely hiding her annoyance. "Rested?" she asks.

"I'm sorry. I guess I was more tired than I realized."

"Well, come on. We've got to get to the police station."

Sloane cringes inwardly but dares not protest. She stumbles into the gargantuan hallway, more of an upstairs landing, really. "Margaret, wait a sec," she calls down the stairs. She wants to check out the room where she'll put Sam. Her black heels click on the hardwood floor that stretches into the beach-facing guest bedroom, peach colored with a queen-size bed covered in white eyelet. Double French doors open onto a wraparound balcony that stretches the entire width of the house.

Those balcony doors remind her of another space, her favorite. She enters the cozy reading room nestled between the guest room and Aunt Millicent's master suite, painted the deepest coral and furnished with a pair of wing chairs, a globe, and her grandfather's antique telescope. How many hours has she spent in here, reading, searching for dolphins in the sea below, or simply spinning the globe, imagining places she'd travel? This room also opens onto the balcony, as does Aunt Millicent's. Because the house boasts a twelve-foot foundation, the balcony is essentially three stories high, offering a princely view of the coastline. Her aunt loved standing out there, staring out to sea like a sea captain's widow.

Margaret is undoubtedly waiting downstairs, growing antsy, but Sloane can't resist. She unlatches the doors and emerges onto the balcony. The breeze is picking up, the view breathtaking. Only a few fishermen and four beach walkers can be seen in either direction, enjoying the wide swath of sand that appears pinkish from this dizzy height.

Like the exterior itself, the railing has been recently painted, its white spindles waging a constant battle against the salt and humidity. Most owners of beachfront property use materials that age naturally, allowing seasons to pass without upkeep. Not Aunt Millicent. Her insistence on pristine white rails is as familiar to Sloane as her formal tea lessons, her tailored suits.

"Sloane!"

She hears the irritation in her sister's raised voice. She locks the balcony doors and hurries to join her downstairs.

Chapter 9

Walking into Millicent's police station, an unexpectedly cheery structure on Main Street, Sloane recalls the night she and Kent Espey were brought in after planting cherry bombs beneath Camp Resurrection's benches.

She must have been drunk to let Kent talk her into it—not because it was wrong or dangerous, but because an arrest would've threatened her ticket out of Millicent. Greenbrier College frowned upon potential Unabombers, so Chief Hartwell's predecessor was treated to Sloane's complete meltdown. Her sobbing bordered on hysteria, and he must have interpreted it as fear of her father's reaction. In a town the size of Millicent, people knew what Robert Cheney was, even as they looked the other way.

Kent was startled by her reaction and fell silent.

As her tears showed no sign of abating, the chief stuttered and fidgeted and finally let the teens go with a scolding. "I'm not going to tell your father, Sloane," was the last thing he said.

Out on Main Street once more, Kent lifted Sloane off the ground and twirled her in a half-circle before they tumbled onto the lawn of Elsie's Diner next door. "Give the girl an Oscar." He laughed.

"I wasn't acting." Sloane willed herself to stop trembling. "If that went on my record and kept me out of Greenbrier, I'd kill myself."

"So you weren't worried about your dad?"

"Hell no, he wouldn't care. He'd think it was funny."

"Your family is weird. Queen bees on one side, lowly shrimpers on the other."

"Tell me about it."

"Well, it worked in our favor tonight."

She can't remember what this lobby looked like that night through a film of snot and tears, but now it's downright inviting. Someone has painted the lobby a soft yellow. The vinyl chairs are navy, and magazines are stacked on the side tables. She elbows Margaret and Robroy. "Mayberry by the Sea-plus," she whispers.

"So you've seen the posters?" Margaret asks.

"Yeah, and Otis would kill to stay here."

Margaret laughs. "Maybe they'll let us paint murals in our cells."

"I keep telling you I was five hours away. In Georgia, for goodness' sake."

Her sister raises an eyebrow. She's getting this Queen Millicent thing down pat.

Chief Hartwell strides into the lobby, followed by two women in pantsuits—one in gray, one in navy—whom he introduces as detectives from the Beaufort County Sheriff's Office. "I'll take this one," he says, nodding at Sloane.

One detective motions for Robroy to follow her, and the other smiles at Margaret. "Mrs. Simpson, we met at the Beaufort Chamber of Commerce."

Sloane rolls her eyes. Why couldn't she get the good cop?

Chief Hartwell ushers her into a small room. She expects dirty walls and a gray metal table, but instead, the room is the same yellow as the lobby, with matching wing chairs and a wooden coffee table strewn with copies of *Coastal Living* magazine. Her anxiety lowers slightly. Surely this isn't the room where they grill suspected murderers—or anyone likely to throw up. A drunken Sloane had spent enough time in tiled emergency rooms during her lost years to appreciate the difference.

"So," the chief begins. "You and your brother stand to inherit your aunt's property. And as I understand it, you've already arranged its sale. For eight point six million."

She swallows dryly and nods.

"I must say, that didn't take long. Did you have the sale lined up before your aunt died?"

Actually, yes. "No, it's not like that," she protests. "The developer—the same one who bought the Baptist camp—had a standing offer with Aunt Millicent. Through Raeford. Raeford Carlisle."

"And?"

"Well, that's it. He'd offered to buy her house and beachfront property five or six years ago. She said no. Other developers came and went, but this one checked in with Raeford every few months, sometimes upping the offer. To what you said. Eight point six."

"That still doesn't answer my question."

She crosses her legs and shifts in her seat. "I never had any intention of moving back to Millicent. I made no secret of that. So when Raeford called to tell me that Aunt Millicent had died..." Unexpectedly, her throat closes, and she has to pause. "When he called, he... he said we could close on the sale at the same time, so I'd have to come only once. For the funeral and the closing."

Chief Hartwell's eyebrows furrow. His tone changes, and he asks mildly, "Why do you detest this place so much? Why the rush to sell and leave?"

Where to start? My violent father. My absent mother. The suffocating business of being a Millicent in the land of Millicents.

"It's not that I detest this place," she lies. "It's just that I've built a life in Atlanta and have so much to do before the end of the semester that it's causing me anxiety."

He leans onto his elbows. "Let's back up for a minute. Burle Jenkins found your aunt delirious on the sofa in her study a week ago and rushed her to the hospital. Did no one call to tell you?"

He's determined to put Sloane in the worst light possible. But she deserves it. "Yes. Raeford called me."

"But you didn't feel it necessary to come then?"

She pauses for a beat, unable to meet his eyes. "No. It didn't sound serious. Raeford said it was dehydration and a urinary tract infection. Plus, Aunt Millicent had Burle, as you said. And Jesse. And my sister Margaret. And Octavia." She takes a deep breath. "The truth is, I thought I had time. I planned to come next week, after the semester ended." The thought did cross her mind. *Would I have done so? I'll never know.*

Chief Hartwell changes the subject, and Sloane wonders if he's trying to keep her off balance. "I understand that you're a writer." Meaning he hasn't read her book.

"Yes. But also an assistant professor at Warner College. So I have grades to post and a graduation speech to write. By tonight. I don't know how I'm going to get it all done, and having to stay here isn't helping."

The chief straightens in his seat. His face displays what she can only describe as dislike. Disapproval. "Miss Cheney, you do understand that your aunt was *murdered*? It doesn't seem to have made much of an impact on you."

She's taken aback by his bluntness. She blinks and tries to speak but can't. Shame, a familiar companion, washes over her. She attempts again to speak, to explain, but nothing comes out. It occurs to her there is no explanation.

She bows her head, and at last the tears burst past the lump that has been wedged in her throat all day. She ugly cries silently, stomach twisting, shoulders heaving, nose running. Aunt Millicent was the one adult in her life who was constant, giving, loving. She understood Sloane's brokenness and the need to distance herself from their hometown. Her aunt's letters were filled with regret, yes, but also with understanding and even encouragement for her niece's new life. Somewhere in her hardened heart, Sloane thought she'd have time to thank her.

But time ran out.

Chapter 10

Despite her earlier nap, Sloane is drained by the time Margaret delivers her and Robroy to the beach house on Monday evening. Her eyes are swollen and gritty, her makeup smeared. She steps wearily into the balmy air, traces of jessamine wafting as its blooms fade. The scent of her childhood, fleeing, just as she did. As her mother did.

Elsie and Jesse have left loads of plastic-wrapped food on the counters and in the refrigerator, and Margaret efficiently whisks some into the freezer and some into fabric bags for her family. She makes sure there is plenty to carry Robroy and Sloane through the week.

Sloane didn't eat much at the reception, so she's famished after the questioning at the police station. She pulls out a casserole that looks promisingly like lasagna and puts two slices of rye bread in the toaster.

"Weird combo," says Robroy, cracking open a beer and leaning against the kitchen counter.

"Don't you want some?"

"Nah. I filled up earlier."

She looks longingly at a drink cart where several neighbors have left bottles of wine. But the last thing she needs is to get sleepy. Instead, she brews a pot of coffee.

Robroy raises the window over the kitchen sink. The breeze lifts the hair that flops over his forehead, and he tosses his head in a practiced move to keep it out of his eyes. They stand for a moment, gazing at the white caps and skittering sand kicked up by the wind.

"The beach seems wider than I remember," she remarks.

"It is," he says, squinting at the view. "Storms have eroded Garden City and Hunting Island and other places. But some beaches, like here and Fripp, are getting the benefit. More sand. At Fripp they've had to build walkways over canals and scrub to get to the beach."

"Huh. No wonder the developer is so hot for this house."

"Yep. It's a prime spot, no doubt about it."

She turns to her brother. "Aunt Millicent really didn't tell you she was leaving you the house? Or half the house?"

"She really didn't. Which is odd because we talked a lot about development. She did *not* want the town developed. And she knew you and I had no intention of coming back here. I guess blood won out."

"Maybe she didn't care about development so much if she wasn't here to witness it." Sloane transfers a plate from the microwave to the table, and Robroy joins her, fitting his tall frame into the bay nook. Up close, his eyes are bloodshot too. She butters the rye toast and takes a bite of lasagna, groaning with pleasure. The island cooks haven't lost their touch.

She doesn't want to talk about what happened to their aunt, doesn't want to revisit the emotions that swamped her at the police station. But they have to. "So, what do you think?" she asks.

He sighs. "About who would kill Aunt Millicent?"

"Yeah."

He shakes his head and rocks his bottle on the table. "I have no idea. The only new element in her life was that Jacksonville developer getting hold of Camp Resurrection after all these years. People knew that you would sell as soon as you inherited. So maybe someone wanted to hurry that sale along?"

Her stomach knots at his frankness, but then something occurs to her. "You don't think Aunt Millicent added you as beneficiary hoping you'd block the sale, do you?"

Robroy leans back and idly scratches a knee. "I think she'd have told me, if that's what she wanted. Did you ever know her to hold back?"

"I haven't seen her in a long time," she admits.

They sit in silence, as Sloane wolfs the lasagna. "At some point," she says, "we also need to talk about Margaret. Do we want to give her a third of the estate?"

Robroy peels the label off his beer. "I'd like to know more about why Aunt Millicent excluded her."

"You don't think it was because she and Joel already have enough money?"

"Maybe."

Sloane peers at him. "What are you not saying?"

"I'm not sure that Aunt Millicent was crazy about Idelle and J.C. Simpson. Maybe she didn't like the idea of her estate going into the Simpson empire."

"Oh. You never know about small towns, do you?" She takes another bite. "Why didn't she like them?"

"I'm not entirely sure. But I was here once when Idelle's picture was on the cover of the *Beaufort Gazette* for the opening of a gas station. Aunt Millicent rolled her eyes and muttered something like, 'Great. Let's attract more trash.' I asked her, 'You mean like in her parking lots?' She said, 'I mean like her.'"

"Harsh."

He shrugs. "They're lifetime islanders. No telling what's in their history."

"But on a practical note, somebody's got to empty this house. We can't expect Margaret to do it while we run off with the money."

"Well, Raeford's the executor. He'll get paid for that, right? So if Margaret empties the house, she will too. Or maybe we hire one of those estate auctioneers." Robroy pauses. "But the fact that Aunt Millicent added me shows that she hadn't forgotten about her will. She actively changed it. And she still didn't include Margaret."

Sloane didn't think of that. She studies Robroy's lean face, a muscle pulsing steadily at his jawline. *Does he know something I don't? Or suspect it, anyway?*

"I tell you what," he says. "While you're working, let me poke around Aunt Millicent's study. I might find some clue to her thinking."

She stands to take her dishes to the sink. "Sounds like a plan."

As Sloane returns the casserole to the refrigerator, she discovers a pitcher of Jesse's iced tea. Nothing is more reminiscent of an island summer than the sugary drink, so she pours a glass and takes it to Robroy in the study. He closes a desk drawer and points. "See that?"

A hardback copy of *Girl, Lost* stands upright on the corner of the desk. It feels like an "attagirl" from her aunt.

Robroy takes his tea to the porch to watch the sun set, while Sloane opens her laptop on the kitchen table and reads over what she wrote earlier for the graduation speech. It's as pedestrian as she remembers.

Her mind wanders to her aunt, lying alone in a room at the island hospital. Chief Hartwell didn't explain exactly what happened, but she overheard other officers at the police station refer to "those killer nurse cases." She'd watched a series on TV, and a nurse had randomly injected killing doses into saline bags. *Did someone target Aunt Millicent using the same method? Did she know what was happening? Was she frightened?*

Sloane tries to concentrate on the speech, but she keeps seeing bland hospital walls and her aunt lying defenseless amid white sheets. *Who would want her dead? The developer who wants this house?* The thought is too horrible to contemplate, and Sloane's mind skitters from it like a Lowcountry lizard.

She jerks her attention back to the speech. Every high school, college, and university has a graduation speaker. That's a given. But why was she specifically invited to deliver the one at Warner College? *Because of my book. So I should include something from the book. Not the traumatic episodes, certainly, but maybe something toward the end. Something hopeful and inspiring from when Murphy has emerged on the other side.* She slumps. *Girl, Lost* is not particularly hopeful, even at the end.

Nonetheless, she ought to take a look. She returns to her aunt's study, light and airy with three walls painted lilac and one given over to white shelves. There's a comfy couch where her aunt napped, and above it, in pride of place, a watercolor portrait of this house. *Millicent House* reads the artist's cursive title. The angled view is from the front, not the beach side, and less tangled vegetation surrounds the house than what currently covers the lawn. Built in 1903 by Aunt Millicent's grandfather, the exterior is the same cool white with coral shutters that her aunt retained. Sloane knows from her tea and history lessons that Aunt Millicent was born in the house, but Sloane's mother, who came along later, was born in the hospital in Beaufort.

She runs her fingers along her aunt's beloved books—kept separate from the century-old collection in the library. These spines are aligned neatly and grouped into biographies, mysteries, and women's fiction. On the bottom row are children's books. Sloane remembers lying on her stomach to pick out *Goodnight, Moon* and *Where the Wild Things Are* and countless Berenstain Bear adventures. On the end, its green, red, and white cover peeling as a result of bumpy travels all over the house and yard, is her all-time favorite, *How the Grinch Stole Christmas*.

Smiling, she tugs it from its perch. A single sheet of paper flutters to the floor.

Last Will and Testament, she reads.

Too shocked to pick it up, she notes the date—April of this year. Four weeks ago. Her eyes dart to the section titled Dispensation of Property.

Disbelieving what's written there, she yells, "Robroy!"

She hears the screen door clatter then her brother's footsteps.

"What? What is it?"

She scrabbles for the paper and hands it to him, her trembling hands causing it to rattle.

He skims it, jaw dropping. "She's leaving everything *to Mom*? This must be old. Raeford said she rewrote her will after Mom had been gone seven years."

"Look at the date."

"Oh." He is silent, an expression of bafflement on his face. "I don't understand."

"How was Aunt Millicent's mind the last time you saw her? Any sign of dementia?"

"No," he says, almost angrily. "Not at all. She was sharp as a tack. You'd know that if..." He stops, but she knows what comes after. One more family member is disgusted by her long absence.

She shoves away her hurt feelings and concentrates on the paper he's holding. It appears to be a standard form obtained from the internet and filled in with Aunt Millicent's tidy handwriting. She has enough of her handwritten letters to know that much.

"Aunt Millicent thought Mom was alive," she says in disbelief. "But why wouldn't she go through Raeford if she wanted to write a new will?"

"No idea."

"We've got to call him."

"Ye-e-s." Robroy is clearly hesitant.

"I hear a 'but' in there."

He runs a hand through his hair. "'But' there goes our inheritance. Four point whatever million dollars each. Poof. Gone."

She studies his face. Surely, he's not suggesting they hide this. But he leads a nomadic, low-earning life. Every penny his band earns goes to travel expenses. The inheritance would mean even more to him than to her. And heaven knows, it would mean a lot to her. She could quit teaching, for one thing. No more Dr. Avery. No more grades. No more speech deadlines. Just writing, free and clear. Precious few writers have that luxury.

She takes a shuddering breath. The money is not what has shaken her about this document. It's the corollary: Aunt Millicent thought her sister—Sloane's mother—was alive. She can't let her thoughts go there.

"Well, dead women can't inherit, can they?" she says flippantly, recalling Raeford and Aunt Millicent's efforts to find her mother in the months and years following her disappearance. "It'll revert to us."

She grabs her cell phone from her pocket before they can go down this dark road that her brother is hinting at. He doesn't protest as she calls Raeford.

Raeford doesn't answer, so she leaves a message. "Hey, this is Sloane. Robroy and I found what looks like a new will in Aunt Millicent's study. Dated four weeks ago." She pauses, trying to remember if the *Grinch* was slightly out of line from the other books on its shelf. *Maybe.* "Um, she left it in my favorite childhood book. I think she knew I'd find it. Anyway, one of us will bring it to you tomorrow, if that's all right. I'll be up late if you want to talk."

Robroy shrugs as she disconnects. "Well, that's that, I guess. It was good to be rich for three days."

"You didn't order a Rolls, did you?" When he doesn't respond, she adds, "Robroy, there's no way Mom is coming back. Not after all this time."

She remembers why she came into the study and snatches her novel from the desk. Beside it lies a copy of Claire Matturro's *The Smuggler's Daughter.* Aunt Millicent recommended this book in her last letter. Set in Florida, its cover features a boat eerily like Robert Cheney's, anchored in a coastal waterway like the one where they grew up. Sloane nipped it to take back to Atlanta. "Millionaire or pauper, I've got to finish this speech," she says. "Poke around all you want."

Robroy's eyes jump from the bookshelves to their aunt's desk. "Yeah, I might."

Chapter 11

Sloane spends a fruitless half hour flipping through *Girl, Lost* without finding a passage to fit into her speech. Maybe this is a bad idea.

She's almost relieved to hear a thud on the house's front porch. It must be her intern, Sam. She carries her coffee the full length of the entry hall and throws open the front door. No one is there.

"Sam?" she calls uneasily. "Is that you?"

A rustle behind a giant magnolia is the only answer. *Where is Sam? For that matter, where is Robroy?* She recalls Mack Sanderson's antagonism and Kent Espey's caution about residents' warring visions for their town.

With the porchlight on, she's in full view of anyone standing in the dark trees that crowd the front yard. Stepping onto the porch, she squints into the gloom of the long driveway and makes out a shape that could be a truck. *But why is it so far away?* She hears another rustle and backs slowly toward the doorway. "Robroy!" she shouts over her shoulder, not taking her eyes off the magnolia.

She hears nothing from within the house. Her heel hits the doorjamb, and she trips, dropping the coffee mug. It hits the porch's old floorboards and bounces, splashing coffee. She glances down, and in that moment, a figure detaches itself from the magnolia's low branches. She screams.

The old man holds up his hands in supplication. He doesn't say a word. He doesn't have to. Her body remembers and goes rigid. Her throat can scarcely utter the word, and it comes out as a choked whisper.

"Dad."

Robroy, drawn by Sloane's second yell of the evening, tumbles through the doorway. He quickly takes them in. "Dad, what are you doing here?"

Their father walks into the circle of porchlight, far below them in the yard. He doesn't have the skin for a shrimper, but rather an Irish fairness that burns and freckles, burns and freckles. His wispy hair is yellow-white, and his face is ruddy and lined beyond his years. His voice carries the rasp of decades of cigarettes.

He coughs and stares at his daughter. "Sloane, you are the spitting image of your mama." He swipes a palm across his eyes. She touches the wild mane piled messily on her head. It's the way her mother wore her hair during the island's hot summers.

They wait awkwardly to see if he's going to answer Robroy, but he doesn't. "I'm, uh, sorry. About your aunt."

Robroy walks down the steps and embraces their father briefly, but Sloane remains frozen. *How long has it been since I touched my father? Decades.*

"What are you doing here?" Robroy repeats.

Their father shuffles his worn boots on the driveway's crushed shells. "I guess I just wanted to pay my respects. I always... admired Millicent."

Robroy turns to Sloane and mouths, "Invite him in?"

She shakes her head in a vigorous no.

Her father must catch the exchange. "Well, that's all I wanted to say. I'll be on my way." He starts up the driveway then turns back to Robroy. "You want to stop by the house? Tomorrow?"

"Yeah, I'll do that."

"Okay. 'Night." With one more glance at Sloane, he heads into the shadows.

She and Robroy enter the house, and she closes the door, leans against it.

Robroy regards her silently. "Not ready to forgive him?"

"No." She lifts her shoulders. "I saw too much. Way too much." When Robroy doesn't respond, she adds, "He robbed us of our mother, you know."

Robroy looks stricken, and she is immediately remorseful. "Look, I know he's the only real parent you've known. And if he was good to you, I'm grateful. Truly and sincerely grateful." She pauses, but she can't leave it at that. "But what he did to her, Robroy. He left her no choice."

Robroy shrugs and returns to the study. But her father's appearance has raised a question, slippery and dark. *Could he know something about the will we discovered tonight?* Because despite her assurance to her brother that their absent mother's inheritance would revert to them, would it? Or would it go to the husband she never divorced?

Chapter 12

Sloane's cell phone song—once pleasing, now irritating—signals that Dr. Avery is calling. Again. It's past ten at night, and she hasn't sent him the graduation speech. Instead of answering, she shoots him an email. "Rough speech is on its way. Very rough. Five minutes."

She has moved some words around but is basically no further than she was two hours ago. Which is no further than she was yesterday. Or the day before.

Oh, well. She's her own worst critic. Maybe it's not as hopeless as she thinks.

Before she can hit Send, there's another thud on the porch. The hair on the back of her neck bristles. *Has my father returned?* But then the doorbell chimes.

She hurries to the door and is met by a golden Lab nudging and pushing at her legs. "Careful, Sophie," Sam calls as he pulls a duffle bag, dog food, and leash from the car. "Her best friend is a Chihuahua, and she thinks she is too," he explains. "She'll calm down in a minute."

Sloane opens the door wide, and Sophie bounds inside. She hears Robroy happily greeting the Lab in the kitchen; their father always had a hunting dog or two around their place.

"Am I glad to see you!" she says sincerely as Sam mounts the porch stairs. His brown hair is unfashionably long, but his face is clean-shaven. Wearing his all-weather wardrobe of flannel shirt, jeans, and hiking boots, he looks like every male grad student at

Warner. She slides his laptop from its grip under one arm. "You can pick a room anywhere you'll be comfortable working."

"I can start tonight," he says gamely.

"No, you've had a monster drive. Let's get you something to eat and a good night's sleep. You can start on those exams in the morning."

Sam drops his overnight bag and stretches. "Sounds good. Where do I sleep?"

"This way." She leads him up the staircase to the peach-colored room she'd inspected earlier. "You can have this one."

"Nice," says Sam, taking in the queen-size bed and bright décor. "This overlooks the beach, doesn't it?"

"Yes, and the sun's pretty bright in the morning. It'll wake you up."

"Okay if Sophie sleeps in here too?"

"Of course. But beware. My brother's a dog lover. He'll try to lure her to his room."

Sam laughs. "He's welcome to walk her if he likes."

"Actually, that's a good idea. We'll meet him in a minute. But first, I want to show you the *piece de resistance*. The reason you'll thank me despite all your hard work."

He laughs and follows her as she throws open the doors to the balcony. Lights twinkle from Shark Island down the beach and from Fripp and Harbor in the distance. A nearly full moon stripes the ocean in undulating bands. "Wow," he whispers. "I see what you mean."

They pass the Adirondack chairs and lean on the chest-high railing to enjoy the magnetic pull of the ocean. Sloane senses a tremor instantly and glances around to see if the palms or the house itself is quaking. She hears a crack and stumbles, off balance, but her mind is more confused than alarmed. Another crack pierces the night, this one louder, and Sloane staggers as the railing jerks from her grasp.

She turns, stunned, to see Sam teetering toward the darkness, arms pinwheeling, mouth open in shock. Too frightened to scream, she hurls herself sideways, grabbing desperately for Sam's shirttail. Her weight is enough to yank him from the precipice, and they land in a heap, watching in horror as the rail gives way and crashes onto the lawn below.

She and Sam lie silently for a moment, their panicked breath the only sound. They hear the pounding of footsteps, and Robroy and Sophie burst through the French doors. "Keep the dog away," Sloane chokes out.

But Sophie noses Sam and whimpers, not venturing to the balcony's edge. Grasping the dog's collar with one hand, Sam rolls off Sloane and inches toward the house, his other hand awkwardly tugging at Sloane's flimsy tank. Robroy clutches her under the arms and lurches into Sam's room, trembling as badly as they are. As soon as they are safely inside, he slams and bolts the doors, his face dead white. Her upper arm, bruised by Mack Sanderson, aches when he grips it, but he looks so frightened she doesn't protest.

"What happened?" he demands, his voice quivering.

"The rail," she says, rubbing her throbbing hip. "It gave way. Sam almost... Sam almost fell."

"Sloane caught me," Sam says, hugging his dog's neck. "I was a goner."

She wants to contradict him, but she recalls his arms flailing, his weight tipping into dark nothingness. He was shaken enough to use her first name. Her breath comes out in a shudder.

"Was it rotten, you think?" says Robroy. "Burle probably hasn't had time to repair things for the season."

She shakes her head adamantly. "I was out there this afternoon, and everything looked freshly painted. Burle wouldn't have painted over rotted wood."

"You're right," he agrees. He blows out a shaky breath. "We can look it over in the morning. A whole section of the railing fell into the yard. I heard it."

Sam smiles gamely and holds out his hand. "It's a little late for introductions, but I'm Sam Kinnecky."

"Robroy Cheney. Man, I can't tell you how sorry I am this happened in your first five minutes here. Or that it happened at all, for that matter."

"No harm done. Thanks to Sloane."

The three of them hobble to their feet and head through the upper hallway and down the staircase. Sophie recovers a massive bone at the bottom of the steps and begins chomping on it. "We found this in the fridge," Robroy says. "I hope it was all right to let her have it."

"It's fine. She's a canine garbage disposal."

Suddenly, the adrenaline that surged on the balcony deserts Sloane, and she sighs with exhaustion. Leading Sam to the kitchen, she shows him the contents of the stuffed refrigerator and urges him to help himself. Then her cell phone rings, and adrenaline and dread spike simultaneously.

"Oh, shit. I didn't send the speech to Dr. Avery." She ignores the phone once more and rushes to her laptop, typing a note of apology above the attachment. Her hands are unsteady, and she has to correct several misspellings. Then she hits Send.

She's not happy with the speech, but her mind doesn't have the space to worry about it.

Chapter 13

Tuesday

The sound of a barking dog wakes Sloane, and she claws to confused consciousness. She glances around her old pink bedroom, a place where she always felt safe. A white desk is topped by a matching bookshelf, stuffed with titles from her middle and high school years. *Are You There God? It's Me, Margaret. The Pinballs. Catcher in the Rye. To Kill a Mockingbird.*

Then reality lands like a grenade: Aunt Millicent is dead. Not only dead but murdered. And she and Sam could've died last night, hurtling from a three-story height and bouncing off a pointed cupola.

An emotion is tugging at her as well. It feels like a wrecking ball on her chest, heavy, unfamiliar, aching. It's an emotion she hasn't allowed herself to feel for years. But she recognizes it: She misses Aunt Millicent in the same way she once missed her mother. She has behaved horribly, staying away for twelve years, thinking she had time to make it up to her. What could have happened to the fierce woman she knew? How had someone gotten past her formidable self as well as past Raeford and Octavia and Burle and Jesse and Margaret and the Simpson clan? And then, of course, the chilling upshot: *Was it me? With my vehement renouncement of the property, was I the impetus for the killer to strike?*

And the railing? What if her aunt had leaned on it, as was her custom during good weather? *Is that exactly what someone intended?*

The question that follows is a black eel that slips in, uninvited: *What if it was one of Aunt Millicent's inner circle, somehow in league with the developer who wants this house?*

Sloane swings her feet to the plush white rug, her hip protesting its smash into the balcony, and gingerly makes her way to the large bathroom between her bedroom and Robroy's. His shaving kit appears to have exploded across the counter, so he's already up. She takes a quick shower and dresses in gray leggings and a sleeveless gray-and-yellow tunic that will be appropriate for police visits, Raeford's law office, a meeting with the developer, whatever else the day holds. She applies sunscreen, mascara, and lipstick and slides into black ballet flats.

In the kitchen, the coffee carafe is full, so she helps herself. She wanders to the back porch and sees Robroy and Sam inspecting jagged pieces of painted wood and gleaming spindles that lie scattered across the grass. Robroy looks up. "It was cut through," he says quietly, picking up segments of wood and showing her two flat surfaces. "When this piece gave way, it pulled that other section that's splintered."

Sam picks up a spindle. "And I don't think these were anchored with screws or glue. I think they were wedged between the boards above and below them."

"Who would do that?" She walks out past the grass and onto the sand then turns to gaze up at the balcony. It looks impossibly high from here, and the rail-less floor jutting into empty space causes her to shiver. She reaches for her phone and hits the number for Police Chief Dan Hartwell that she entered yesterday.

"He wants us to leave everything exactly as it is," she informs Sam and Robroy after speaking with the chief. "He and those detectives were already on their way to search the house."

Robroy takes Sam's dog for a gallop on the beach, while Sam returns to his place at the dining room table, notebook pages spread around him. "Three down, nineteen to go," he announces, pulling his hair into a low ponytail.

"You got an early start."

"Yeah, it was easy with that sun glinting off the ocean." He reaches for a folded newspaper lying on a dining room chair. "Robroy said you'd want to see this."

It's *The Greenbrier Herald,* which she wouldn't have expected down here. Sam taps the section headed *Lowcountry Edition.* At the top is a picture of Aunt Millicent, dressed in a lavender suit and matching hat, taken at what must have been a ladies' luncheon in Beaufort. Or maybe Charleston. She looks regal, even a touch haughty.

Sloane smiles. "That's my aunt to a T." She picks up the paper, and out of long habit, scans the byline. *Can that be right?*

"Robroy said you know the writer," Sam says.

She does. Elijah Cartwright. Her college boyfriend.

E li's family lived in the farming community of Pickens, an hour outside Greenbrier. They took Sloane in for holidays throughout freshman year, never probing as to why she wasn't going home, never making her feel anything but welcome. The summer after that first year, she took a job on the obit desk of the *Herald* and rented a cheap apartment on Greenbrier's unfashionable south side; the subsequent part-time hours during the school year allowed her to keep it all through college.

Eli eventually followed her onto the *Herald* staff, but unlike Sloane, he stayed and made a career of it. From the number of his bylines on this section front, he is possibly the *Herald's* entire Lowcountry bureau.

"Beach town Millicent's matriarch murdered" reads the headline. Millicent Roundtree may not have been a biological matriarch, but she was mother to the entire town. Eli's story has more information than Sloane learned yesterday.

He hits the development angle hard. Developer Ryan Carbonier is headquartered in Jacksonville, Florida, and Eli lays out his successful campaign to get Camp Resurrection from the Baptists and his desire to make the historic Millicent House a boutique hotel. Millicent Roundtree resisted, and now that she is dead, her heirs will decide the fate of the sleepy seaside village.

Eli quotes a Charleston city planner on responsible development in other island communities. Folly, Edisto, and Sullivan's Islands have kept a semblance of character, in the planner's opinion, while Isle of Palms and Fripp have gotten too crowded, too pricey, too generic. Who knows which way Millicent will go?

Eli acknowledges the quaint vision of Carbonier's Mayberry by the Sea but points out that a picturesque downtown will not prevent adjacent areas from out-of-control growth. *Once the camel's nose is in the tent...* and so forth.

Sloane skims back to a section that quotes Chief Hartwell. He tried to be cagey, but Eli got him to acknowledge that Aunt Millicent's death was almost assuredly murder and not medical error. She reads the article through again.

"That must be awfully good," Sam remarks.

"No. Yes. Well, it's got some stuff I didn't know." She grabs her coffee. "So, are you all right with these, or do you need help?"

Sam holds up the handwritten instructions she'd left with the test papers. "You were pretty clear about the points you want to see. But feel free to check behind me."

Already her mind is moving away from the finals. She trusts Sam. There was a single student in each of her classes who showed genuine writing promise, and she'd already given them extensive feedback. These grades are the last hurdle until graduation on Saturday.

She plans to spend the day on revisions for her second novel, revisions that were originally due at the end of March. When her editor granted a two-month extension, it had sounded like a lifetime. But now she's staring at a deadline less than two weeks away and a manuscript that refuses to submit.

Her editor had initially suggested a sequel to *Girl, Lost*, but that's not what Sloane wrote. She didn't want to return to that bleak time or to her self-obsessed protagonist, Murphy. Despite the character's surprise success in both literary and commercial circles—and Sloane doesn't take either for granted—she is a part of Sloane's past that she's ready to relinquish. Indeed, Sloane has seen flashes of her on this trip—and in Jesse's eyes. She doesn't want to be that girl.

She turns back to the kitchen, eager to reenter the northeast Georgia setting of her new manuscript but knowing she's got to deal with this broken rail business first. The doorbell rings. "I'll get it!" she calls to Sam and makes her way down the dim, cool hallway. Chief Hartwell stands with the two sheriff's detectives from yesterday. Behind the white SUV with navy lettering that proclaims Millicent Police Department, a gray Cadillac SUV rolls up. Raeford.

The three officers wait for Raeford to follow them up the porch steps. His gait is slow, but his posture erect. Surely, he's here about last night's phone call, but he doesn't mention it in front of the officers. Instead, he asks, "Both the Millicent Police *and* the Beaufort County Sheriff's Office are looking into Millicent's death?"

"I requested their help," says the chief, leading the way as the deputies' eyes rise appreciatively to the grand staircase. When they pass the dining room, Sloane introduces Sam. They hear a commotion in the kitchen and find Robroy wrestling to clean the sand off Sophie's paws. The Lab happily noses the detectives, who smile for the first time.

"What do you want to see first?" Sloane asks.

"Let's start with the railing," says the chief. "Then we'll get to Miss Roundtree's study and bedroom."

"Railing?" says Raeford. "What's this, Sloane?"

Chief Hartwell indicates that she is to fill everyone in, so she recounts last night's near-miss then leads them into the yard where the wooden pieces reveal that some have been cut and some ripped. Chief Hartwell turns to one of the detectives. "Could you find Burle Jenkins and see if Miss Roundtree hired any contractors recently? He would know. If not, did he work on that balcony himself?"

Sloane starts to sputter in defense of Burle, but Chief Hartwell waves her words aside. "Miss Cheney, we're going up to look at the balcony. We'll be right back."

Sloane stares after the officers. "Don't worry," Raeford assures her. "Chief Hartwell is the real deal. He came to us from Charlotte, where he was well respected. We've found him to be levelheaded. And fair."

"But Burle? He can't think Burle did this."

Raeford's rumbling drawl is reassuring. "He's not going to railroad Burle, Sloane. I can guarantee you that. But you want him to keep an open mind."

Robroy pours the lawyer a cup of coffee, and the three gather at the kitchen window.

Raeford lowers his voice. "Can you show me the document you found last night?"

"You don't want Chief Hartwell to see it?" Sloane asks.

"No, he'll have to. But I want to get a look first."

"I left it on Aunt Millicent's desk," Robroy says. "Let me grab it." He returns within seconds, the paper in his hand.

Raeford reads it, his face blanching. "Annie?" he says in disbelief. "What made Millicent think we could find Annie after all this time? Or that she's even alive?"

"Beats us," Sloane answers. "Aunt Millicent never gave you any hint she was changing her will?"

"None at all. This is most unlike her."

They hear footsteps overhead, then Chief Hartwell rejoins them in the kitchen, his brow furrowed. "We're not sure what we're dealing with yet regarding that railing," he says. "Criminal negligence on the part of workmen or an earlier attempt on Miss Roundtree's life. But we'll get to the bottom of it. For now, we need to search the house."

"One more thing, Chief," says Raeford. "Sloane and Robroy found this."

He hands the one-page will to Hartwell, who skims it quickly. "You found this when?" he demands.

"Late last night," Sloane answers. "It was in my favorite children's book."

"So that's why you're here, Raeford? You knew about this?"

"I didn't until Sloane called me."

"This contradicts the will Miss Roundtree had you draw up, correct?"

Raeford nods solemnly. "She and Robert Cheney had Annie declared dead. Years ago."

The chief eyes Sloane and Robroy. "What do you two make of this? Have you been in touch with your mother?"

Robroy's eyes widen, and Sloane starts to stammer. "Not a word," she swears, hearing the bitterness in her tone. "Not a single word in twelve years."

The chief remains silent, so she offers to show him to the study. He demurs. "I know where it is. Your aunt had me out here this winter."

Raeford looks as puzzled as Sloane feels. "What about?" she asks.

The chief's black eyes stare a hole in her, and she fights to hold his gaze. Finally, he relents. "She wanted me to find your mother. She said she'd made a terrible mistake and Annie Cheney was alive."

On one side of her, Robroy gapes. On the other, Raeford protests, "Not possible."

But Sloane's heart is spluttering with a feeling it hasn't had in years. Way past the anger, the disbelief, the hardness, a tiny flicker of something else. She recognizes it as hope.

"Why?" she demands. "What made her think that?"

"A letter," he says. "She claimed to have a letter. That's what we're looking for."

Chapter 14

Sloane rushes to the doorway of Aunt Millicent's study, Chief Hartwell close behind. One deputy, wearing plastic gloves, is painstakingly removing each book from her aunt's shelves and shaking it. The other is going through a wooden filing cabinet. "Nothing yet," says the latter.

Sloane whirls to face the chief. "Did you see it? The letter? Did she show you?"

"No."

"Why not?"

He runs a hand through his hair. "I wish now I'd insisted," he admits. "But Miss Roundtree was adamant. She said the letter was personal. But she gave me the return address, your mother's Social Security number, things like that."

Robroy speaks, his voice tight. "And did you find her?"

"No. I made calls and went back to the file from the private investigator your aunt hired twelve years ago. Even called him. But no, we didn't find anything. The return address was a fake, belonged to an elderly woman in St. Louis who'd never heard of Annie Cheney."

"But what did the letter say?" Sloane's voice rises. "What did the writer want?"

The chief shrugs. "Your aunt kept saying it was personal. I gathered her sister wanted to come home, but that was a guess."

Raeford shakes his head. "I wish Millicent had confided in me. We could've tried another investigator."

Sloane turns to Robroy, not caring who hears her. "And you didn't find anything in her desk?"

The chief looks up sharply. "So you two have been through her study?"

"Slightly," she replies. "After we found that will, we wondered if there was anything to back it up."

Robroy shrugs. "I only made it through two desk drawers. Nothing there."

Chief Hartwell speaks to his colleagues. "You two keep going. Yell if you find anything. I'll start on her bedroom."

Sloane silently leads Dan Hartwell up the staircase then left onto the landing. Aunt Millicent's bedroom takes up the entire beach-facing left side of the hall, twice the size of the guest room Sam occupies. She stands in the doorway, staring at the old-fashioned wallpaper of climbing lilac that echoes the color of the study. Beyond the double glass doors, the ocean sparkles and yellow police tape flaps against shards of broken wood. Chief Hartwell heads straight for Aunt Millicent's bedside table.

"Do you want any help?" she asks.

"No, please leave everything as it is. Everywhere. If we don't find what we're looking for, we'll extend the search to other rooms."

"Got it."

Sloane walks slowly down the staircase, thinking hard about her father's visit the night before. *Could he know about the will naming his wife as beneficiary?* That would be a huge motive for wanting Aunt Millicent out of the way. When she locates Robroy and Raeford in the kitchen, she's made a decision.

"You still going to see Dad?" she asks her brother. "I need to go with you."

Chapter 15

They take Robroy's vintage van that could only belong to a rock 'n' roller. Or a drug dealer.

After winding through the low-lying interior of Millicent Island, the tide at times within feet of their tires, they pull into a sandy drive marked by a giant water oak. A hound dog, black and tan and white, bounds out to greet them as they approach their father's fishing shack. "Bubba!" Robroy shouts. "Where's your sister, big boy?"

Sloane raises her eyebrows, and he explains, "Dad got him and his sister Lily from the same litter. They're always together."

Bubba barks and races along the side of the house. Unpainted and ramshackle, it sits on the tidal creek that meanders through the island. The yard is sandy, pockmarked with scrub oak and one early blooming oleander in hot pink.

"Man's trash can't overcome God's beauty," Sloane whispers, hearing her mother in her head. "When did he move out here?" Their childhood home was no great shakes, but it was better than this.

"Soon after Mom left. Turns out our old house was Roundtree property that Mom and Dad were renting. Dad said he wasn't living on her family's charity."

Sloane is struck by a vision of her ten-year-old brother in this hardscrabble yard. "Robroy, you lived here?"

"It looked a lot better then," he assures her. "And I spent a lot of time with Jesse and Burle's families, and at Margaret and Joel's. And a lot of nights with Scotty Espey. His mom and dad were great."

Sloane recalls that the Espeys weren't at Aunt Millicent's funeral reception. "But you had some kind of disagreement with them?"

Robroy turns to look at her. "Where'd you hear that?"

"Kent."

He relaxes. "Yeah, that was much later. Scotty and I fought. Over a girl." He grins. "The delectable Rachel Abercrombie. Whatcha gonna do?"

Sloane returns her attention to the derelict shack. Her expression is so stricken that Robroy elbows her.

"It's all right, Sloane. Honestly." He smiles again. "But now you see why a coupla mil looked so appealing."

"Yeah, I get it." She gazes around the scraggly property, noting that windchimes have been placed incongruously in the trees. "Does someone live here with him?"

"From time to time, I imagine. He had a bartender girlfriend for several years. But she finally left."

"So where is he? I thought he asked you to come by today."

"Well, his truck is here." Robroy points to the far side of the yard. "And he's not on the boat without Bubba. He must be inside."

They climb the warped wooden stairs. The right handrail is sun-cracked and splintering, the left gone entirely. Sloane treads carefully, fearful of plunging through the floorboards.

Robroy laughs. "If they hold Dad, they'll hold all of your hundred pounds."

"More than that," she murmurs, crossing the porch and opening the screen door. It takes a moment for her eyes to adjust to the dimness of the kitchen. An outdated calendar picturing a shrimp boat is the only adornment on the walls. An empty bottle of Woodford Reserve sits on the table, and a chair is overturned.

Robroy eyes the bourbon. "He's upped his brand. He usually goes for rotgut Rebel." He moves toward the bedrooms at the rear of the shack, calling for their father. He's back in moments. "He must be down at the dock."

They exit the way they came and circle the house. Another oleander struggles to provide beauty, but Robert Cheney's fish-cleaning table, two broken boats, and assorted engine parts spoil the attempt. Sure enough, Bubba is pacing the aged dock, where their father's shrimp boat is tied up. Another hound, presumably Lily, sits motionless in the yard, almost at the water line.

When they see Robroy, both animals whine deep in their throats. Bubba springs toward him then goes to Lily's side. Robroy reaches for Lily's head, patting gently. "What's the matter, girl?"

Sloane shades her eyes from the sun glinting off the inland waterway and watches a heron take off from high grass on the other side. The great white's body is reflected in the water, but then the bird is gone, and the reflection remains. She bends closer and realizes that the white in the water is hair, splayed out and floating gently. Then she sees the blue shirt. Their father is face down in the saltwater creek, not two feet from his own yard. She freezes, and Robroy pushes her out of the way.

"Dad!" he yells, splashing in and grabbing him around the torso. "Dad!" Sloane grabs a leg, and together, they haul him into his sandy yard. Bloated and gray, he is so clearly dead that even Robroy doesn't try resuscitation. He drops heavily and puts his arms around Lily, burying his face in the dog's fur. In a moment, his shoulders start to heave.

Sloane recalls the empty bourbon bottle and overturned chair. "He looked bad last night," she says. "Was he having liver issues?"

Robroy raises his head and blinks back tears. "No." He is nearly shouting. "No. He always drank, but he could handle it."

She sits beside her brother, feeling only detachment as she gazes at the drenched remains of Robert Cheney. He was the reason her mother left. He was the reason this island is no longer her home. He was the reason she treated Aunt Millicent so appallingly. She carries responsibility for that, surely, but if he had been anything like a normal father, perhaps she could have salvaged a normal life. She waits for the black hatred to descend, and for a moment, it does. But then it recedes, and she is left with only numbness, tiredness.

She drags out her phone, but instead of dialing 9-1-1, she locates Chief Hartwell's number on her list of recent calls. Still at Millicent House, he answers immediately.

"Chief Hartwell, this is Sloane. Robroy and I just found our father. It looks like he drowned in the inlet behind his house."

"Your *father*?" The chief's voice is disbelieving, but he apparently forces himself to calm down. "I'll send an ambulance, just in case. You two wait for me outside. Don't go in the house."

"We already did. We looked for him there first."

"Don't go back inside. We'll be right there."

Disconnecting, she stares at her father's unmoving form. Above them, the sky is blue, cloudless, gorgeous. A gull shrieks. A pelican dive-bombs for a fish. Beside her, Robroy takes a shuddering breath. "Is this family cursed?" he croaks.

Her laugh sounds harsh even to her own ears. "You have to ask?"

Chapter 16

Three hours later, Chief Hartwell, his officers, the coroner from Beaufort, and the ambulance have come and gone. Margaret, Robroy, and Sloane pull rickety kitchen chairs onto the front porch so, for Robroy's sake, they aren't facing the inlet. They have caught Margaret up on last night's near fiasco with the balcony railing, the puzzling new will, and today's discovery of their father's body. The tide has retreated, and the stink of pluff mud reaches them.

"Did you see Dad often?" Robroy asks Margaret.

"No. I could count on one hand the times he's met my girls."

"Damn, I'da thought you'd run into him at the grocery store more than that."

"Or the liquor store," she mutters. She turns to her brother, and something passes between them. "I'm glad you can grieve him," she says carefully. "But he was a nightmare to me and Sloane. I can't pretend otherwise, and I doubt she can either."

"Amen. He was no father to us in any real sense."

Robroy sighs. "Yeah, I know. But I guess he'd gotten old by the time I came along. He wasn't going to win Father of the Year, but he was okay. When he was sober." He swipes a hand across his eyes. "He bought me my first guitar."

The three of them stare into the early afternoon heat. A mosquito bites Sloane's arm, and she slaps it. A line of sweat trickles down her back, and she raises her humidity-plumped hair off her neck and holds it atop her head. This place is as miserable as Millicent House is grand. For the first time, she wonders what her father thought of his wife's family and their valuable holdings on the island. *Was he envious? Resentful? Was that behind his violence toward our mother?*

"The question is," she poses, "what did he want at the beach house last night? Could he have known about the will leaving everything to Mom?"

"I don't see how," Robroy says. "Not even Raeford knew."

"You didn't tell him?"

"When?" he cries. "I found out thirty minutes before he showed up!"

"You could've called him."

"But I didn't. Damn, Sloane, what is wrong with you?"

Margaret interjects before she can apologize. Or explain. Or make up an excuse. "Sloane makes a good point: Did he know about the will?" She looks sideways at her sister. "Is that why you came here with Robroy? I was wondering."

"Yes," she answers. "I thought it was too coincidental that he came by to 'pay his respects' last night. Then it turns out that Aunt Millicent supposedly received a letter from Mom and changed the will to give Millicent House to her. I think he found out. And if Mom is dead—or *still* dead," she adds sarcastically, "he thought he'd be next in line. Because they never officially got divorced."

Margaret wrinkles her brow. "Could he have been in touch with Mom?"

"No," Sloane says flatly. "He was the reason she left. He's the last person she'd contact. Besides, she must be dead. Just because Aunt Millicent was taken in by a fake letter doesn't mean we have to be." Despite her resolute words, her mind is at war and her stomach flips. *Which is worse? That my mother is dead? Or that she is alive and never contacted me?*

"One other thing," Margaret says, eyeing Robroy. "The railing."

Sloane catches on immediately, but Robroy doesn't. "What about it?" he asks.

"Dad?" is all she says. All she has to say.

Robroy's face crumples. "No way," he says softly. His gentleness is almost worse than his anger of a moment earlier. "He'd never do that."

"Aunt Millicent would never have let him set foot in the house," Sloane admits.

"But if she wasn't there?" asks Margaret. "It's pretty isolated."

"I suppose," she says slowly, "but Dad was not a planner. He just struck out in drunken rages, don't you think?"

Margaret sighs, dropping the subject. "So, what's next? I really don't feel up to another funeral extravaganza."

Sloane stares at her in alarm. "No, no, no, surely we don't have to do that again."

"Of course we do," Robroy interrupts. "Maybe not the whole reception thing, but some sort of service." He looks at them plaintively. "Please, Margaret."

She sighs. "I'll ask the rector. Dad wasn't a member of St. James, but he was married to a Millicent once upon a time."

Sloane thinks of all those disapproving faces from yesterday. And of Sam's body so nearly pinwheeling into space. She's not anxious to gather with the neighbors when she doesn't know who can be trusted. "Could we do something smaller? Maybe a graveside service?"

Robroy considers, and for the first time in hours, his face brightens. "Actually, that's a good idea. Dad never set foot in a church. It makes a lot more sense to have the whole thing outside. I'd even hold it on his dock, except for..." His shoulders sag.

Margaret grabs her chair to carry it back inside. "It's decided then. Graveside service. Family only. I'll try to schedule it for Thursday."

Nodding, Sloane picks up Robroy's chair along with hers. Margaret holds the screen door open, and she drops the chairs onto the old plank floor with a clatter. "Where's the bourbon bottle?" Sloane asks.

"What bottle?"

She looks in the trash can. "There was an empty bottle on the table when we got here. The police must've taken it."

"Why would they?" Margaret asks. "The autopsy will tell his blood alcohol level."

"Right," Sloane says slowly, swiveling to look around the depressing room. "They must be looking for something else."

It's a relief to leave their father's shack. With any luck, Sloane will never have to see it again.

She trails after Margaret as her sister heads to her glistening white BMW. "You know, it's great that you know all about buying and selling real estate from building your gas stations. Won't that make it easier to sell this place?"

"In other words, you expect me to deal with Dad's so-called 'estate.'"

"Well, it would make sense." Sloane sounds like she's kidding, but they both know she's not. "You *are* the oldest. *And* you live here."

"Sloane, can we get the man in the ground first?"

Margaret's words sting like a slap. She didn't like their father any more than Sloane did, but maybe she's perturbed about all the work they're foisting on her—first Aunt Millicent's estate and now their father's. Raeford can handle the legal transactions, but there will be furnishings to parse, cleanups to oversee. Sloane clamps her lips and nods. "Sure."

But she flips frantically through her mental calendar. If they bury their father on Thursday, that leaves only two days until she has to be in Atlanta for the graduation speech. *The one that isn't finished.* She doesn't dare tell Margaret what she's thinking. Her sister is annoyed enough as it is. And Robroy is seated, unmoving, in his van, grieving their father in a way she and Margaret won't.

She runs to join Robroy.

Maybe she can think more clearly back at the house. She believes that until the moment they pull into the driveway to find the Alleged Baby Stompers.

Robroy hops out to greet his bandmates, whose names Sloane confuses unless they're with their instruments. Sean Barnstable, bass guitar. Derek something, keyboards. Arturio Jenkins, drums. But why is she trying to remember their names like some inane hostess? *What the heck are they doing here?*

"Sloane!" her brother shouts. "Since we had to cancel this week's dates, the boys need a place to stay."

Her shock must show because Arturio jumps in. "Just until Friday, Sloane. Then we've got a two-night gig in Charleston. It comes with an apartment."

She looks at Robroy's face, alight at seeing his friends. Their three faces are turned to her, similarly expectant. Sweet Sean, quietest of the bunch. Bearded Derek, in ripped jeans and a shapeless black T-shirt. And the one she'll always think of as Little Arturio from his days trailing behind his great-uncle Burle at the Seafood Shack. There's certainly plenty of food for them.

"Yeah. Whatever." She stops. "But Arturio? You're not staying with your people?" *Listen to me. Your people. Twenty-four hours in this place and I'm talking like a Millicent.*

Arturio is the only other islander in the band, and she doesn't want to get on the bad side of his mother. "Not that you're not welcome," she adds. "I just don't want Miz Nadine coming after me."

Arturio grins. "Mama's got a full house. Her people are here from Philadelphia."

"Well, in that case, make yourselves at home. Robroy, you need to find them beds and clean sheets." Contrary to her words, she hears the unwelcoming flatness in her tone as she mounts the steps to the front porch. Of course, it sails right over the heads of the young men as they grab their suitcases and instruments and lean in to hear Robroy's news about his father.

She goes in search of Sam to warn him of the horde descending on them.

Chapter 17

Sloane locates a huge bowl of cut-up strawberries, pineapple, cantaloupe, and blueberries in the fridge and pairs it with chicken salad and wheat crackers. The chicken salad has walnuts and is no doubt Elsie's recipe from the diner. Robroy's friends are out on the beach with a cooler full of beer, a giant box of Cheez-Its, and the frisbee-loving Sophie. Murphy from *Girl, Lost* would've joined them. But it is Elle from As-Yet-Unnamed Book who has Sloane's attention.

Man, she loves this character. Unreliable and broken narrators are all the rage, and Murphy was certainly part of that trend. But Elle is healthy and wise, even witty, everything that Sloane is not. She loves spending time with her.

Sloane reads over a few chapters that *do* work before hitting the problem spots her editor has identified. Elle is rural Georgia born and bred. She's Sloane's age, 30, working in Atlanta as a commercial interior designer, practical and down-to-earth. She's kind, settled, happy in her work and relationships. She's who Sloane wants to be. Well, until the bomb goes off.

The idea for Elle's novel came from her friend Leah after the publication of *Girl, Lost*. "Have I got an idea for your next book," she'd said as they slid onto barstools for a mid-summer happy hour. Leah all but bounced on her backless seat. "Ready to hear it?"

Sloane was busy with interviews and readings and signings and hadn't done much more than contemplate where a sequel might take Murphy. Settling in with a spicy margarita, she played along. "Shoot."

"Well, last weekend, I went back home to visit my aunt in a nursing facility so my cousin could get a break. You remember where I'm from, right?"

"Americus?" Sloane said, naming a town in Georgia's endless midsection.

"Right. So I'd sit in her room for a while then go for a walk outside. It was nice out and kind of depressing inside, you know."

Sloane nodded, doubting she would set a novel in a depressing nursing home in Nowhere, Georgia.

"So, it's a triple room, and my aunt is in the bed by the window. A really old woman was in the middle, and the bed by the door was vacant when we arrived." Leah smiled conspiratorially and took a sip of her drink. "But then the nurses returned with the woman who had the bed by the door. She'd been getting tests or something. The nurses left, and the two women started talking. It sounded like they were old friends. Maybe even related. Or maybe they'd just been together in the nursing home for years. I don't know. But the one by the door started wailing, 'I miss my daddy!'"

Sloane set her cocktail on the bar. "These were very old women?"

"Yes. They couldn't have had living fathers for years. Decades. But she's crying, 'I miss my daddy! I miss my daddy!' On and on and on. The nurses didn't respond, which made me think they were used to it."

"So far, this is a ghastly story," Sloane said.

"It gets worse. So after about ten minutes, I couldn't stand it anymore and went outside and walked around. When I came back, the wailing woman had calmed down a little, but every few minutes, I'd hear, 'I miss my daddy.' Clearly, the poor soul had dementia."

Leah flicked her eyes around to make sure no one was close enough to hear her next words. "And the woman in the middle bed, the non-wailing woman, said, 'Didn't you tell me your daddy killed a whore?'"

Sloane choked on her drink, dripping orange dots on her white blouse. As she dabbed at it with a napkin, she demanded, "She said *what*?"

Leah nodded vigorously. "You heard it right," she said. "So, the wailing woman says, 'He did! He did that. He threw that girl off a bridge.'"

Leah sat back, slapping the bar.

"So then what?"

"Then nothing."

"They had no more conversation?"

"Well, more of the same. The wailing woman said, 'I know that ain't right, what he did. It weren't right! But I miss my daddy! I miss my daddy!' And we were back to that soundtrack."

Sloane sat up straight, appalled. "Did you report it?"

"To who?"

"I don't know. The nursing home owner? The sheriff? I don't know," she repeated.

"I thought about it, believe me. But if the woman's daddy did such a thing, he was long dead. And who knows how reliable her memory is? It could be a product of her dementia."

"Wow," Sloane said. "That is awful. But intriguing."

So intriguing, in fact, that it stayed with her. She had no desire to revisit Murphy, so she gratefully accepted Leah's gift. In her version, stable, good-hearted Elle visits her grandmother in a nursing home in their hometown of Royston, Georgia. She overhears the story Leah shared, but now all the participants are from one little town, and Elle believes it's possible to track the story down. In uncovering this murder from the 1940s, she comes face to face with a mystery that permeated her own family.

Now Sloane shivers as she rereads the chapter in which Elle meets the great-granddaughter of the murdered woman. Elle is confident in her own motives, sure the woman's descendant will want the truth revealed as much as she does. But it doesn't turn out that way.

The women's explosive encounter works, according to her editor. But Elle's subsequent swerve into self-doubt goes on for too long. Sloane hunkers down and begins the painful process of cutting, every excised sentence like a painful scrape of skin off her knuckles.

Her head is deep inside the dynamics of a family in northeast Georgia when Sam puts a hand on her shoulder. She startles and whips around, momentarily confounded by her surroundings. "Didn't you hear the doorbell?" he asks softly.

"Uhm, no. No, I didn't."

"The police chief is back."

"What? I spent all day with him."

Sam tilts his head to indicate Chief Hartwell standing in the kitchen doorway, well within hearing range. She sighs and stands, the deaths of Aunt Millicent and her father crashing back into her consciousness. "Sorry, I didn't mean to be rude." She waves a hand vaguely at the laptop. "I was—"

"We need to talk," Chief Hartwell says. "Privately."

Sam ducks into the dining room, and she trails the chief into the study, her head still swirling with images of the cotton fields and train tracks surrounding Royston, Georgia. The little town is as firmly Deep South as Millicent, but different too. Rural Georgia and coastal Carolina look different, sound different, even the heat feels different. But when it comes to the deep chasms of family secrets and dark repercussions, are they really that dissimilar?

One look at Chief Hartwell's face as he perches on Aunt Millicent's sofa halts her meandering thoughts. He looks angry.

"Sit down," he orders. She takes a striped club chair, puzzled at his abruptness. He wasn't like this at her father's shack just hours ago.

"Is this about... my father?" she asks.

"No. Well, eventually, yes." She must look perplexed because he starts again. "But that's not where I want to begin. First, we have learned that your aunt died of a lethal dose of digoxin. Do you know what that is?"

"I... I... think that's what that killer nurse used on the TV series?"

"Exactly. So you are familiar with it?"

"No. I mean only from watching the show."

Chief Hartwell stares unblinkingly. "I'd like to talk about where you were last week."

His quick change of subject bewilders her. "Last week? I was in Atlanta, teaching classes and administering final exams and trying to hold my head above water."

"No travel?"

She goes still. "Oh, well, yeah. I forgot. A one-day trip for a speech. Several book clubs got together to invite me."

"Not exactly," he says, pulling a paper from the folder he carries. "You stayed overnight on Thursday. In Savannah."

"That's right. It was too far to drive from Atlanta and back all in one day. The organizers paid for a hotel room."

Chief Hartwell's face remains unchanging. "Savannah is forty-five miles from Millicent. Did you know that?"

"No," she says slowly, feeling her way over the tripwires. "I've never driven it." *Technically true.* Familiar shame washes over her. He's going to ask why she didn't visit her sick aunt. *How can I answer?*

"Are you sure you've never made that drive?"

"Yes, I'm sure." She fights to keep her face blank. "Why are you asking me?"

He leans forward, his words punching the air like fists. "Because you spent Thursday night in Savannah, forty-five miles from Mercy Hospital in Millicent. The night your aunt was murdered."

Chapter 18

Upon hearing Chief Hartwell's words, she leans back and stares at the ceiling of Aunt Millicent's study, her heart pounding. Raeford called her on Friday, hours after she'd arrived back in Atlanta. He reached her at the college as she was rushing between classroom and office, trying to catch up from her lightning trip to Savannah. But there was no question of murder at that point.

"I... I... Okay. I guess I was nearby." She doesn't understand what the chief is getting at. *Or do I?* "Wait a minute." She blinks at him. "Do you think I drove to Millicent and killed my aunt? That's insane."

"Is it?" he asks. "Any more insane than being forty-five miles from your sick aunt and *not* coming to see her?"

There it is. Her mouth opens and closes soundlessly. Self-loathing grips her. Did she think of her aunt even once during the initial stages of that trip? Or was she so focused on her presentation and then the afternoon tea with fans that she never considered how close she was? But then there was the unexpected encounter. The encounter that most definitely made her think of Aunt Millicent.

"Look," she tells him. "I am guilty of being a shitty niece. I think everybody knows that by now. I cop to it. But I did not set foot in Millicent or the island hospital last Thursday."

The chief remains silent, staring. "What if I told you we have video from the hospital's security cameras?"

Her breath catches. *He must be bluffing. He must.* Bravado is the only way through this. "I'd say, 'Great!'"

The chief slaps his folder against his leg and rises. Does that folder contain information about her movements, her speech? Pictures of her in the hotel in Savannah? *What else does he know?*

"I'm concerned that you withheld information," he says curtly. "You're a smart woman. I can't imagine that you didn't realize your little trip to the coast on the night of the murder was important." His black eyes blaze. "Then there's the matter of the quick sale to a developer. A sale already in the works at the time your aunt died."

"I've explained that."

He continues as if she hasn't spoken. "And of course, you were in town when your father died."

"My father?" Her voice is squeaky, nearly breaking. "Surely you don't think..." She can't even finish the sentence. "My father... my father..." She's gasping and can't get her thoughts straight. She leans over and places her head between her legs until she calms down. When she lifts her head, Chief Hartwell's face is as stony as before. Mustering as much dignity as she can, she whispers, "My father... was a drunk."

"A drunk who managed *not* to drown himself for what, fifty-nine years?"

She simply stares. *Why does this man hate me? Does he see me as the bringer of chaos to his little island?*

Reluctant to provide him with more ammunition, she's too curious to resist. "Why did you take the bourbon bottle from his house?"

He squints and doesn't answer.

"Were you looking for—what did you call it? Digoxin?"

"What do you know about the drug?"

"Nothing!" She throws up her hands. "But you said that's what killed Aunt Millicent. And the bottle on my father's kitchen table was missing after you left. It doesn't take Sherlock Holmes to figure out you're looking for a connection."

He waits for several beats. "It contained only ninety-proof bourbon whiskey."

"So it was—what?—a drunken accident?"

Chief Hartwell shrugs. "Maybe. There was Valium in his system, but pills in his bathroom cabinet too. So we assume they were his. And there were lumps on the back of his head. The coroner thinks he slipped on the dock and hit his head before falling into the water."

"Sounds reasonable."

"What kind of sports do you play, Miss Cheney? Do you lift weights?"

"*What?*" It's her turn to gawp before answering. "I-I ride a bike. In Atlanta. I walk around campus. But no, I don't lift weights. Why would you ask that?"

He stands. "Just curious." He throws a final comment over his shoulder as he exits the study. "Don't leave town, Miss Cheney."

She waits to stand until she hears the front door close because she's not sure her legs will support her. Sam meets her at the door to the study. "Are you alright?" he asks.

"How much did you hear?"

He looks embarrassed. "Voices carry in this house."

"Yeah, well, it seems I'm a suspect. I guess I shouldn't be surprised, but I am."

"I am, too," Sam says loyally. "Surprised, I mean."

"But what was all that about sports?"

Sam hesitates.

"What?"

"He was probably wondering if you could've dragged your daddy to the canal."

"Oh my God! Are you serious?" She takes a shaky breath and follows Sam into the kitchen, where he pours two glasses of Jesse's sweet iced tea. The sugar courses through her bloodstream like a shot of adrenalin.

She needs time to process Chief Hartwell's accusations. Or suspicions. Or whatever they are. Does he really think she could've killed Aunt Millicent and her father? *For what?* She pauses. Clearly for money. Lots of money. From his perspective, it does make sense.

But why now? Aunt Millicent's will—the one in Raeford's office, anyway—has been the same for years. If she wanted the money, wouldn't she have made a move before now? Clearly, Chief Hartwell hasn't been privy to her life. There were years and years—when waiting tables and writing *Girl, Lost*—that she lived hand-to-mouth, struggling to pay rent, eating exclusively from oversalted noodle packets and restaurant leftovers, driving her old Jeep as it spewed smoke and dripped oil. Now, with the book published and the Warner College teaching job, she has a measure of stability. So why would she have waited until now?

By unspoken consent, she and Sam exit through the screen door. "Sophie's found her piece of heaven," Sam says, nodding down the beach to where the Lab is running into the waves with Derek. Or maybe Sean.

"Feel free to take some beach time," she says, plopping into a rocking chair. *Do I want Sam here, or do I want to be alone?* Her nerves are taut.

Sam tentatively takes a seat. "I will. I want to finish these grades first."

"That's good." She can't deal with the grades.

Sam takes in the beach, vacant except for Robroy, Sean, Derek, Arturio, and his dog. "But I'm here if you need to talk," he says, not meeting her eyes, giving her space. "Did you grow up in this house? It's magnificent."

She breathes a bit more calmly. Maybe it's best to talk. "No, we lived on the inland waterway about a mile that way." She jerks a thumb behind them. "But my mom lived here before she married.

And Margaret and I spent lots of time here. With our Aunt Millicent."

"It's funny when you meet people as adults, you have no idea of the places that shaped them. I would think that a place like this would have a huge impact on who you turned out to be."

"For better or worse," she murmurs.

"What do you mean?"

"Well, I haven't set foot on the island in twelve years, if that tells you anything." *Not exactly true, but close enough.*

Sam stares at her. "Really? Why? I would assume you'd spend all your vacations here."

"It's a long story."

He is tactfully silent, allowing her to decide how much of that story to tell.

She speaks haltingly. "My father was a bastard, a drunk. He beat my mother." She waves an arm to indicate the house. "She sent my sister and me to stay here with Aunt Millicent when it was especially bad."

"But not Robroy?"

"He was much younger than us. And my dad liked him in a way he didn't like me and Margaret. Took him out on his shrimp boat. Hunting. Fishing. Stuff like that."

She takes a deep breath. "The night I graduated from high school, my mom left. Just disappeared. Margaret was married, and I was leaving for college that fall. Robroy was only ten, but I guess Mom thought he was safe with my father. And there were other people looking after him too. My sister, Margaret, and her husband. And this couple Burle and Jesse, who own the Seafood Shack you passed on the way in. They worked here sometimes, too, catering and yard work and repairs and housekeeping."

"The guy the police chief wants to talk to about the balcony rail."

"Right. But believe me, Burle had nothing to do with that. He loves this place and loved Aunt Millicent."

Sam's brow is furrowed. "So, your mom. Did she leave on her own?"

"Yeah, she left a note."

"And you're sure it was real?"

She glances at him. "Yes. I didn't tell you the other part. Mom changed after Robroy was born. She got quieter, more distant. Never took us places or did things anymore. In retrospect, I'm sure she was depressed, but as a kid, you don't recognize that. We started spending lots more time here with Aunt Millicent."

"And she's never gotten in touch with you?"

"Nope."

Sam cringes. "Still, that seems weird. With the history of your father's violence, didn't anyone think she might have been killed?"

"Well, no, because of the note, which was clearly in her handwriting. And she spoke to Robroy, told him she was leaving on a trip. Dad wasn't even home. He was out overnight fishing, which gave her time for a head start."

"She left Robroy alone?"

"Yeah, but she knew I'd be home the next morning, and he knew how to call Margaret or Burle. It's a tight community."

Sam sits back with a low whistle. "That's devastating. I guess I can see why you haven't been back."

"Yeah, I kept looking for her all that summer. I thought 'a trip' meant there would be a return, you know? I was sure she'd be here to send me off to college. But we literally never heard from her again. I have imagined her living in Louisiana, Nevada, or even Mexico or the Caribbean. I have pictured her as a waitress, a librarian, a teacher, a nurse, a grad student, even a mom with a whole other family." She swallows painfully. "But mostly, I imagine she must be dead. Surely, surely, surely, she must be dead. Otherwise, wouldn't she have contacted us as adults? Once she was standing on her own, apart from Dad?"

"Once she read your book," Sam says quietly.

"Well, yeah, that too." She doesn't tell Sam about the letter Chief Hartwell claims Aunt Millicent received, allegedly from Sloane's mother, or about her aunt's new will that indicates she thought her mother was alive. She doesn't believe any of it.

Unless. Unless. She feels the old stirring once again. Unless her father's death is the one thing that could lure her mother from hiding. *If she is hiding. Which she's not, because she's dead.*

Chapter 19

Sloane feels like she's living in a frat house. Robroy's bandmates are sprawled downstairs, sleeping or waiting for dinner. "You guys are on your own," she calls, pulling a chicken-and-dumpling casserole from the refrigerator. "Eat with us or get anything you want."

Arturio strolls into the kitchen. "That looks like Mama's," he says with a nod at the casserole dish. "It'll be good."

She raises the dish above her head to see Nadine's name taped to the bottom. "Yep. Good choice. You want some?" She places the dish in the microwave.

"Absolutely." He circles the kitchen, unwrapping a platter of wheat rolls to go with it.

"And there's salad," she says, pointing to a refrigerator shelf.

"And peach pie." He finds it under aluminum foil. "The neighbors done good."

Robroy comes in and locates plates and silverware for four. He's subdued, and Sloane places an arm around his waist for a quick hug. He can't quite muster a smile. "It's just us and Sam," he says. "Sean and Derek are asleep. Sun wore 'em out."

"And beer," says Arturio.

"Goes without saying."

When they settle at the dining room table, Arturio takes several huge bites of his mother's dumplings and refills his tea glass. "So I've been wanting to ask you guys," he begins. "About your aunt."

"The sixty-four-thousand-dollar question," says Robroy.

"But how was she killed in our hospital? Aren't there doctors and nurses around all the time?"

"You ever been in there?"

"No."

Sloane pauses with her fork in mid-bite to hear Robroy's response. "Well, it's not like a level-one hospital. There are nurses on duty, and maybe a doctor sleeping somewhere, but not a whole staff working third shift. The patients are perfectly able to sleep through the night."

"How do you know that?" she interrupts.

He holds up his left arm. "Let's see. Broken arm. Strep throat. Two cracked ribs. Bronchitis. Broken collar bone." He glances down at his body. "I think that's it. Aunt Millicent used to joke that I got the family's money's worth out of her donation."

Sloane eyes her brother, not knowing how to ask. "Those injuries." Her voice sounds tinny.

Robroy doesn't respond, so she clears her throat. "How did you get those breaks?"

"Different ways. Broke my arm falling out of a tree. Broke my collar bone making a diving catch at shortstop. Cracked the ribs on Scotty Espey's four-wheeler."

Arturio stares at his plate. He doesn't meet Robroy's eyes until he's sure he's finished his litany of injuries. "I get that it's not a full-fledged hospital, but there had to be people around. How was your aunt killed?"

Robroy shrugs, so Sloane inserts, "Chief Hartwell says she was poisoned with digoxin."

Robroy's fork scrapes his plate. "When did he tell you that?"

"Oh, sorry. He was here this afternoon, while you were on the beach." She pauses. They're going to find out sooner or later. "He was grilling me about being in Savannah on the night of the murder."

Robroy and Arturio look at her. "What were you doing in Savannah?" asks Robroy.

"And why does the chief care?" adds Arturio.

She tells them the same half-story she told Chief Hartwell. "I was there for a book speech, and the organizers paid for a hotel room. Apparently, the chief thinks I took the opportunity to drive to Mercy Hospital and kill Aunt Millicent."

The young men gape, then Arturio says, "Oh, to hurry up your inheritance, right?"

Robroy and Sam look at him in horror. Arturio holds up his hands. "Hey, I'm not suggesting it. I assume that's what the chief was suggesting."

Sloane's shoulders slump. "Precisely."

Arturio glances at her brother. "Robroy and I have talked about this. The islanders are split on this whole development thing. My folks don't want it. The shrimpers don't want it. The turtle ladies don't want it. But a lot of the downtown business owners do. From what Mama has told me, Town Council meetings have gotten heated. People yelling. Accusing each other of being greedy or being backward. It's gotten ugly, Sloane."

"And Aunt Millicent was the final barrier," she muses. "Kent Espey told me this house was critical to the whole deal."

"The part that doesn't make sense," says Sam, "is where did your aunt stand? If she was the 'final barrier,' as you say, why did she leave the house to you two"—he nods at Sloane and Robroy—"knowing you were going to sell?"

She and Robroy look at each other. "Good question," he says. "Sloane made no secret of the fact she wasn't coming here to live. And I didn't even know I'd inherited, too, until Raeford called over the weekend."

"But the bigger wrinkle," says Sloane, "is a handwritten will we just found, leaving everything to our mother. Our *long dead* mother."

This time, Arturio's fork bangs against his plate. "*Miz Annie?*" He stares at Robroy. "Is Miz Annie alive? Mama won't believe this."

"I... maybe I shouldn't have said anything, Arturio," Sloane responds. "I'm not sure Chief Hartwell wants that out yet."

"But Sloane," he says, "don't you see what this means? Uncle Burle and Mama and Daddy—well, a lot of people—are going to be excited to hear there's still a possibility of blocking this development. They all gave up when they saw you at the funeral."

She pushes her plate away. So she wasn't imagining the looks and whispers.

The doorbell peals its demanding ring. Sloane pictures an elated mob of native islanders on the front porch, ready to dance through Millicent House in celebration. She rises and walks to the door, dreading what fresh hell she will find.

Her sister stands on the porch. Slightly behind her, a man has his back to Sloane, scanning the trees and vines and shrubs that threaten to overtake the yard. He turns, and her stomach flips.

Elijah Cartwright. Her old boyfriend.

Chapter 20

Wordlessly, she walks into Eli's embrace. She has thought so often of doing this very thing, wondered at what she discarded so carelessly years ago. He holds her close for a moment, but he's the first to break away. She blinks and notes Margaret's incredulous glare.

"Okay," she says, walking past Sloane. "Not as awkward as I feared."

Sloane steps back reluctantly. "Eli. It's good to see you."

And it is. Eli's light-brown hair is shorter than he wore it in college, but his deep aquamarine eyes—the color of the ocean, she always told him—are the same. He's wearing khakis and a blue-and-white-checked dress shirt, sleeves rolled to mid-forearm, the unofficial reporter's uniform. He's skinnier than she remembers, undoubtedly due to replacing the college's carb-heavy fare with a bachelor's kitchen. And she knows from late-night Facebook browsing that he *is* a bachelor.

"I'm here about the development-slash-murder story," he says, his voice sweetly familiar as they walk toward the dining room. "And I'm sorry for your loss, Sloane. I met your aunt several times and liked her a lot. She was a character." He smiles for the first time. "Like you."

"How'd you meet her?"

"This Mayberry by the Sea business has been going on for a while." That makes sense. His *Herald* story had too much background to have been gathered on the fly.

Margaret turns to them. "He came to my house looking for comment. But since you and Robroy are the official heirs, I thought you should do the commenting." Her tone is even, but Sloane considers again that she may not be pleased about Aunt Millicent's will. She tries to put herself in Margaret's place—rich in-laws, plenty of money, reputation as a sharp businesswoman, heiress, if not to Millicent House, at least to the Millicent name. But maybe there's a sting to being the sole Cheney sibling excluded from the will.

Before Sloane can respond, Robroy sees Eli. His face breaks into a smile and he rises to shake his hand. "Gentlemen," he says to Sam and Arturio, "meet Eli Cartwright, Sloane's old boyfriend and the best reporter in the state."

Eli's neck colors, and she feels hers doing the same at the "boyfriend" label. "Robroy, I'm sorry about your dad, man. And your aunt. Tough times."

Robroy sits back down as Sloane finds her manners. "We're eating some of Miz Nadine's chicken and dumplings. Can I fix plates for you two?"

Margaret waves her away and pours iced tea for herself and Eli.

"Nothing for me, thanks," he says. "Ya'll finish, and then I can talk to the three Cheneys, if that's okay."

"Not on deadline?" Sloane asks.

"No, this is for a longer piece." He takes his tea to the kitchen. "I'll wait on the porch so you can eat your dinner in peace."

Sloane assumes he wants to get a look at the property everyone is fighting over. *Or has he already been here with the developer? Or even with Aunt Millicent?* She carries her plate to the sink and starts to follow him. But the doorbell rings again.

My God. What happened to quiet, sleepy Millicent?

"Margaret, can you get that?" Without waiting for an answer, she slips through the screen door. Eli is standing beneath a cupola, gazing over the purpling sea. Far up the beach, the sun is a bright red ball heading for the horizon, turning the clouds riotous shades of pink and orange and lavender. "This place is magical," he says. "I have more questions than ever."

The breeze whips curls into her eyes, so she grips her hair over one shoulder. "Then why did you head to Margaret's?"

"Because I had no idea you'd be here."

"Oh. Well, I came for the funeral. And to sign papers."

Eli flings an arm out to indicate the breaking waves and breathtaking sunset. "Why didn't you ever want to come back here?" He smiles wryly. "Or more importantly, why didn't you want to bring me here?"

Why didn't I? Standing this close to Eli, recalling her off-campus apartment where he practically lived, it's hard to recall why she didn't want to share this too. She grasps for a reason. "I guess because your family was so much more normal than mine."

He turns a withering look on her. "What the hell is a normal family?"

"Something besides mine, I can tell you that."

"Sloane, that's absurd. From what I learned of your aunt, she was spectacular. And Margaret and Robroy seem normal enough."

"Yeah, they were. Are." She hesitates. "But when we were dating, my mother was gone, and I didn't want you to meet my father." There. She'd said it.

"Because?"

She shakes her head miserably. "Let's just say he was a painful part of my life. And during my time with you in Greenbrier, he was very much alive. I guess..." She swings her gaze away from him and rushes through the next words. "I guess I was afraid you'd think less of me if you met him."

Eli catches her shoulders and turns her to face him. Her hair escapes her fist and blows wildly. "Did you think less of me because my dad is a redneck farmer, and my brother is two steps away from being Ku Klux Klan?"

She laughs. "Jacob? He is not."

"Maybe not a card-carrying member. But he flies a Confederate flag."

"Really? I didn't know that."

"Exactly. But you know *him*. While you never let me meet anyone but Robroy, and that was by accident when I showed up at your apartment."

"Okay. Okay. I was a bad girlfriend. I get it."

"Don't do that, Sloane. That's not what this is about."

"So what is it about? Why are you here?"

His eyes search her face. "Well, right now, for a story. Are you really going to sell this property to Ryan Carbonier?"

"Sure. It's no secret. In fact, I'd already signed when we learned Aunt Millicent had been murdered. That put a kibosh on the sale. Temporarily, anyway." She considers telling him about the sabotaged railing, too, but she doesn't want their family name all over the news any more than it already is.

Eli pulls out a digital recorder. "May I?"

She nods reluctantly.

"This is a big deal, at least in the Lowcountry," he says. "The last undeveloped beach in the state."

"People keep saying that. But there are beachfront state parks at Myrtle and Hunting Island and Edisto. Aren't those undeveloped?"

"Yeah, technically. But those are tiny stretches for camping. This is an entire town, which is going to turn from fishing, shrimping, and farming to unrestrained tourism overnight. Don't the tourists have enough places on this coast?"

"I thought you were supposed to be objective."

He sighs. "You're right. I am. But damn if I don't hate to see Millicent go the way of Myrtle, North Myrtle, and Isle of Palms. Almost all the stories I do down here are fights over eroding beaches, re-plenishing sand dunes, and building seawalls. Threatened lighthous-es and seabirds. Polluted waters when hurricanes hit. Can't we leave one beach that can heal itself?"

She stares out to sea. He has a point. She imagines this beach overrun with fat, sunburned tourists, boomboxes blaring. But if saving it means she has to live in Millicent, the cost is too high.

Eli is not finished. "If your dad was truly the issue, doesn't it make a difference now that he's gone?"

How can I explain how my father has tainted this place? Every-where she looks she sees signs of his cruelty. Signs of her missing mother.

"Eli, I..." The screen door thumps against the house's wooden wall. Chief Hartwell looms large against the lit kitchen. His face is flinty. *Geez, what is with this guy?*

"Mr. Cartwright, I need to speak with Miss Cheney. Alone."

Eli clicks off his recorder. "I'll wait inside."

The chief regards her in silence. If he's waiting for her to say something, she'll oblige. "What now?"

"The hotel cameras. In Savannah."

Her heart sinks, but she tries to keep her face from reflecting dread.

"Obviously, they can't show us whether you drove to Millicent last Thursday. But they do show you in the downstairs bar. Meeting with Ryan Carbonier."

Chapter 21

Sloane bows her head out of shame, surely, but also hoping for a moment to think. Instead, her mind blanks.

"Y-Yes," she admits. "Ryan Carbonier found out I was speaking in Savannah and drove up to meet me. From Jacksonville."

"He wanted to talk to you about buying this property?" The chief indicates the house and beach with a flick of his head.

"Yes."

"He wanted to talk to you even though the property's owner was alive and well at that point."

She cringes and doesn't answer. Anything she says is going to make her look bad. The truth is, she *should* look bad. She has behaved despicably.

"Miss Cheney," says the chief, "you do understand how this appears? You met with the developer who very much wanted to buy this property. A few hours later, your aunt, who was just forty-five miles away, was killed, clearing the way for him to buy it. From you."

She swallows convulsively. "I know how it looks. But I swear I didn't set up that meeting in Savannah. Ryan Carbonier showed up at my speech. He introduced himself afterward and invited me for a drink. One drink. And he reiterated that his latest offer to Raeford was eight point six million." She shrugs. "I thought he'd just keep going up and up and up until Aunt Millicent died, fifteen or twenty years from now."

Chief Hartwell's skepticism shows on his face.

"But you knew your aunt was sick. Raeford Carlisle had called you."

"Yes, but I already told you I didn't think it was serious. Dehydration and UTI, he said. And apparently, he was right. It wasn't serious or she wouldn't have been in Mercy Hospital. She would've been in Beaufort."

Nothing she says is going to convince the police chief she's innocent. And maybe he shouldn't be convinced. In all the ways that matter, she is not innocent. She's been ungrateful and ungracious to the one person who gave her love and sanctuary. But if he arrests her, she'll lose her position at Warner College, no question about it. Dr. Avery will pounce on the scent of scandal and convince the board she is a poor role model. And with the inheritance held hostage for who knows how long, she can't lose her job.

"Why aren't you looking at all the developers who want into Millicent?" she asks desperately, then just as desperately, she wants the words back. The last thing she needs is for the chief to look into Ryan Carbonier.

"Oh, believe me, we're looking at everyone." The chief turns and opens the screen door. "Don't even think about leaving town."

"But it's..." She clamps her lips shut and doesn't tell him she will be in Atlanta in four days, come fire or brimstone. He can't forbid what he doesn't know. "I'm working from right here," she says instead.

She follows the chief into the kitchen, where Eli is deep in conversation with Margaret and Robroy, his recorder on the kitchen-nook table between them. Chief Hartwell lets himself out as she busies her hands refilling a glass and listens to her siblings share memories of their aunt and this house. Margaret's bridge lessons. Robroy cleaning fish with Burle for church suppers.

"Robroy, I didn't know you stayed overnight," she interrupts.

"Sure," he says. "Especially when Burle and Jesse were working here or when Dad was out overnight on his boat." She realizes how much life she has missed in this house, on this island. Her life has been one continuous journey of loss. Her mother. Eli. Aunt Millicent. Not her dad, exactly, but any kind of real father. She studies her brother and sister and thinks of her nieces. If she keeps going the way she is, for all practical purposes, she will lose them too. Is that what she wants?

She thinks of her character Murphy and the chaotic mess that was her life, then she thinks of Elle and the solid family she created to sustain her. For the first time, it occurs to her how close Elle's name is to Eli. *Well, of course.* Why is she throwing away the good parts of her history, her family, her loves? Especially now that her father can no longer hurt them.

Her next breath comes as a shudder. "I need to tell you all something."

Chapter 22

From where they sit at the kitchen table, they spin to look at her—Margaret, Robroy, Eli. Sam has slipped away to give them privacy, and she can hear him murmuring to Sean and Derek in another room. Arturio plants himself at the open refrigerator door, unnecessarily rearranging its contents. He's practically family, so she doesn't object.

Swallowing some iced tea to relieve the dryness in her throat, she leans against the counter and begins. "Last week, on the Thursday night Aunt Millicent died, I was in Savannah speaking to some combined book clubs. There was a man in the audience, expensive suit, slicked back hair, professional looking. Book clubs are mostly women, with maybe a few husbands they drag along, so he stood out. I actually thought—hoped, I guess—that he might represent Netflix or HBO." She feels her face flush. "But he didn't. It was Ryan Carbonier."

Eli's eyes widen, and Margaret inhales sharply. Only Robroy is silent, his face questioning. They recognize the name.

"You'd never met him?" asks Eli.

"No. I'd heard his name from Raeford, and he'd called me several times. But I had no idea what he looked like." She clears her throat of an aggravating tickle. "Anyway, he asked me to have a drink in the hotel bar. As you might expect, he wanted to talk about the house. He repeated his latest offer. He said he knew Aunt Millicent was sick, and it might be close to time."

"What?" exclaims Margaret. "She had a UTI!"

"That's exactly what I said. But he seemed to think it was more serious and wanted to know if I was ready to move immediately."

"And what did you say?" Margaret demands.

"Not much. I just kind of reiterated that I hadn't changed my mind about moving here but that I was sure Aunt Millicent was going to be around for another couple of decades." She hangs her head. "I still thought... I thought we had plenty of time."

She waits for their reactions. *Will they be angry? Suspicious? Chief Hartwell sure is.*

Robroy stands to clear his plate from the table. "We all thought we had more time," he says flatly, clanging his cutlery into the sink.

"Anyway, that's what Chief Hartwell wanted to talk about," she says. "He seems to think Mr. Carbonier inspired me to rush to the hospital and kill Aunt Millicent."

"Don't kid about that, Sloane," says her sister. "It's not funny."

"I know!" Her voice inches toward a wail. "I know. But don't you see? Ryan Carbonier was within forty-five miles of the hospital that night." Her eyes flick to each face. "He was the one so hellbent on getting this house. For him, a decade or two might have been untenable."

She readies herself to voice the fear that has haunted her since Octavia's announcement at the church. "Telling him she was going to live that long, telling him I would sell as soon as she was gone..." Her voice slides to a whisper. "I might as well have handed him the poison."

Arturio slams the refrigerator door. "Damn Florida cracker. Why doesn't he go and ruin his own damn beaches?"

Margaret and Robroy look at each other, undoubtedly assessing who will speak first. As usual, it's Margaret. "I'm the last one to grant you a pass for the way you treated Aunt Millicent," she says. "But if Ryan Carbonier killed her, that's on him. You have been nothing if not constant, Leo." Her sister's use of the old nickname disarms her; she's offering an olive branch.

Robroy nods. "She's right. We might not agree with how you've avoided us and the whole town, but you have been entirely upfront. Aunt Millicent knew that and left the house to you anyway."

"And to you," Margaret tells him pointedly.

"Well, yeah. That was a surprise."

"Was it?" Margaret seems to remember Eli is in the room and stops. "Never mind."

Robroy bites off a reply. Something lies just under the surface between those two, but Sloane shoves her curiosity aside for now. She's been given a reprieve.

Eli looks from Margaret to Robroy, but when they say nothing further, he gathers his recorder and notebook. "I think you have an excellent point, Sloane. Surely, Chief Hartwell's crew is looking at Carbonier's company, no matter how farfetched it sounds. I doubt the big man himself crept into Mercy Hospital and put digoxin in your aunt's IV, but..." He shrugs and rises to leave.

Pushing off the counter that has been supporting her, she trails behind Eli. "It still seems impossible," she says when they reach the front door. "I keep thinking the medical examiner is going to come back and say, 'I made a mistake. It was a heart attack.' I mean, who could be a murderer in Millicent?"

"That's the key, isn't it?" Eli says. "Someone who had no use for this last little beach town."

Chapter 23

Wednesday

Sloane wakes early with a hip still aching from her awkward landing on the balcony Monday night. The moment she is conscious, two women war for her attention—Octavia and Elle. With all the drama and visitors of the past two days, she hasn't gotten back to her aunt's best friend. As for Elle, as occasionally happens upon waking, Sloan's mind suddenly presents a solution for revising a problematic scene in her novel-in-progress. *So, edits? Or a visit to Octavia?* She's been awake for less than a minute, and her heart is already racing with anxiety.

She slips on a bra, brushes her teeth, and runs fingers through her tousled curls while gazing in the mirror. Her green eyes remain slightly bloodshot, and new freckles sprinkle her otherwise pale face. She needs to double up on sunscreen today. Without changing from her T-shirt and pajama pants, she heads downstairs. Edits first.

Sam and Robroy's bandmates lounge around the dining room table, coffee and pancakes in front of them.

"Who cooked?"

"Robroy," answers Arturio. "We saved pancakes for you."

She slides two onto a plate and drowns them in syrup, her mind already on her manuscript. She longs to retreat to the kitchen nook with her laptop, but decides it would be rude and instead takes a seat next to Sam. His duffle bag is in the hall, along with Sophie's dog food and leash.

"Heading out?"

"Yep, all the exams are finished. I'm sorry I can't stay for your father's service, but I have one last seminar tomorrow."

"I don't know how I'll ever thank you," she says. "You really saved me."

"My pleasure." He reaches for the morning newspaper, which is open to the obituary page. "You'll want to see this."

He points to two inches of copy with the heading "Robert Elroy Cheney."

"Robroy, did you put this in?" she asks in surprise.

"No. Margaret, I assume."

She reads it quickly. Lifelong Millicent resident. Shrimper. Widower of the late Millicent Ann Roundtree Cheney. Father of Margaret, Sloane, and Robroy. Grandfather of Emma Sue and Sarah. *So much vileness hidden in so few words. How could one person wreak such havoc?*

But as she watches Robroy laughing with his bandmates and thinks of Margaret secure in her family, she realizes that it's only her and her mother who couldn't get past the destruction he wrought. Or maybe it's only her. Maybe her mother is happily preparing pancakes in some far-away kitchen for some new family. Or maybe she's heading into a high-rise office in Columbia or Raleigh or New York, briefcase swinging, without the burden of a husband and children.

And only Sloane Cheney's life is an all-black kaleidoscope, the pieces clicking and sliding with each turn of her wrist but revealing nothing but a void every time.

"Sloane, are you okay?"

She wrenches her eyes from the obit to meet Sam's, then she notices Robroy, Arturio, Sean, and Derek watching her as well. She pushes away the newspaper.

"Sure. Yes." She attempts to smile at Sean and Derek. "Did you two get dinner last night?"

The young men assure her they did then return to their discussion of playlists and dates and accommodations. She retreats to the kitchen.

After seeing Sam off, Sloane spends a fruitless two hours wrestling with Elle's problems before giving up and calling Margaret.

"Will you go with me to see Octavia and then to Mercy Hospital?"

Margaret is silent.

"The girls are in school, aren't they?"

Her sister sighs. "Yeah." More silence. "Octavia, fine. But why do you want to go to the hospital? You think you're going to find something Chief Hartwell and those detectives missed?"

"No, nothing like that." How does she explain what she's not even sure she understands? "It's just that..." Her heart pounds painfully. "I guess it's what I was trying to say last night. That I might have triggered this. Inadvertently. I need to see where it happened."

Margaret gives another breathy sigh fraught with disapproval.

What a fine thing it must be to live so above it all.

"Okay," she relents. "I'll pick you up in fifteen minutes."

Sloane wanders into the parlor where the Alleged Baby Stompers straggle about and hang over sofas and lounges. It's as if these young men don't have spines. "Robroy, do you want to come to Mercy Hospital with me and Margaret?"

Her brother looks up in horror. "What? No! Why are you going there?"

"I feel like I need to."

He all but shudders. "Well, count me out. That's ghoulish."

"No, it's not. I want to see how it could have happened."

"Suit yourself."

Arturio lays aside the drumsticks he's been clacking together and stands. "I'll go with you, Sloane."

"Really?"

"Yeah. My Auntie June is a nurse there, and she told Mama to send me over while I'm home."

"Great. Margaret's on her way, so meet us outside. Oh, and we're stopping at the post office first."

The post office on SC 900 resembles a playhouse, a miniature brick structure where Octavia Hargrove reigns. They find her sitting motionless behind the counter, no customers in sight.

When Octavia sees Sloane, Margaret, and Arturio, she rises slowly, unsmiling. She's wearing the same black dress she wore at Aunt Millicent's service. Or maybe she has a closet full of them. "I was expecting you yesterday," she says.

Margaret takes over. "I guess you heard about our father. We were tied up with that."

Octavia nods. "I don't suppose it's necessary to give my condolences." She turns to Arturio. "I'm surprised to see you, Arturio. What brings you along?"

He leans across the counter to give her an awkward hug. "The band's staying at Millicent House this week, and Sloane wanted to go the hospital. I thought I'd visit Auntie June."

"I see. And what do you girls hope to find at the hospital?"

Sloane can't hold back a moment longer. "We want to know what happened to Aunt Millicent, Octavia. I don't understand what's going on. You obviously know something, and we're hoping you'll share it with us."

As Octavia observes her coolly, Sloane continues, "She must have said something to you. How did you know she was murdered when the police didn't suspect it?"

"Let's sit." Octavia walks through the opening between the counter and the lobby, where three chairs line one wall, awaiting patrons. "I promised Chief Hartwell I'd be circumspect, but you deserve to know." She sighs. "But first, I have to say, Sloane. I'm disappointed in you. You hurt your aunt."

"Yeah, I'm hearing that loud and clear," Sloane murmurs. She glances sideways at Margaret, whose arms are crossed.

"You know," her sister interrupts, her voice tight, "I'm getting a little tired of everybody piling on Sloane."

Sloane's head snaps up. Even Octavia looks surprised.

"I've been here the whole time," Margaret continues. "I stayed on this damn island. I saw Aunt Millicent—and you, Octavia—at least once a week. Sometimes more. If there were all these secrets that needed to be dealt with, why didn't you guys let me in?"

Arturio slides into a seat along the wall, no doubt anxious to get out of the line of fire.

Octavia purses her lips and sits beside him. "You're right, Margaret. In fact, I often asked Millicent why she didn't confide in you. Let me assure you it had nothing to do with you. It was..."

"Idelle?" Margaret seems resigned.

"Yes. Idelle."

"What was it about Idelle?" Curiosity causes Sloane to interject.

"Idelle and Mom were friends," Margaret says, never taking her eyes off Octavia. "Best friends."

"So?"

There's an uncomfortable silence. Margaret and Octavia stare at each other. Prickles run down Sloane's spine, and it dawns on her that something's coming. Something big.

"Two years ago," says Octavia, "Millicent learned that Annie had been in touch with Idelle. All that time she'd awaited word, all that time she'd had a private eye looking for her, all that missing and regret and thinking her sister was dead..."

"And Idelle knew she was alive," Margaret whispers.

Sloane whirls on her sister, practically screeching. "You knew?"

But Margaret shakes her head. "No, but now some things make sense. All I knew was that Aunt Millicent developed a great animosity toward Idelle, and I couldn't figure out why. I thought she just hated Gas 'N' Such, how our business catered to travelers and tourists."

"But Mom?" Sloane cries. "Mom was in touch with Idelle? Mom's alive?" Her legs begin to quaver, and she falls heavily into the last remaining chair.

Octavia slides her chair around to face her, showing a little more warmth. "I'm sorry, girls," she says. "After Millicent found out, she didn't feel it was her place to tell you. She thought it was up to Annie."

"But where is she?" Sloane demands, recalling fantasies of her mother in far-flung cities, in various occupations. "Does she have a new family? Is that why she didn't come back?"

Octavia and Margaret look at her with incredulity. "Don't be silly," barks Octavia. "She didn't come back because of your father."

In her mind's eye, Sloane sees her father's white hair and blue shirt floating in the canal's high tide, sees the white heron lifting into the sky. Things shift, change shape. All that she has known for twelve years jiggles and dissolves. She feels Arturio's hand lightly touch her shoulder.

Her voice emerges scratchy and raw. "And now?"

"Now," says Octavia, "she's on her way home."

Before Sloane can process Octavia's statement, they are interrupted by the jangle of bells hanging on the post office door. Elsie from the diner walks in and speaks to each of them, and Octavia hustles behind the counter to retrieve a package. It's an excruciating five minutes, but their strained answers to Elsie's polite questions persuade her to move on.

As soon as the door closes behind her, Margaret says, "Where? Where is Mom coming? Your house? Idelle's?"

"Millicent House," says Octavia. "She wants to join all of you there."

Margaret looks stunned, unable to say anything further.

"When?" Sloane asks.

"She said late afternoon. She's driving from... well, I'll let her tell you everything."

The three of them stumble from the post office, squinting in the bright sunlight.

Arturio seems to be the only one capable of speech. "I assume you don't want to go to the hospital," he says. "Want to go to the diner and debrief? Or would you rather be alone?"

"There's nothing you don't already know," Sloane says. "Let's go to the diner."

Margaret, looking as shellshocked as Sloane feels, climbs into her BMW without a word.

Sloane takes the back seat, giving Arturio the front. But then she remembers: *We didn't get what we came for.* She steps back out onto the tiny square of concrete parking lot. "Wait for me," she commands.

Shoving open the post office door, she speaks before Octavia can. "I almost forgot what we came for. The murder—how did you know?"

Octavia sighs and leans against the counter. For a moment, grief flashes across her wizened face. "For the past two years—after she learned Annie was alive—Millicent agonized over her will. What to do with the house. Developers were circling like vultures, especially that Ryan Carbonier from Florida. She wanted to leave the house to Annie, but Annie never tried to contact her."

"Then how did Aunt Millicent know she'd been in touch with Idelle?"

"Pure accident. Millicent and Idelle were at some luncheon in Charleston. They were at the same table. Millicent said something, and Idelle replied, 'You sound just like your sister.' Of course, Millicent jerked around and said, 'What do you mean?' And instead of Idelle laughing it off as though she meant she was remembering Annie from years earlier, she turned fire red, according to Millicent, and fled to the restroom.

"Millicent couldn't get anything more out of her that day. But she was convinced Idelle knew something, and it turned out she was right. It took another year and a half of badgering to convince Idelle to tell the truth. Millicent blamed Idelle, but I always thought she was misplacing that anger. Annie was the one making the decision not to contact Millicent. Or come home, for that matter."

"Because she was scared," Sloane says. "Of my dad."

"So she said."

She peers at Octavia. "What do you mean?"

Octavia pauses, considering her words. "I mean, Annie was a grown-assed woman with no children to protect. Why, exactly, was she so scared of a washed-up, drunken fisherman?"

Sloane recoils at the scalding words. Her defense of her mother is automatic. "You don't know, Octavia. You don't know what it was like living in that house."

"You're right. I don't. And maybe Annie did what she had to twelve years ago. But sometime in there, she could've grown a backbone."

Sloane stiffens. Perhaps Octavia's comments echo the ones in her own head a little too closely. But these aren't questions for outside the family. "I don't want to argue about this," she says. "What I still don't understand is why Aunt Millicent was killed and how you knew it?"

Octavia visibly releases her ire, and weariness once more washes over her. "Like I said, developers were circling. Millicent's behavior, I thought, was getting a little erratic."

"How so?"

"She'd been talking about leaving the house to Annie, but then she suddenly added Robroy to her will. And left you in, obviously. She insisted you loved the house and hoped you'd change your mind about selling when push came to shove."

"And she didn't even tell Robroy."

"Hmm," she mutters. "I guess not."

"Anyway, Aunt Millicent? In the hospital?"

"I got there her second day, and she was all over the place. Called me Annie. Gripped my arm and said, 'I left the boat for you.' Raeford was there and said she had a UTI, which I know can mimic dementia. So I wasn't overly worried." She pauses, her eyes filling with tears. "I should have been."

"But how could you have known?"

She pulls a tissue from her sleeve and wipes her eyes. "Because when I went back on Thursday, she looked right at me—her eyes were clear—and she said, 'Annie, people want me out of the way for our property. I think they'll kill for it.'" Octavia continues to wipe her face, her anguish clear. "But I didn't believe her."

"Octavia, she thought you were my mother! She clearly wasn't in her right mind." Sloane's own mind is racing. "But she said, '*They'll kill for it*'? Not 'he'? Or 'she'?"

"Right." Octavia pauses. "Anyway, Raeford and I assured ourselves it was the UTI talking, and Millicent would be better once the antibiotics had more time to work. But she died that night. Raeford thought the infection caused the strain on her heart. But I wasn't so sure. I thought about it for a few days then called Chief Hartwell. You know the rest."

Sloane slumps against the counter, picturing her delirious aunt thinking in her last moments that her beloved sister had returned. Imploring Annie to save her as she'd so often tried to save Annie.

Her mind is reeling, pounded by more questions than when she arrived. "Thank you, Octavia," she says weakly. "For being her friend."

She leaves the old woman sagging against the post office counter, her aged back bent.

None of them speak during the drive to the diner. Sloane gazes out the car window until she hears sniffles from the front. Margaret's shoulders tremble beneath the blanket of her honey-blond hair.

"Do you need me to drive?" Sloane asks.

A sob erupts, but Margaret clears her throat. She doesn't answer, only waggles her head.

Arturio looks back at Sloane, his dark eyes filled with worry. "Miz Annie," he muses. "How long has she been gone?"

"Twelve years exactly." Sloane wonders if her sister feels doubly betrayed—by her mother, certainly, but also by her mother-in-law, who kept such an important secret from her. Margaret's shoulders straighten as she struggles to regain her composure.

They pull into the parking lot of Elsie's Diner, only half full, before the lunch crowd arrives in earnest. Arturio leads them to the farthest booth, which offers a semblance of privacy. They sink into its red vinyl, which squeaks with a sound so familiar that Sloane catches her breath. She'd been in this diner with Kent Espey after school. With Margaret and Robroy when their mother was too sick or too tired or too—who knows what?—to cook. And on cheerier occasions, with her mother and her aunt.

Nothing has changed, not the coffee pots on burners behind the counter, not the homemade pies under pristine glass covers, not banker Mack Sanderson, grasping a heavy white mug with thick fingers. He looks at the trio but doesn't speak; Margaret's thunderous face likely prevents it.

"What more did you learn?" Arturio asks.

Where to start? She fills them in, concluding, "The main thing was that Aunt Millicent was hallucinating and thought Octavia was Mom. Oh, and she told her she 'left the boat' for her. Whatever that means."

Margaret laughs mirthlessly. "Weird."

Sloane's phone rings, and she grabs it, anxious to tell Robroy about their mother's impending visit. But it's not her brother; it's John Avery. Cringing, she slips out of the booth and answers.

"Sloane," he snaps. "I got the speech. I'd say it needs work."

It's the same thing she'd thought, but his reproach rankles. "I know. I'm rewriting it."

"Something else," he says. "The trustees want to meet with you."

Her stomach curdles. *Do they hate the speech too? Are they rescinding the invitation?* Her fortunes have changed drastically over the last hour. She will no longer inherit Millicent House, at least not anytime soon. Her book advance won't be available until—or unless—she finishes the damn thing. The job at Warner College represents her sole income.

"Uh, when? And why?"

"Well, it seems you have some real fans on the board," he says, his distaste evident. "They want you to have dinner with them the night before graduation."

Relief washes over her, followed by anxiety. None of her family entanglements will be resolved by then, and Chief Hartwell may send a squad car to fetch her if he learns she's gone to Atlanta. *But what the hell?*

"Friday night. I'll be there."

"Be in the trustees' dining hall by six o'clock," Dr. Avery commands. He hangs up without saying good-bye. Her stomach gives a final lurch as she returns to the table to find Caesar salads for her and Margaret and a juicy hamburger for Arturio. "I'd have preferred that," she says, pointing at Arturio's burger but then picking a handmade crouton off her salad.

"You know," says Arturio, slicing off a quarter of his burger and placing it on her napkin, "we need to find out who was in the hospital with Miz Millicent last Thursday. I mean, besides Miz Octavia and Raeford."

"Surely Chief Hartwell is looking into that," says Margaret.

"You'd think," Sloane says. "But he must not be coming up with anything if he keeps harping on me sneaking over from Savannah."

"That's only because he thought you were inheriting. Everybody did."

"But so was Robroy. Why's he not hassling him?"

"Way to throw Little Bro under the bus," remarks Margaret.

Arturio stops eating. "Thursday. Last Thursday." He snaps his fingers. "We played North Charleston that night."

"I thought you stayed with Aunt Millicent or your folks when you were on the coast," Sloane says.

"Sometimes. But this club had an apartment. Much more convenient. It takes a good two hours to make the drive from Millicent to North Charleston."

No one says anything, so Sloane changes the subject. "So, Margaret. Mom's coming? Can you believe it?"

"No," she responds abruptly.

Sloane eyes her sister, trying to figure out if she's sad or angry.

Margaret takes a deep breath. "You know, when I met Joel and learned what a healthy family looked like, it made me resent what we'd been through." She stabs a bite of lettuce.

Angry, Sloane decides.

"Then when Emma Sue was born, and I thought about what it would take to make me leave her... well, I can't imagine what Mom was thinking. It wasn't so bad for you and me, I guess. I mean, I was grown, and you were too. Mostly. But Robroy? Who leaves a ten-year-old? That's cold."

Sloane starts to defend their mother as she has on so many occasions, but Margaret stops her. "Don't. I know what you're going to say. She was traumatized. She was abused. Blah, blah, blah."

Sloane sits back, shocked. This is a side of her sister she's never seen.

"She stayed in touch with Idelle," Margaret continues. "Idelle! Not me or Aunt Millicent or you or Robroy or her granddaughters or any of the people who were hurting. She blew up my relationship with my in-laws and with Aunt Millicent. They were all kinds of coy and distant. I knew something was wrong, and I thought it was something I'd done. I can't tell you how many nights I sat with Joel, trying to figure out what in the world I'd done wrong."

She shoves her salad aside and takes a big gulp of water. Her eyes glisten. "And you. Look at you. You wanna tell me she didn't derail your life?"

"I would've said Dad derailed it."

She barrels on. "Robroy is the only one who seems to have escaped without damage. And he was raised by Dad, not her. You think that's a coincidence?"

She's wandered into cuckoo land now. Even Arturio is looking at her with incredulity.

"I get that you're mad about Mom being in touch with your mother-in-law instead of you," Sloane says. "But Margaret, I always thought you were like Robroy. You created a healthy family of your own. You didn't let Mom *or* Dad pull you down."

She sniffs. "Maybe." She looks out the window to the parking lot filling with the town's lunch crowd. "How do you feel about seeing her?" Her voice is tremulous.

How do I feel? How often have I dreamed of reuniting with Mom? "Excited. Sick to my stomach. Mad. Dying of curiosity. All of the above."

Beside her, Arturio snorts.

"What would you know?" Margaret frowns at him. "Miz Nadine is the world's greatest mom."

"That she is," he concedes. "I think I'll go see her after we hit the hospital."

"We're not still going there, are we?" Margaret protests. "Haven't we had enough drama for one day?"

Sloane imagines pacing the beach house all afternoon, awaiting their mother's arrival. "Might as well. Better than hanging around the house."

As they walk to her car, Margaret asks, "Should we call Robroy? Give him a heads-up about Mom?"

"No, let me tell him in person," Sloane says.

Margaret nods, and they head out.

Chapter 24

Mercy Hospital is a neat one-story building with a circular driveway and white columns that line a welcoming portico. Its flower beds are bright with purple lilacs as well as perky yellow daylilies. Even Margaret smiles. "Looks like Mad Gardener Millicent had a hand in landscaping."

Arturio hops out of the car and heads for the front door. "I'll meet you back in the lobby," he calls.

Sloane and Margaret wander around the grounds, skittish about going inside. Finally, they head toward the same door Arturio disappeared through. Inside, the sisters are greeted by a watercolor portrait of Aunt Millicent in the same lavender regalia she wore in yesterday's *Herald* photo.

Margaret laughs. "Wow. How long did Aunt Millicent wear that suit?"

"'Don't follow trends if they don't suit you,'" Sloane quotes their aunt, knowing Margaret can also recite the mantra. "'Find your own style.'"

"That she did."

The receptionist is elderly, and Sloane hesitates to announce their relationship to Aunt Millicent, fearing it will get them whisked away by some poor underling. Margaret has no such compunction. Within moments, a young Black woman in a white coat, not an underling but the medical director, strides toward them, expressing condolences. They accept her offer of a tour.

"We fall under the rural hospital system," explains Dr. Erin Rasmussen, leading them along a wide curving hallway dotted with watercolors of island flora. "We make no pretense of treating exotic diseases or even accepting high-risk pregnancies. But for non-acute needs—non-life-threatening illnesses, infections, normal deliveries, diabetes, broken bones, or fishhooks embedded in a lip—we're fine."

"Ouch," Margaret says. "Been there. Not in the lip, but the foot and hand."

"You wouldn't be an island girl otherwise," the doctor says with a laugh. She holds out a palm to indicate a question-mark-shaped scar. "We all have them."

"I thought you looked familiar," says Margaret. "But the Rasmussen was throwing me. Are you Jayroe Martin's sister, by any chance?"

"I am. You know Jayroe?"

"I graduated Beaufort High with her and still run into her occasionally."

"She's a pharmacist in Augusta," the director explains to Sloane. "We see her quite a bit."

Is she making a statement about me? Heck, am I offending people I've never met?

"Miss Roundtree talked about you both," she adds. "And your brother."

They come to a stop in front of an empty room, beige upon beige, the bed crisply made.

"This was your aunt's room."

"Yes, I visited her here," Margaret says. "Her doctor initially thought sepsis from the UTI had caused heart failure."

"That *is* what we assumed at first," says Dr. Rasmussen.

"But obviously, that's not what happened," Margaret presses. "What can you tell us?"

"Unfortunately, I can't say much more because of the police investigation." She meets their eyes. "But your aunt made sure I got this job despite my age. It was important to her that the director understood our island, and she had enough clout on the board to make it happen." She pauses. "So I will tell you that she was finally responding to the antibiotic. She probably would have gone home in three or four more days, especially if Burle and Jesse Jenkins were moving in. As I understood they were."

They wait.

"I can't tell you what happened after that because I don't know," the director continues. "I can only tell you how sorry I am, how devastated we all are that this happened in our hospital."

"Could it have been someone on your staff?" asks Margaret. Dr. Rasmussen looks as surprised as Sloane is by the blunt question.

"I don't... I guess it's..." She stops. "I really can't say anymore, Mrs. Simpson. Only that I am deeply sorry."

Sloane makes a lame attempt to follow up. "And Chief Hartwell is interviewing the staff about Aunt Millicent's visitors?"

"I would assume so. I really can't speak to what he is asking, but yes, he's been talking to staff."

Sloane isn't quite ready to quit. "Chief Hartwell told us that digoxin was introduced into her IV. Is that something you stock?"

"Every hospital does."

"So it was taken from your supply?"

Dr. Rasmussen is so clearly uncomfortable that Sloane starts to feel bad. Guessing at the source of the director's discomfort, she inserts, "We would never sue this hospital. This is Aunt Millicent's legacy. Chief Hartwell assured us it wasn't medical error."

Dr. Rasmussen nods, without smiling. "But it's more than that. It wasn't even negligence. We keep digoxin in a locked cabinet in a locked storage room. When we went back and inventoried, there were no missing vials."

The sisters look at her blankly.

"Someone brought in the drug from the outside?" Margaret asks.

"Apparently so."

They spend another ten minutes walking the corridors with Dr. Rasmussen, but their conversation all but ceases when they move on from Aunt Millicent's room. Margaret has gone silent, and Sloane's mind whirls with confusion, imagining someone creeping these same halls with a deadly vial already pocketed. *That's about as pre-meditated as it gets.*

When they circle back to the lobby, the director spots Arturio and cries out in delight. He rushes to hug her. "Auntie June tells me you lured her from the hospital in Beaufort."

"My proudest moment," she laughs. "She's teaching me as much as I learned in medical school."

Sloane marvels at the relationships that run so deep and knotted in this place. *What have I given up for my independence?*

The three make their way to the parking lot, where the early afternoon sun beats bright and hot. Arturio waits until they're in Margaret's car to drop his bombshell.

"Auntie June spoke to Raeford and Octavia Thursday when they visited Miz Millicent," he says. "But after they left, she had another visitor."

Sloane and Margaret look at him expectantly until he produces a crumpled newspaper photo from his jeans pocket and shoves it onto the center console.

Sloane stares into the handsome face of Ryan Carbonier.

For a few seconds, the sisters are silent, then they raise their heads simultaneously. "This proves it!" Margaret cries, waving the newspaper clip in jubilation.

Sloane wishes she could join in her sister's elation, but guilt over-whelms her. If Ryan Carbonier did this terrible thing, it is her fault. "What about your aunt, Arturio?" she asks. "Will she talk to the po-lice?"

"Already has. She said Chief Hartwell was at the door when she got to work this morning."

"I wonder why Dr. Rasmussen didn't mention it," Margaret says.

"She admitted she couldn't comment on the investigation," Sloane offers. "I bet he told her not to." Her mind goes back to last Thursday. She left Ryan Carbonier in the hotel bar in Savannah around a quarter of six. After hearing her cavalier estimates that Aunt Millicent would live many more years, he circled back. Was he al-ready in possession of the digoxin? If so, will his computer or phone reveal where he got it? Or, despite what Dr. Rasmussen claims, did he find the drug at the hospital?

Margaret wants to call Chief Hartwell to ask if he's arresting Carbonier, but they decide they don't want to get Arturio's Auntie June in trouble.

"It's almost two o'clock," Sloane says. "Should we go back to the house?"

"I'll drop you off," says Margaret. "I need to get the girls settled after school before I come over. I don't want them to meet their grandmother quite yet. Sparks may fly." Her voice has regained a measure of humor, and Sloane is relieved.

"And I'll drive the van to visit my folks," says Arturio. "I'll take Sean and Derek, too, if you want the house to yourselves."

"Good idea," Sloane says, her body taut with nerves over what awaits them.

Sloane can't tell what Robroy feels about their mother's impend-ing visit. He grew quiet and took a soft drink onto the beachfront porch when she told him. She wants to join him, but emails crowd her inbox. Both her agent and her editor want to talk about edits.

She feels herself edging toward hysteria. *The edits that haven't been done? Not unlike the graduation speech that hasn't been written?* Her body thrums with anxiety. For the fifth or sixth time, she walks to the foyer and peers out. Still no Annie Cheney.

She paces to the kitchen window then back to her laptop, where she pounds out an email to hold her editor and agent off for another day.

Ladies, I'm sorry, but there are unexpected developments surrounding my aunt's death. Turns out my mother—whom I've told you was dead—isn't and, in fact, is on her way to see us. Needless to say, I'm having trouble concentrating. Begging for your mercy.

Sloane

She crosses the kitchen and shoves the screen door too hard, wincing as it bangs against the outside wall. She intends to join Robroy but is too edgy to sit. It's after five o'clock, which certainly qualifies as "late afternoon."

"Nervous much?" her brother asks.

"Aren't you?"

"I hate to say this, but I didn't know her as well as you and Margaret did. I guess I missed her"—he lifts his shoulders—"but I think I missed the *idea* of her more than her specifically. If that makes sense."

She flops into a rocking chair. "Yeah, it does. They say that children grow up in the same household, but we really didn't. I missed her. Specifically." She gazes out to sea, picturing her mother holding her hand as she jumped into the waves. *Did that really happen? Or was it Aunt Millicent's hand I grasped so tightly?*

"Sloane, do you think she'll really come?" Robroy's voice is almost forlorn.

"Yes! I mean, she told Idelle and Octavia she would." She hears the alarm in her tone. "You don't think she will?"

Her brother flips the hair out of his eyes. "It's been an awfully long time."

She jumps to her feet.

"You got more pacing to do?" Robroy teases.

"Ha. Ha." She lets the screen door slam behind her, as if making noise somehow accomplishes something. As if stomping around makes the time pass more quickly.

What will I call her? Mom? As I called her during my last year in high school?

She speaks to herself, testing it on her tongue. "Hi, Mom. Is that you, Mom?" *When did I stop calling her Mama?* She doesn't remember. She was never *Mother.* She tries again. "Hi, Mom."

What am I doing? Am I focusing on her name so I don't have to think about the deeper stuff? About why she abandoned us? Probably.

She makes another lap around the downstairs then stops to peer through the parlor window. Still no Annie Cheney, but she is rewarded by the sight of Margaret's BMW crawling into the driveway. Sloane throws open the front door as her sister mounts the steps, her heels brittle as a hammer on the hard surfaces. She has changed into a dress and open-toed sandals. Her expression is grim as she pushes past Sloane.

"So, where the hell is she?"

Part Two

Chapter 25

Annie

She thought she was ready to face her children, but the closer she gets to Millicent House, the tighter the band is around her chest. She swerves abruptly into the parking lot of the Seafood Shack, spewing gravel onto the side of an empty pickup truck. She glances around to make sure the truck's owner hasn't registered the dinging. No one runs out of Burle's grocery, so maybe she's safe.

Annie spends a lot of time thinking about that—her safety. It's become second nature.

Take, for instance, this rusty Chevy Impala—not a 1950s classic or a gleaming 2020s newbie, but an unmemorable 1999 model. For more than a decade, she's aimed for unmemorable. She was pretty sure Millicent and Raeford would send a private investigator when she fled, and she intended to stay off his radar. Her sister and attorney meant well, she knows they did. But they weren't able to protect her before, and they never would have. She's learned to protect herself.

She sits until her heartbeat slows, until her breath ceases hitching. After checking the rearview mirror to make sure there are no surprises, she yanks it to change the angle and inspect her reflection. Her reddish curls reveal no gray, courtesy of a high-end colorist, and her green eyes are surrounded by gentle wrinkles. But a lifetime of hiding from the sun has paid off: Her alabaster skin is smoother than most fifty-three-year-olds', especially those living under a blistering Southern sun.

Sloane is the child who looks most like her. Though Annie hasn't seen her younger daughter for twelve years, she's watched her on YouTube interviews and recorded library readings. She's seen her picture staring from bookstore shelves. Her heart begins to hammer again. Within minutes, she'll see Sloane. And Margaret. And Robroy, whom she'd never even recognize were it not for videos shared by his fans.

She has missed her children terribly. Achingly. *But will they reject me? Will they understand the fear that drove me from this place?*

She shoves her car door closed and walks briskly into the Seafood Shack before she can change her mind.

Jesse is wrapping a shrimp purchase for a customer. She looks up idly, then her jaw drops, and she gasps. "Miz Annie?"

Burle whirls around from the frozen food case. A gigantic grin splits his face, and he rushes around the counter to lock her in his huge arms. "Miz Annie!" he exclaims. "You're a sight for sore eyes."

He pulls away, holding her at arm's length. "We didn't know if you were dead or alive!" He pats her shoulder. "You just wait 'til you see your Sloane. She's the spitting image of you. And Margaret and her girls. And that rock star son of yours."

Her throat catches, and she can only nod. "And how are you, Burle?" she finally chokes out. "And you, Jesse?"

The old woman remains rooted behind the counter, using the interaction with a customer to avoid Annie's eyes. "We're fine. We held Miz Millicent's homegoing on Monday." She adds pointedly, "Two days ago."

"Yes, I know." *Should I explain why I didn't attend? Impossible, since I can't explain it to myself.*

Burle is watching her. "Of course, she knows, Jesse. And she knows that Mr. Robert's service is tomorrow. Ain't that right, Miz Annie?"

Jesse accepts her husband's rebuke. They knew Robert Cheney. Everybody in town knew Robert Cheney and his savage temper and cruel fists. For years, in fact, Burle and Jesse had encouraged Annie to leave him, had offered transportation and financial help from their church. But their escape plans included Sloane and Robroy. What she's witnessing in Jesse's coolness is disdain for a mother who would save herself and not her children.

She swallows painfully and backs out of the store, apologizing. "I'm on my way to Millicent House, and I just wanted to stop and..." *And what? Say sorry? Say I need a minute before facing my children? Say I'm a miserable excuse for a mother, sister, and friend?*

Burle raises his massive hand. "No need to explain, Miz Annie. You know where we are if you need us."

Ten minutes later, she is still sitting in the parking lot outside the Seafood Shack. She can picture the driveway, not far down the road, where iron seabirds rise from Millicent's stalwart fence and, at this time of year, flowering vines run riot. She'll always think of it as her sister's house, though she grew up there too.

Their father, Jasper Roundtree, was an attorney, first in Millicent, then in Beaufort as his practice expanded. He was a good bit older than their mother as well as stern, proper, and humorless. When their mother died, her sister stepped in, not only to raise Annie, but to serve as Jasper's hostess for political meetings and formal dinners, all the functions that went along with owning the most prominent property on the island.

By the time Annie started school, her father was spending most nights in Beaufort. Millicent shielded her from the fact that he had what amounted to a second family there, though there was never a marriage. His widowed lover had money of her own, so there was no threat to the Roundtree fortune.

Her father's dour superiority and her sister's exacting airs combined to create an airless household. No wonder then, at seventeen, she sought out the island boy most likely to upset them. Though Robert Cheney was hardly a boy. He was twenty-three and already living on his own along the tidal creek that runs through the island, shrimping for an older brother and saving for his own boat.

His wildness and disdain for Annie's lineage, and okay, his rock-hard body, excited her. The young men—fishermen, boat mechanics, farmers—who hung around his cabin were loud and funny and pro-fane, opposite of the boys at school. None of them gave a whit about the family their town was named after. For the first time, she was simply Annie, and she basked in it.

Her pregnancy brought the party to an abrupt stop. The men still came around, but she was too tired to be sociable and retreated to the single bedroom at the back of the cabin. She started her senior year at Beaufort High, but before long, Baby Bump Margaret was visible. Despite the school board's enlightened stance that allowed girls to attend to term and return after giving birth, she was too self-conscious to do so. A semester shy of graduation, she dropped out. Four months later, her father died. Two weeks later still, on her eighteenth birthday and with infant Margaret asleep in a carrier, she and Robert drove to Beaufort and were married by a notary public.

Meanwhile, Robert panicked that his dream of owning a shrimp boat was dissolving into a morass of medical bills and onesies, diapers and wipes, bottles and baby food. The night she protested that her sister would happily pay for anything related to their Roundtree baby was the night he first hit her. She never saw his fist coming, only found herself on the cabin floor, a lump rising behind her right ear and bile threatening to spill from her throat.

She rushed out to her yellow Mustang and fled home with her newborn. Of course, she did. Robert called every hour—tearful, sobbing, apologetic. In her other ear, her sister assured her that they would raise this baby together, that she could return to school, attend college, have a career.

Along with the cajoling came a warning: "Annie, once a man has shown you who he is, believe him."

Stupidly, Annie lashed out at Millicent: "Is that why you don't have a man at all?"

Her sister recoiled, a look of deep hurt on her face. Of Annie's many regrets, that's one of the sharpest.

After a week, sick with indecision and the specter of single motherhood, she bolted once again from her stifling home. True to her sister's prediction, Robert showed her over the next decade and a half who he was. He didn't bother restricting his blows to her torso or back or other places that clothes could hide. That would've required forethought. No, Robert lashed out in blind, drunken rages, never caring or calculating where his knuckles landed. After a while, he didn't even apologize.

Did she think about leaving him? *Only every other week.* But the humiliation, the thought of admitting her failure to Millicent—and to the town—kept her from doing so.

The one thing she managed to do was protect her girls' inheritance. Robert was out on his boat the morning she went into labor, so he never saw the birth certificate, never saw the *Millicent* the nurse wrote between *Margaret* and *Cheney*. And six years later, he never saw the *Millicent* penned before *Sloane Cheney*. To Annie's mind, she was securing her daughters' future at the same time she was ensuring their present safety. For she had learned that it was at least partially her lineage, her privilege, her family name, that infuriated her husband. He was not a fit match for Millicent Ann Roundtree, and he knew it.

As her daughters grew, she bided her time. Her sister provided them occasional sanctuary, so they didn't see the worst of Robert's wrath. Or so she told herself. Millicent warned that Margaret and

Sloane knew more than she imagined, that they were terrified of Robert and hated him for what he did to their mother. She begged Annie to move back to the homeplace, promised that they would hire private security.

But Millicent didn't understand the oily black bottom of Annie's fear. She didn't know about Chelsea Cheney. Robert's sister.

Annie cranks up the old Impala and creeps across the Seafood Shack parking lot to the road that will carry her to Millicent House. But instead of turning left toward the house and the ocean, she swerves right. She needs a few more minutes of aimless driving. A few more minutes to settle.

But there's no settling her racing mind, no blocking the memories that rush her like rogue waves. It is as if the memories are released by the very trees, monstrous and looming, by the draping moss, by the briny smell of the nearby marsh.

In the months after Margaret's birth, when Annie believed that Robert's initial blow was a one-off, never to be repeated, she drove her Mustang convertible to meet his mother. All she knew of his family was his older brother Ian, who picked him up at their creekside cabin to go shrimping six days a week.

Robert had pointed out his mother's house the previous summer, when they'd taken Ian's boat on an inland waterway cruise. She knew the island well enough to locate the house by land. It teetered on stilts above the tidal creek, off a deserted, unpaved road.

Eileen Cheney was suspicious of her visit. "And you married which of my boys?" she asked, peering into Margaret's carrier but not touching the baby. The question flummoxed Annie. Did his mother have so many sons she couldn't keep up?

"Robert," she answered.

His mother's face darkened. "I see. Does he know you're here?"

"I... I... don't think I mentioned it to him, no."

"Probably smart."

"Why is that?"

"It's just that he might not like you meeting me."

"But why?" She was genuinely curious. Maybe that's why she and Robert had been drawn to each other. Both of them were misfits in their own families. Her mother-in-law didn't answer, so Annie's eyes flitted around the small living room, seeking something to spark a conversation. Perched on a shallow credenza was a photo of three boys holding beers aloft on Ian's boat. Robert had told her about his brothers, Ian, two years older, and Elliott, a year younger. But beside it was another photo, one of two teenage girls with the same brassy blond hair and wide smiles.

She didn't know Robert had sisters. "Are those your daughters?"

Her mother-in-law stiffened. "Yes. Chelsea and Sierra."

"Do they live off island?" Surely, she would have heard of them otherwise.

The older woman looked wary. "No."

"Do they live here? With you?"

Robert's mother bowed her head. "Chelsea died shortly after that picture was taken. Drowned right out there," she said, nodding toward the tidal creek.

"Oh my gosh, I'm so sorry," Annie stammered. "I didn't know. Robert never... um... mentioned her." Her face grew hot. *Did I just make things worse?*

"No surprise there," his mother said bluntly.

What does that mean? In the face of Mrs. Cheney's cold reserve, Annie wasn't sure how much she could ask. "And Sierra?"

"Sierra does live off island. With my sister. In Columbia."

Annie didn't know what else to say. Clearly, there were bad feelings between Robert and his mother. But then she hadn't introduced

Robert to her father or sister either. Their marriage was a rebellion of sorts against their respective families.

After a few more awkward minutes, Annie rose and told Mrs. Cheney goodbye. "Probably best if you don't mention to Robert that you was here," his mother said. "Probably safest for you and that baby."

Later that evening, she and Robert were eating meatloaf and mashed potatoes in their tiny kitchen, Margaret asleep in her crib. Robert was talking about the day's catch and asked what she'd done all day. Ignoring his mother's warning, she told him she'd been to meet her. He froze, but Annie was too naïve to notice.

"You never told me you had sisters," she continued, sipping her iced tea.

"What did you say?"

Foolishly, she didn't recognize the change in tone.

"I saw their picture. Chelsea and Sierra."

She never saw the plate coming. The next thing she knew, she was on the floor, meatloaf and potatoes and gravy warm on her face, her lip bleeding, and a tooth chipped from where the tea glass had rammed her mouth. She rolled into a ball, clutching her still mushy tummy.

Her husband stood over her, swaying. She thought he was going to bend down and pick her up, cry, apologize, as he'd done the first time. Instead, he said stonily, "Don't. Ever. Say. Their. Names. Again." And he banged out the screen door.

Annie had never considered herself a proud person. But the thought of returning home, of admitting to Millicent what a mess she'd made of her life, was worse than the mess itself.

The one thing that made life with Robert tolerable—if you could call her existence tolerable—was that at least once a week, he and Ian traveled miles beyond the barrier island and stayed out overnight. For Annie, that meant two days and one night of freedom.

Following the plate-throwing incident, she made an appointment with a dentist in Beaufort to fix her chipped tooth. Afterward, with baby Margaret in tow, she went straight to the Beaufort County Library and asked the librarian for help in accessing *Beaufort Gazette* obituaries. Chelsea had looked to be in her mid-teens in her mother's photo. To throw a wide net, Annie started searching in 1980. Nothing. 1981, nothing. Then in January 1982, more than five years previously, there it was. Chelsea Cheney, sixteen, drowned behind her family home on Millicent Island. There was not only an obituary but also a news story.

Chelsea had been discovered in the water by her brother Elliott. The family reported that she liked to swim off the dock, though the writer pointed out that the day in question was fifty-five degrees. The reporter hadn't been able to glean much more from the family, but her friends at Beaufort High were effusive. Chelsea was "lively, fun, beautiful, talented." She'd starred in the school's production of *Grease*. She'd planned to move to Los Angeles to pursue acting as soon as she graduated.

Then Annie noticed the final paragraph. Chelsea was the daughter of the late Ian Cheney Sr. and Eileen Cheney. Sister of Ian Jr., Elliott, and Sierra. She went back and read it again. She hadn't missed it. Robert wasn't listed in the news story or the obit. The writers would have relied on the family to provide names. *Why had they left Robert out?*

She sat back. Chelsea had died when Annie was in middle school. It said something about her isolation at Millicent House that she'd not heard of the drowning. *And Sierra? Why did she go to live in Columbia?*

Clearly, Robert wasn't going to tell her. But she couldn't stop thinking about these mysterious sisters, both of whom were whisked from his life.

Annie drives all the way to the bridge that would carry her over the inland waterway and back to the mainland. Instead of crossing it, she wrenches the wheel and enters the parking lot of a Gas 'N' Such owned by her best friend, Idelle, and Idelle's husband, J.C. And of course, now, by their son, Joel, and Annie's daughter Margaret. Trusting that none of them will be in this location, she enters the store to buy a Diet Pepsi and crackers she doesn't really want. But maybe they will calm the turbulence in her stomach that these memories have unleashed. She knows she's putting off the moment she will see her children. It's hard to separate them from their family history, their lives with Robert Cheney.

After Margaret's birth, Annie often met Idelle at the newly opened Elsie's Diner. Her friend was headed to college that fall, so they knew their time together was limited. Annie's sister-in-law, Ian's wife, Caroline, was a waitress there and let the teens sit for hours, even if their only purchases were Cokes and fries.

Annie's time at the diner kept her from going stir crazy; she was eighteen, stuck at home with a baby, increasingly fearful of which husband would return each evening—the jovial, sexy man she'd fallen in love with, or the moody, sarcastic man who had surfaced as his goal of boat ownership receded. Fortunately, Margaret was a content baby and sat happily in her carrier while Annie drank creamy coffee and gossiped or read the *Gazette* cover to cover.

When Idelle wasn't around, Annie's sister-in-law would slide into her booth to chat during breaks. Caroline and Ian were having trouble conceiving, so she doted on Margaret, prying her out of her carrier, lifting her to a shoulder, visibly inhaling her sweet baby scent.

Elsie didn't complain because she was rather besotted with Margaret too.

In the beginning, Annie had hoped that Ian would learn of Robert's violence and step in. But Caroline had seen her clumsy attempts to hide black eyes and purple bruises, and nothing changed. Robert's older brother, like the rest of the town, understood what was happening and let it.

That was hardly fair. Munching a peanut-butter-filled cracker beneath the Gas 'N' Such sign, Annie can see that now. She was the only one who could have changed her situation. But at the time, immature and ashamed and frightened, she thought her decision to marry Robert was irrevocable, her waking nightmare no less than she deserved.

With baby Margaret creating a bond between Annie and Caroline, her sister-in-law began to reveal tidbits about the Cheney family. Ian had no more contact with his mother than Robert did. Their brother Elliott fled the island as soon as he was old enough.

"And Sierra?" Annie asked.

Caroline suddenly got busy and claimed to hear Elsie calling from the kitchen. It was enough to make Annie wonder what had gone on in that house by the tidal creek. *Had Robert learned violence at the hands of his late father? Or even his mother?* She recalled enough from her high school sociology class to entertain the thought.

The next time she was alone with Caroline, she brought up Sierra again.

"She lives in Columbia," Caroline said abruptly, handing baby Margaret back to her. "That's all I know."

"Does the family ever get together? Like at Thanksgiving or Christmas?"

Caroline's laugh was harsh. "Not since I've known them." She spun around to check her other tables. "I have to run."

Finishing the Diet Pepsi, Annie throws the can into a recycling barrel. If she's going to Millicent House, she needs to go now. There's nothing to be accomplished by this senseless procrastination.

She pulls the Impala to the road and resolutely turns left. Every mile uncovers another memory, carefully buried these past dozen years. For much of her life, SC 900 carried her from Beaufort High to Millicent House. To church. To Idelle's house.

When Idelle left for the University of South Carolina, Annie felt more bereft than ever. She wondered how she had ever thought that leaving her family and having a husband and a baby was a great adventure. As far as she could see, she had only added bars to her island prison.

One morning when Margaret was nine months old and beginning to protest confinement to her carrier, a handsome man with sandy hair, ruddy skin, and an affable grin slid into the diner seat opposite her. Caroline stood by the booth, smiling nervously.

"Annie, this is our brother-in-law, Elliott. Elliott, this is Annie, who I was telling you about."

Elliott looked like Robert, but cleaner-cut—and better smelling. He wore a button-down shirt with no tie, rolled up sleeves, and the Old Spice cologne her father had favored. A wave of wistfulness rolled over her.

"So nice to meet you, Annie. And this little one," Elliott said as he gently tugged Margaret's foot. She rewarded him with a vigorous kick and a giggle.

"What are you doing in town?" Sloane asked. "Are you here to see Robert?"

"Robert? Oh, no." There was something in his voice she couldn't pinpoint. *Disgust? Trepidation?* Hard to know. "I'm here on business for my mother."

Her face must have looked quizzical because he added, "I'm a banker in Columbia. I handle Mom's account."

She nodded, having no understanding of banking or investments or anything financial. He glanced up at Caroline. "I'll have coffee and a stack of those pancakes you promised. With blueberries, if you've got 'em."

"Coming right up," said Caroline, giving Margaret's tummy a final pat.

Elliott turned his attention to Annie. "I won't beat around the bush. Caroline told me you've been asking about Sierra. And I take from that, about Chelsea."

She gulped and nodded. "You found her. In the creek that day."

"How'd you know?"

"The *Beaufort Gazette.*"

"Oh, you *are* interested, aren't you?" His gaze was friendly but sad.

She felt herself blush. She was glad she had no bruises to hide. Robert had been surprisingly calm that month, which had made the optimist in her hopeful. Pathetic, she knew. "It's just that no one—not your mother or Caroline or Robert—will talk about your sisters."

He nodded, toying with the salt and pepper shakers. "There was a time I wouldn't have either. But being away, I've come to realize that Robert is nothing but a small-town bully." Her eyes must have widened because he hastily added, "No offense to you, Annie."

She made the leap, hoping it was too big and too absurd. "Robert had something do with Chelsea's drowning?" Her voice sounded squeaky.

"Yeah. We're pretty sure. We never could prove anything."

"But what happened?"

Elliott took a deep breath. "When she was sixteen, Chelsea was raped. I was her favorite brother, closest to her in age. She told me and Ma, but we couldn't get her to tell us who'd done it. We assumed it was someone at school."

Annie tensed, not sure she wanted to hear the rest of the story, but Elliott forged ahead.

"Understandably, her behavior changed. She grew angry, started throwing things around the house, storming out, then staying out all night. Ma and I begged her to let us take her to the police, but she said she wouldn't tell them anything. She'd say we were lying. And then she made a cryptic comment like, 'Believe me, you don't want to know anyway.'"

He sighed. "In retrospect, it didn't go on that long. She told us around mid-November. On that Christmas morning, she gave us all gifts as usual. Except Robert. He made some crack about not getting a present. Chelsea didn't say a word, but she was shaking and got up and went to her room.

"A week later, on New Year's Day, I found her in the inland waterway. We called the police and all those things you do. But hours later, I went into the boys' bedroom. Ian had already moved out, and Robert and I shared the room. I could see that Robert's bed was soaked, like he'd thrown a ton of wet towels on it. I guess in the back of my mind, I was already suspicious. So I put my fingers on his spread to taste the wetness. It was salt water, not water from our shower. Robert had not been around Chelsea the whole time I was pulling her out and yelling and calling the police. So when had he gotten so wet with sea water?"

Annie stared, unsure if he was actually seeking a response.

"You think..." Her voice gave out, so she coughed and started again. "You think Robert killed her?"

"I think Robert raped her and then was afraid she was going to talk, and so he drowned her. Things that hadn't made an impression before started to. You saw how small that house was. But when Robert entered a room, Chelsea would take Sierra by the hand and pull her into their bedroom. They ate their meals in there. But the most telling thing was she started riding the school bus to Beaufort rather than riding with me and Robert in his car. It took her an extra two hours a day. Working back in my head, I remembered I'd stayed home sick for a couple of days in early November, so it was just Chelsea and Robert who had driven to school. I think that's when it happened. Probably in Robert's car."

Annie reached for her coffee but felt physically sick and realized it might come back up. "And so you and your mother sent Sierra away," she said. "To protect her. From her own brother."

The coffee already in her stomach burbled sourly. Margaret started to fuss, so she pulled her from the carrier and held the baby close, mind racing. Her fear of Robert's rages had been misplaced. He had committed murder not in a drunken fury but in cold blood. He'd promised more than once to kill her and Margaret if she tried to leave. Suddenly, the idea that he would follow through on that moved from possible to probable.

She gazed at Elliott in horror. "Thank you for telling me. But why are you? After all these years?"

He shrugged. "I was seventeen when it happened. Robert was a year older, and I guess I was scared of him. I know Ma was. But it's been over six years. I worked my way through college, got a good job, and realized he's nothing to be afraid of. Just an angry, uneducated fisherman who drinks way too much. Again, no offense."

Caroline brought his pancakes, and he attacked them with vigor. As Annie was processing what she'd heard, he leaned in. "But Annie. What made you marry him? I mean with your family?" He waved his fork in a circle to indicate the Roundtrees' standing in this town, her legacy as a Millicent.

She shook her head miserably. She had no good answer, not then, and not now.

Chapter 26

Annie

Driving once again toward Millicent House, Annie passes the Seafood Shack for a second time and looks longingly at the building where Burle and Jesse are working. It's time to face her children. *Will they be glad to see me? Angry? Bitter?* She has no idea.

She can smell the ocean, or the tidal creek, or whatever it is that creates the distinctive scent of the Lowcountry coast. The smell of home. A smell that accompanied all the days of her life until twelve years ago.

After Elliott's visit to Elsie's Diner, years passed, some more bearable than others. She and Robert and Margaret moved into a slightly larger house on the inland waterway. Robert bought his damn boat, which seemed to satisfy him for a while. Until the price of shrimp fell, or the dock needed repairs, or she wore too much makeup, or—who knew?—maybe the moon waned. Then the fists flew.

She got her GED, which unexpectedly caused Robert to react with pride. He bought cheap champagne at the grocery store and demanded they celebrate. That night, she got pregnant with Sloane. Only in retrospect did she suspect it was Robert's way of tying her more inexorably to him.

Yet, with Robert on his boat most days, Annie was free to join her sister and Burle and Jesse at Millicent House and let the girls run and play on its beach. Millicent made up a bedroom for her daughters and urged her to let them stay over, especially when she had injuries to hide. The girls knew intuitively not to talk about their aunt's

142

hospitality in front of Robert, and Annie knew to never bring up her family name. Looking back, it was an insane way to live. She understands that now, she truly does, and she doesn't expect anyone but another abused woman to comprehend the absurdity.

Her original plan, encouraged by her sister, was to get Margaret to college then take Sloane and escape. She'd borrowed Millicent's computer to map things out, calculating distances and prices for food, housing, and transportation. The problem was she had no marketable skills. But she was playing a long game, and her sister put Annie's name on one of her bank accounts. She told her she was free to empty it when it was time to flee.

"And remember, Annie, this house is as much yours as it is mine," Millicent told her frequently, though their father had left it entirely to Millicent. He'd said there was no way he was risking Millicent House falling into the hands of Robert Cheney. Even Annie understood the wisdom of that.

She also understood there was no way to sever Robert's future claim on Millicent House by getting a divorce. He'd kill her before he let that happen. She knew that as surely as she knew he'd killed Chelsea.

Still, still, she began to believe there was a way out. As Margaret grew into a self-assured young woman and Sloane became her funny little Mini-Me, Annie's spirits inched upward. She renewed her friendship with Idelle, though watching her and J.C. build a successful business prompted a jealousy that surprised her. Pushing the feeling aside, she imagined Margaret safely in college and out of Robert's reach, and herself and Sloane forging a new life in St. Pete or Fort Lauderdale or Corpus Christi. Annie was still young, so young. She'd be only thirty-five when Margaret went off to school; surely, she could re-invent herself, preferably in another beach town.

And so her days unspooled as she watched and waited to make her move.

That's what she was doing right up until the night Robert raped her and she became pregnant with his son.

Passing through the gates of Millicent House, Annie shivers despite the late afternoon heat. Her tires crunch on the same oyster shells Robert's truck used to churn up. She sees the side yard he stomped through to find her. Though this was her home, his unwanted presence is everywhere, distorting, disturbing, disrupting. She blinks to clear away the ghosts. Shame floods through her, and she hopes the children she is about to meet are free from the fear and degradation that have steered her life.

But I'm finally making a stand, aren't I? Decades too late, admittedly. There will be things Margaret and Sloane and Robroy can never know. But *she* will know that she, Millicent Ann Roundtree, fought her way back.

The ring of her cell phone interrupts her reverie. She glances down to see *Babe,* the endearment she has nicknamed the caller.

"Hey, babe," he says, echoing the identification on her phone. "Are you at the house yet?"

"I'm sitting in the driveway."

"Getting your courage up?"

"You know it. And getting swamped with memories before I even go in."

"You've got this. I love you, and I'll see you tomorrow."

The front door of the house opens, and her heart skips. Sloane walks out first, red curls piled messily on her head, skin as fair as her own. Then Robroy, taller than she'd imagined, handsome but bewildered looking. Then Margaret, crisp, blond, professional, frowning. *Goodness, she reminds me of Idelle.* They line up shoulder to shoulder across a porch laden with orange, pink, and yellow blossoms. Robroy reaches for Margaret's hand, and the movement pierces Annie. He's like a little boy, waiting to cross the street.

Sloane breaks the solidarity of their line and bolts toward the car.

"I've got to go, Ryan," Annie says.

Chapter 27

Sloane

They are seated in the formal parlor, sweating glasses of iced tea on coasters before them. Sloane, Margaret, and Robroy trade nervous glances, and their mother's hand trembles as she reaches for her glass. It's all Sloane can do not to touch her. She hugged her the instant she got out of that old Impala, and she longs to pat her shoulder, her hair, her hand. But Margaret and Robroy are holding back, so she resists as well.

As usual, Margaret dives right in. "So," she says, sitting erect and crossing her legs as if she's interviewing a manager for Gas 'N' Such, "do you want to tell us where you've been?"

The question is as good as any, though Sloane wants to shout, *And why? Why did you leave us?*

Their mother appears to consider the question seriously. "I moved directly to Corpus Christi for that first six months. Then New Orleans because it was still chaotic years after Hurricane Katrina, and I figured I could avoid anyone sent by your father or your Aunt Millicent. Then after a few years, I felt safer, and moved to Florida. That's where I've been ever since."

"Where in Florida?"

Did she just hesitate slightly? "St. Pete. Mostly."

"How did you live?" Margaret is persistent on these nuts and bolts, and Sloane shoots her an exasperated glance.

"A little nest egg from Millicent to start with. Waiting tables. Then in New Orleans, I met two guys who ran a bed and breakfast.

They wanted to travel, and they entrusted me with running the place for weeks at a time. Things worked out so well they moved to St. Pete and bought another huge house, and brought me in to run it as a B-and-B." She smiles tremulously. "Is this really what you want to know, Margaret?"

Sloane bursts in. "What I want to know is why. Why you left us." She bites her lip but can't stop the flood of words. "I was sure you were going to come back before I left for college. I was so sure of it. And Robroy. Mom, he was only ten years old, and you left him with... with Dad."

Their mother gazes at Robroy for a long time, but his eyes are on the floor. "That's the crux of it, isn't it?" she asks softly, never taking her eyes off him. She sighs. "I've had this conversation so many times in my head, but now that I'm here, I hardly know where to start."

Her eyes rove over the genteel parlor, as if seeking an answer among its fabrics and antiques. "First of all, it's no secret that I was scared of your father. You girls saw that. Robroy, I'm sorry, son. I'm not sure what you saw. Everything kind of blurred after you were born."

She sighs again, takes a drink of tea. "I say this in no way as an excuse, but as an explanation. In retrospect, I think I sank into depression, postpartum or garden variety, I'm not sure. It was no reflection on you, Robroy. You were a good baby, a sunny little boy, truly a joy to be around—if I'd been capable of experiencing joy." She stares at him, willing him to look up. When he does, she adds, "More importantly, I was convinced your father loved you. Loved spending time with you."

She catches herself and adds, "I'm not saying he didn't love you girls, but let's just say he didn't know how to show it."

Sloane laughs bleakly. "You don't have to apologize for him. Margaret and I aren't under any illusions."

"Well, whatever. Sloane, I'm sorry I wasn't here to send you off to college." She gives her the barest wisp of a smile before returning to Robroy. "But my deepest regret concerns you, Robroy. I was too afraid to take you with me. Afraid of what your father would do. Now that I'm in a healthier place, I see what a poor decision that was. But at the time, I couldn't see past my own… my own—I don't even know what. Needs? Fears?" She smiles sadly. "All I can say is I am truly, truly sorry. Sorry I deserted you. Sorry I left you with him. Sorry I missed seeing you grow into the handsome young man you've become." Tears glisten in her eyes. "But I *have* seen you, you know. All those videos online of you and your band. You're extremely talented."

Robroy's reserve is melting, Sloane can tell. Their mother wipes her eyes. "But in my defense—and believe me, it's my only defense—I knew that your Aunt Millicent and Margaret and Joel and Burle and Jesse would look out for you."

Robroy nods. "They did." He places an arm around Margaret's shoulder and squeezes.

Her sister's eyes are still frosty. "You have grandchildren, you know," she says stiffly.

Their mother lights up. "I know! Emma Sue and Sarah! Idelle sent me pictures."

If their mother thinks this is the way to win Margaret over, she quickly recognizes her mistake. Margaret's expression is incredulous. "And all this time you were in touch with Idelle? What the hell?"

Their mother looks taken aback. "No, I wasn't. I mean, not the whole time. I didn't get in touch with Idelle until maybe two and a half years ago. She managed to keep it secret from Millicent for a while." Her eyes skitter around the room. "I wanted to reach out to all of you. And I know you would never intentionally have told your father. But this town, this island is so small. I just couldn't take the chance. I'm sorry."

The poor woman has apologized repeatedly. *What will it take for us to believe her?* Margaret remains stonily distant. Robroy is staring at her with the guilelessness he brings to all his relationships. And Sloane, she's somewhere in between.

A cell phone rings, and their mother jumps. She rummages through her purse, glances at it and switches it off.

"Are you staying here?" Sloane asks. "And coming to Dad's service tomorrow?"

"No!" she says. "Not that. But yes, I will stay here if there's room." She smiles, almost girlishly. "But Robroy, don't you have the Baby Smashers staying here?"

"Alleged Baby Stompers," he corrects her with a grin. "But we didn't let them have Aunt Millicent's room. You can sleep there. Right, Sloane?"

It's more than fine with Sloane. They have so much to catch up on. "But don't go onto the upstairs balcony," she warns. "You'll see the police tape."

"Police tape?" Her mother's brow furrows.

Sloane doesn't know how much to say and doesn't want to scare her off. "The porch railing gave way."

Robroy and Margaret remain quiet.

"Since Aunt Millicent's death was under investigation," Sloane continues, "the police responded and taped it off."

Their mother seems to accept the explanation. "It's been over thirty years since I slept in this house," she muses. "I was younger than you, Robroy." She rises to her feet and again wipes her eyes.

"I'll get your suitcase," he says, heading for the door.

By nightfall, their reunion turns into a raucous party. Joel brings Emma Sue and Sarah over to meet their grandmother. Octavia, Idelle, and J.C. join them, Idelle carrying a platter of fried chicken from her closest convenience store. Arturio arrives with Sean and Derek.

Their mother doesn't recognize Arturio at first; he couldn't have been more than twelve when she left the island. But as soon as he speaks, her head cocks, and she says—loudly, for she's had several glasses of cabernet—"Little Arturio! You're Nadine and Randall's Arturio? And Burle's?"

He laughs. "Yep, I belong to all of them. It's good to see you, Miz Annie. Mama says to come see her when you get settled."

"I sure will." She shakes her head in amazement. "Little Arturio. I didn't even recognize you on the band's videos."

Their mother plays guest of honor, squealing delightedly with Emma Sue and Sarah, linking arms with Idelle, calling out requests for Robroy's band. Sloane and Margaret serve as hostesses, pulling cheeses, raw vegetables, and hummus from the fridge, heating up croissants, locating the last lemon pound cake in the freezer.

"When's the last time Millicent House had a party like this?" asks Sloane as they hear a warm-up riff from Robroy's guitar.

"No telling. I doubt Aunt Millicent booked the Alleged Baby Stompers for her garden club." Margaret yanks gold-rimmed plates from a cupboard. She hasn't thawed yet.

"So, what are you thinking?"

"I'm thinking," Margaret says, banging cutlery on the counter, "that she's on a make-up tour." Sloane doesn't have to guess who *she* is. "She's figured out who's most upset with her, and she's picking you off, one by one."

Sloane gapes at her sister. "Are you serious?"

"Tonight's target is Robroy. Officially the most sinned against. Notice her inroads via his music. 'Oh, Robroy, can you play us something? Wherever did you get your talent? It certainly wasn't from me.' Cue trilling giggles." Sloane stops with a wine bottle in mid-air, while Margaret barrels on. "Next up: You. I imagine the path will be your book. She's either already read it and is prepared to discuss, or she'll grab it from Aunt Millicent's study and read it as you watch. Anxiously. Dying for her approval, which, of course, she will dispense with utmost gravity."

"Margaret!" Sloane is in equal parts shocked and intrigued. "What about you? What's her inroad to you?"

"You don't hear it?" A sudden squeal of laughter echoes through the kitchen. "My girls. She thinks she'll get to me through my girls." Margaret pulls the croissants from the microwave. "Though she doesn't really need to win me over."

"Why not?"

"Because I'm not in Aunt Millicent's original will. I wouldn't be the one fighting the new will."

Sloane stares at her sister.

"Close your mouth," Margaret says. "You'll catch flies."

"But... but..." She puts the wine bottle down harder than she intended. "Margaret, you act like you didn't witness her life with Dad." Even now, it's hard for her to call him that. "Do you not remember that at all?"

Margaret sniffs. "Sure, I remember. Probably better than you. But I just find all this rather convenient. Her showing up the week that Aunt Millicent died and mysteriously left a new will naming her as sole beneficiary."

"Also the week that Dad died," Sloane points out. "He was the one keeping her away all this time."

"Maybe."

Sloane fingers some plastic wrap lying on the counter. "Are you sure you're not mad because she reached out to Idelle and Aunt Millicent, and not you?"

Margaret pauses to consider. "That may be part of it," she concedes. "But I swear to you, Sloane, part of it is not wanting to see you and Robroy get hurt."

"How could Mom hurt us?"

Margaret looks at the floor. "By pretending to be someone she's not. Or at least, that she is no longer." She raises her eyes to Sloane's face, which must look confused because she continues. "I hate to keep playing the mother card—you know, 'I'm a mother and you're not'—but honestly, there are things about a mother-child relationship that are hard to put into words. I guess the best way to say it is that I don't want to be Emma Sue and Sarah's friend. I want the best for them. I want them to realize every bit of potential they have. But I don't need them to think I'm 'the coolest mom' or 'the most fun mom' or 'the life of the party.'" More childish laughter erupts from the parlor, and Margaret sweeps an arm toward the sound. "Exhibit A."

Sloane is not sure how much of Margaret's suspicion is warranted and how much is simple jealousy—first of their mother's confiding in Idelle, then of Emma Sue and Sarah's excitement over meeting their grandmother. Margaret senses her uncertainty.

"I know what you're thinking," she says flatly. "Why can't I just accept that Mom was a horribly abused wife who was scared to death of Dad and came home the minute he died? End of story?"

"Well, yeah." Sloane hears the wistfulness in her voice. "I've missed her, Margaret. I really have."

"I know you have, Leo. I have, too." She starts to say something else then stops.

Sloane waits, but Margaret shakes her head, so she grabs a tray of cheese and crackers and heads into the parlor. Robroy has finished tuning up and launches into a toned-down version of an original ballad. Sean and Derek are perched on folding chairs, Arturio behind them on a single snare and hi-hat. Their mother sits on a floral sofa, a granddaughter tight against each side. Her eyes fill as Robroy sings, and afterward, their extended family erupts into applause.

Sloane takes a moment to bask in the scene she's dreamed about for a dozen years. Scores of questions for her mother crowd her mind, but there will be time for all that. Plenty of time. She envisions a quick trip to Atlanta to deliver her speech and pack for an extended vacation. Then she'll join her mother at the house for a month, or heck, maybe the whole summer, editing Elle's story, eating seafood, walking the beach. She'll take her nieces to the aquarium in Charleston. She'll chat with Burle and Jesse, Kent, and Octavia and mend some of those fences her absence has broken. She and her mother will discuss their inheritance—or rather, her mother's inheritance. She'll get Eli to update her mother on the development issues swirling around the old homeplace. Her chest flutters with one more possibility: Maybe Eli can spend some vacation days out here too.

The boys launch into another song, a cover of Old Crow Medicine Show's "Wagon Wheel." Robroy reaches the chorus with "Hey, Mama, rock me," and his face is alight, as it often is when he's playing. But tonight, there's something more. He's happy. He's carefree.

Their mother pulls Emma Sue and Sarah to their feet, and they raise their arms in the air and dance with the uninhibitedness only seven- and eight-year-olds can muster. But her mother comes pretty damned close, and Idelle, laughing, rises to join her. The girls giggle at both their grandmothers behaving with such abandon.

The parlor is filled with so much noise that Sloane sees rather than hears her mother's cell phone vibrate on the table beside the sofa. Someone identified as *Babe* is calling. The idea that her mother has a boyfriend intrigues her.

She looks closer and sees that the number carries the new area code recently assigned to northeast Florida. She's got several contacts of her own whose numbers changed—a college friend, a fellow author, a newspaper book reviewer. Something about this number looks familiar.

She reaches for her phone and taps it in. Sure enough, a name pops up.

Ryan Carbonier.

Chapter 28

Thursday
Annie

Though she's been living in Florida and is well accustomed to heat, there's a difference to this barrier island air. Annie feels it on her skin, can almost picture the humidity seeping into her hair, making her curls even more crazy. She lifts her thick mane off her neck and rocks on her childhood porch, drinking coffee and enjoying the languid morning.

Her children and Robroy's friends are at Robert's funeral. She thought about going with them but knew that, standing over his grave, she'd feel triumph rather than sorrow. Best not to let her face broadcast such unseemly feelings.

She did tell Sloane to invite Robert's brother Ian and sister-in-law Caroline and any other Cheneys back to the house. Robert's mother is dead, and she wonders how many of his siblings will attend the service.

There's close to a whole lemon pound cake and a key lime pie left over from Monday's spread. She'll rouse herself to brew more coffee before they arrive. *Keep it simple.* Not nearly what was served after her sister's service, from what she heard.

She gazes up the beach, wide and vacant even on this gorgeous spring day. Florida never has such vacant stretches, certainly not near Jacksonville, where she lives and which she avoided mentioning to the children.

It's strange to be back in this house. She visited her sister, of course, during her marriage, but the fear of Robert always hung over those visits, the fear of what she might face when she returned home to their tidal-creek cabin. Being reminded that he was married to a Millicent, even a lesser one, sometimes enraged Robert. And sometimes not. That was the thing about being married to him: The uncertainty was almost worse than the volatility.

Sleeping last night in her sister's old room, which had once been their father's room, was unnerving. She didn't open the balcony doors, but the porch light illuminated the flimsy police tape, the only thing standing between her and the wide-open ocean. Despite her exhaustion, she tossed for hours before falling into a sleep laden with dreams of drowning. Being back on an island can do that.

She tries to remember the time before Robert, the time growing up in this house. She can't recall her mother at all; she died when Annie was a toddler. But she can scarcely remember her father in this house either. By the time she started school, he was living mostly in Beaufort, caught up with his new love. It was just Millicent Rose and her, rattling around in this big old place, beautifully furnished but empty of life. The best memories are the sleepovers her sister allowed, when she and Idelle and a handful of girls would unroll sleeping bags on the porch and cook s'mores over a fire on the beach and drink liters of Coke. Her friends would ooh and aah over the grand beach house she got to live in. She sought their envy more than their pity, so she didn't tell them how lonely it was.

She leans back in the rocking chair and closes her eyes. *Would things feel different if I lived here now? Surely.* Margaret and Joel and their daughters live nearby. Sloane and Robroy would likely visit. Idelle and J.C. and Jesse and Burle are still around. She senses an anxious flutter in her chest over this notion she hadn't previously considered. She hadn't been honest with her sister about her plans, but Millicent's words, her assumptions, had apparently trickled into Annie's subconscious. She'd have to let Ryan know. She'd probably have to let him go.

A flash of dread impales her, and she's startled by it. She pauses to consider its origin. Is it the thought of telling Ryan that she doesn't want to sell Millicent House after all? *That can't be it.* Ryan is not violent. Ryan is no Robert Cheney.

But if I thwart his decade-long plan for developing this property, this town? No, no, no. I have not chosen another monster. She thrusts the thought away.

Ryan didn't know who she was for months after they met. Annmarie Crossland was the name she was using when he stayed at her bed-and-breakfast in St. Pete. Then he extended his visit while she showed him the hidden treasures of that city.

He'll simply find someplace else to develop. He'll visit her here and enjoy the private charms of Millicent House. *And if he doesn't?* She's been alone before and doesn't fear being alone again.

She checks her watch. Time to make the coffee in case Sloane brings the Cheneys to the house. She wonders if Sierra will come. Despite her long-ago obsession with Chelsea, she never did meet Sierra. She's thought so often of those sisters, of Robert's rampage through his family.

She pictures Robert in the waterway, bloated, that horrible white-yellow hair floating like seaweed. He died as Chelsea had, forty-one years earlier. *How fitting.*

In the kitchen, she rummages for dessert plates and places the pound cake and key lime pie on pedestal stands. Her sister was always prepared for guests; she'd give her that.

She hears the single slam of a car door and listens for more. Then the doorbell rings. Puzzled at the ensuing silence in the driveway, she heads into the cool dimness of the foyer. This house was built before air conditioning became common, and its deep shade and high ceilings serve it well.

Raeford Carlisle stands on the porch in a crisp white shirt and those delightful navy suspenders she used to tug on as a child. "Millicent Ann," he says, drawing her into a hug. He gently returns her to arm's length and shakes his head. "Your Sloane," he says. "The resemblance is uncanny."

"Raeford, how good to see you." Raeford was her father's law partner, brought on to handle the island office when her father moved to Beaufort. Her father had hoped that he and Millicent would marry, but they remained only trusted friends.

"You look fantastic," she says. "Very old-school. Very posh."

He laughs. She wants Raeford on her side. Requires it, in fact, if things are to go smoothly.

"We need to talk," he says. "Is this a good time?"

"Well, Margaret and Sloane and Robroy may bring people from Robert's service," she explains. "But until then, yes. Come to the kitchen and I'll pour you some coffee."

Raeford is already extracting papers from a briefcase and begins talking before they are seated. "I'm not sure how much you know?"

She hands him a delicate cup from her sister's rose-covered china and fills it from the steaming coffee pot. "Sloane said she and Robroy signed papers to sell the property after you told them they inherited it. But then they found another will?"

"In a nutshell," he agrees. He looks at her steadily. "The newest will—which Millicent Rose *didn't* file in my office—was written four weeks ago. On a form she apparently printed off the internet." He says this with distaste, clearly offended by the thought. "Do you know why she would leave everything to you? Five years after having you declared dead?"

Her stomach flips. Is he saying her sister's new will is invalid? *Why* didn't *she file it with him? Was she having second thoughts?*

"Well, yes, I guess I do know. She found out from Idelle Simpson that I was alive. And Idelle convinced me to reach out to Millicent. Which I did."

"In person?"

"No, in a letter at first. This past Christmas."

"Chief Hartwell tried to follow up on that letter and said the return address was no good."

"I... I ... wasn't ready for anyone to know where I was. I made up a return address and had someone mail it from St. Louis."

"How did you manage that?"

She sticks to the truth when possible so her lies won't trip her up. "Pretty simple really. I was running a bed-and-breakfast in St. Pete, Florida. We had guests from St. Louis. I asked them to mail the letter when they returned home."

Raeford looks at her pensively, and she can't tell what he's thinking. "I see." He pauses, reading from a sheet of paper. It's upside down, but she can read "Last Will and Testament" across the top and lines filled in with her sister's neat handwriting. Her heart speeds up. It's exactly what Millicent promised.

"Well," he continues, "the handwriting seems authentic, as far as I can tell. But since murder is involved, Chief Hartwell is having it examined."

She nods, saying nothing.

"We should be able to verify everything by Friday and file in probate court. I already have the death certificate." He pauses. "Have you decided if you're going to stay or sell? The town is in a real turmoil about it."

"Is it? I've been away so long..." She leaves her answer vague, open-ended. She needs time to think. Ryan is waiting in Beaufort, but she's not sure she's ready to see him. Obviously, he expects her to sell, take the money, move, all the things she agreed to. He's even mentioned marriage after everything is settled, but she's too smart to count on that. *Besides, with four-plus million dollars, who needs marriage?*

Before Raeford can press further, multiple car doors thump in the driveway.

"That's the kids and maybe some of Robert's family," she says, standing. "I hope you'll stay."

Actually, she doesn't hope that at all. The old lawyer is looking at her a bit too curiously, making her wonder what her sister shared with him.

"No," he says. "I need to get back to the office. I'll speak to Sloane and Robroy on my way out."

Chapter 29

Annie

Her sister-in-law Caroline is the first one through the door. Annie is happy to see her, and a smile splits her face. But then she notes the somber expressions of Ian and Elliott and recalibrates.

"I'm sorry for your loss," she murmurs to Robert's brothers.

She looks over the small crowd and glimpses the woman she's seeking, a female version of Robert and Elliott, tall, white blond, and freckled, toned arms visible in a black sundress. Sierra is beautiful, even in her fifties.

Annie makes her way across the parlor to where she's standing. "Are you Sierra?"

The woman smiles. "Yes. And you must be Annie. I met Sloane at the service. She's lovely. Margaret, too."

They take each other's measure. Annie knows the impact Robert had on Sierra's life. *How much does she know about me?*

Sierra glances around the parlor, from overstuffed sofas to floor-length draperies and coastal paintings. "Beautiful home. I remember seeing it when I lived on the island."

"Your mother told me years ago that you'd moved to Columbia," Annie says.

"It was my salvation."

Annie is slightly taken aback. "Really?"

"Yes. My aunt and uncle were great, and Columbia wasn't so incestuous." She colors. "Metaphorically, I mean. It was bigger. More anonymous. Everyone didn't know your business."

Annie wonders how much Sierra's family has told her about Robert. About Chelsea. She doesn't have to wonder long. "I'm sorry for your loss," she says tentatively.

Sierra's laugh is stark. "Are you? I'm not sorry one bit." She leans in conspiratorially. "The only reason I came was to make sure he's dead."

If the situation weren't so horrible, Annie would laugh. "So you knew. Why you were sent away."

"Not at first," she concedes. "But yeah, Elliott told me when I was still a teenager. When he left the island, he didn't want to risk me visiting Ma and ending up alone with Robert." She eyes Annie. "The ones I felt bad for were Chelsea, obviously. And Ma." She hesitates briefly. "And you."

Tears prick Annie's eyes, and she doesn't answer.

"I understand you left too," Sierra says. "Years ago. And are back only now?"

Annie manages to nod, and Sierra continues. "Was it because Robert is gone? Is that why you came back? I can only imagine what your life was like with him."

Annie meets her eyes. "It wasn't good. But it's behind me. My goal now is to rebuild my life with my children. I'm afraid I've made a mess of things."

Sierra grasps her forearm. "I hope you know—and they know—it wasn't your fault. You've got to make them see that." She lets go and pats Annie's arm. "If not, send them to their Aunt Sierra. I'll set them straight."

Annie swallows past the scratchiness in her throat, grateful for Sierra's kindness. Sloane approaches, carrying a tray of cake slices on dessert plates. Annie hasn't seen her daughter since she disappeared from the party last night, before Margaret and the others left. She supposes Sloane was exhausted by all the festivities.

"Long-lost Aunt Sierra," Sloane now says jokingly, "may I offer you some lemon pound cake?" She turns to Annie. "Margaret and I thought she was an urban myth. We are thrilled to find out we were wrong."

Sierra laughs. "I truly regret not meeting you and Margaret earlier. I have business in New York quite often and took my other nieces. I'd have loved to show you the city."

"That is truly tragic," Sloane says. Annie's daughter looks like she wants to ask more but hesitates. Probably she, like Annie, recognizes there are undercurrents in this family best not explored. Instead, she offers, "Cake, Mom?"

Annie takes a slice, using the time to get her emotions under control. Sierra and Sloane continue to chat, and she excuses herself to see if Margaret needs help in the kitchen. Once out of the parlor, she instead ducks into her sister's study to catch her breath. Robroy is seated on the sofa beneath the watercolor of Millicent House, his head in his hands.

"Taking a break?" she asks softly.

He raises his head, and his eyes are red. If he's been crying over Robert, maybe his childhood wasn't as bad as she feared. Or maybe she's only postponed blowing up his life. She holds out her cake, and he takes it.

"Uncle Ian and Aunt Caroline told me they took in Dad's dogs," he says. "Bubba and Lily. I was so out of it when we left his house, I didn't even think about them."

Neither did she. "Did you meet your Aunt Sierra?"

He nods. "She looks like Dad, don't you think?"

"I suppose. But I hadn't seen your father in a long, long time." *What's one more lie in the string I've been slinging?* Tentatively, she sits beside her son and places an arm across his shoulders. He shudders and leans into her.

"I don't think Aunt Sierra liked Dad," he says.

Her response is a noncommittal murmur. She has thought so often of Sierra and Chelsea, the sister who escaped the island and the sister who didn't. Robert's first victim, until he found his wife.

Were Chelsea and I alike somehow? Too young and too intimidated to stand up for ourselves?

Sierra was lucky to have her mother and Elliott step in to protect her, along with a stable aunt and uncle to take her in. But didn't Annie have Millicent who did everything possible to protect her? It was her own willfulness, her own stubbornness, that did her in. And later, later, leaving Robroy to the same monster who ruined Chelsea and her. She's repressed it for years, but seeing this place again, seeing innocent, sweet Robroy again, she's not sure she can live with the knowledge that she abandoned her children.

I've made a step toward penance, but is it enough?

Chapter 30

Sloane

The extended Cheney clan is gone, *thank God,* and her mother is napping upstairs. Sloane still hasn't found a moment alone to ask her about Ryan Carbonier's phone number appearing on her cell. And not just appearing but marked *Babe.*

Her imagination is running wild. Most obviously, is her mother in a relationship with the developer? Is that what's behind the new will naming her as beneficiary? *Did she and Ryan Carbonier collude to trick Aunt Millicent?*

She thinks back to Ryan Carbonier's first call—*what was it? Four years ago? Five?* He was always cordial. "Hello, Miss Cheney, just checking in to tell you I'm still interested in the Millicent House property." And then a monetary offer that sometimes was the same as before, and sometimes an increase of a hundred thousand dollars.

So was he hedging his bets by enlisting her mother? Was the purchase not moving along fast enough? Or had he been involved with her mother *before* he contacted Sloane?

Suddenly Margaret's misgivings hold a lot more credibility. Sloane heads to the kitchen to help her sister and brother with the cleanup but resolves not to mention Ryan Carbonier until she talks to their mother. Maybe there's an innocent explanation. *Yeah, maybe.*

"I thought we weren't going to do this again," Margaret says. "Graveside service only, you guys said. Remember?"

Sloane dries a china plate. "That was before Mom came home."

"And it was *her* idea to bring in Dad's family," adds Robroy. "Why did she want them here anyway?"

"Honestly?" Sloane responds. "I think she wanted an excuse to meet Aunt Sierra. They were huddled when I came in. I enjoyed meeting her too. Didn't you?"

Margaret shrugs. "Whatever."

"She classes up the family. Can you imagine if she'd taken us to New York in high school, Margaret? How cool would that have been?"

"I didn't get there 'til my mid-twenties," Margaret concedes.

"Robroy and I haven't made it yet."

"Ah, but the Babies will stomp through the Big Apple soon enough," he says.

"Were you happy with the service?" Sloane asks her brother. "It was for you, you know."

"Yeah, I do know. It was good. And it was a bonus, seeing Uncle Elliott and Aunt Sierra. I expected Uncle Ian and Aunt Caroline but not them."

The phone in Sloane's pocket vibrates and flashes Dr. Avery's name. She dares not ignore him again so answers with as much cheeriness as she can muster. He informs her that a parent is upset about a student's grade and insists upon speaking to her. She takes down the number and tells him she'll return the call immediately. She doesn't tell him she'll have to read the student's exam for the first time and contact Sam to get his input.

"Work calls," she tells Margaret.

Her sister folds a tea towel and hangs it over the handle of the oven. "Can I tell you one quick thing first?"

She glances at her watch. "If you promise to make it quick."

Margaret gestures toward the vacant oceanside porch. Sean and Derek have entered the kitchen, and Robroy is gathering lunch meat, cheese, and mustard for them.

Margaret checks to make sure the window over the sink is closed then chooses a chair at the porch's far end.

"What's up?" Sloane asks, settling into a rocker.

"Did you ever hear of Dad's sister Chelsea?" Margaret's voice is low.

"What? No. I thought it was three boys and Sierra. The urban myth."

"There was another sister. Older than Sierra."

"Was she stillborn?"

Margaret frowns irritably. "No. She drowned. When she was sixteen."

Sloane sits back, disbelieving. "Where did you hear that?"

"Idelle told me. Last night."

"That can't be right."

"She assumed I already knew," continues Margaret. "She said Grandma Cheney had a picture of both girls in her house."

"I never saw it."

"Me neither. You think she moved it when we came over?"

Sloane shrugs. "Maybe. I only remember being in her house two or three times, period."

Margaret leans forward urgently. "Anyway, Idelle let it slip that Mom always thought Dad had killed Chelsea. That's partly why Mom was so terrified of him."

Sloane is stunned into silence, but Margaret is on a roll.

"Apparently, it was in 1982. The police had no suspicion the drowning was anything but an accident. But here's what made Idelle think Mom was right: Grandma Cheney sent Sierra to live in Columbia. To get her away from her brother. From Dad."

Things start to make sense. The way Aunt Caroline froze whenever their father was around. The fact they'd met their uncles, albeit infrequently, but never the mysterious Sierra. And something she overheard Aunt Sierra say only an hour ago.

She clutches Margaret's arm. "I heard her talking to Mom. She said, 'The only reason I came was to make sure he's dead.'"

"My God," Margaret murmurs. "It could be true." She shakes her head. "I'm glad I didn't know while he was alive. I hated him enough as it was."

Sloane's phone vibrates. It's Eli, but the call reminds her that she needs to deal with an irate parent. "Let me take care of this college business," she says. "We'll talk more later."

It's a good thing Sloane knows she's not inheriting Millicent House. It gives her the motivation to exude patience with her student's whiny mother and explosive father. If she thought she was going to be an instant millionaire, she might hang up on them. As it is, she politely considers their entreaties. In fact, after consulting Sam, she discovers the student was straddling the line between a B and a C. She raises her C-plus to a B-minus, which satisfies the parents.

Within minutes, Dr. Avery calls again. "I took care of it," she informs him.

"That's not why I'm calling." *Sheesh, does he call all his instructors this often? What now?*

He waits a few beats then says impatiently, "Your speech."

"Oh. I thought you understood it will be rewritten before I deliver it. But I can't get the revisions to you ahead of time." She cringes, awaiting his raised voice.

Instead, it is icy. "And why not?"

"We buried my father today."

"*Your father?* I thought you were down there to bury an aunt."

"I was. We did. But then..." She feels her voice cracking and lets it. It may work in her favor. "My father drowned the very next day. My brother and I found him."

Dr. Avery is silent. Apparently, he can't deal with this cracker island voodoo. His tone remains cold but at least he retreats from his demands. "But you're going to make the board dinner tomorrow night?"

"I'll be there," she promises. She has to keep this job at Warner. Ryan Carbonier's money for the sale of Millicent House won't be coming her way.

Before she can hang up with Dr. Avery, the doorbell peals. *Where is everybody?* She hastens her supervisor off the phone and hurries to the foyer.

Her heart leaps at the sight of Eli. Beside him is Chief Hartwell.

Before she can say anything, Eli jumps in. "We aren't together. We just drove up at the same time."

But now a truck is pulling up between the brick posts at the entrance to the driveway. They watch it rumble to a stop beside Eli's Honda Civic, lumber extending past its open gate. Burle steps out with a wave then approaches solemnly.

"Sloane, I hardly know what to say about that railing," he begins. "I was too busy to get to it in April like Miss Millicent asked, so I recommended Bud Randolph. He does real good work." He glances at Chief Hartwell. "I'd like to take a look to see what happened."

The chief nods, so Sloane tells Burle he can access the balcony through the reading room on the upper floor. "I think Mom's sleeping in Aunt Millicent's room."

"I'll do the sawing out here," he says, pointing at the side yard.

"You know your way around. And Robroy is putting out lunch stuff in the kitchen. Help yourself. You, too, Eli."

She leads the chief to Aunt Millicent's study then perches on the edge of the sofa. "I'm glad you realize Burle couldn't have had anything to do with that railing."

"Nothing's off the table," the chief replies. "But we've spoken to Bud Randolph, and he swears he replaced and painted much of the wood last month and left it in solid shape. He's been a loud opponent of development on the island. Damned if I can see why he'd want to harm your aunt."

Again, she remembers Sam—arms flailing, weight shifting—and winces. Was her aunt targeted? Or was the target someone who's inside the house now?

"Your father," he continues, holding out a sheet of paper. She jerks her attention to what he's saying. "The toxicity report shows four times the legal limit of alcohol. And some diazepam, or Valium, which was consistent with what we found in his medicine cabinet. So I suppose it's clear what happened out there."

"And pretty standard for him." She hands the sheet back.

"Unless..." He pauses intentionally, and her mind struggles to follow. "Unless it was all of a piece."

Aunt Millicent's death. Then her father's. Nothing could be worse than her father inheriting the house by some quirk of marriage and her mother's declared death. *Did someone step in to prevent that very thing?* The chief seems to be implying it.

"What's not so clear... is how you spent your time in Savannah," he says, and she hears the warning in his voice.

Her breath grows shallow. She struggles to keep her face unresponsive. *He can't know. He's bluffing.*

The chief's voice is conversational, but she's on high alert. "You see, we've been looking for the young man who was working the hotel desk last Thursday night. He left for vacation the next day, and my officers ran into some confusion about where he was and how to reach him. But he returned to work. Today."

Sloane wills her face to show nothing but polite interest.

"I hope I'm not being politically incorrect," he continues, "but the thing about being an attractive young woman is that people notice you, Miss Cheney. This clerk certainly did. He says that at about six o'clock on Thursday you got into a car, and you didn't return until after nine."

She closes her eyes. *He doesn't know. He doesn't know.*

But it seems he does. "Even more interesting is who you got into a car with. Ryan Carbonier."

Chapter 31

Annie

Burle's buzzsaw is giving Annie a headache, so she's happy to join Arturio for a trip to his mother's house in the band's claptrap van. *The Robroy Cheney Band* is written in 1960s psychedelic colors along the side. She's grateful that the boys don't use the vehicle to promote their Baby Stompers identity. "Alleged, Mom," Robroy reminded her when she teased him. "No babies were actually harmed during the naming of the band."

"Ha. Ha," she told him drily. She can't get enough of her son. The compliant ten-year-old she left has grown into an endearing young man. She invited him to accompany them to Nadine's, but he said he had things to do before tomorrow night's concert in Charleston. She has no idea what road life for a band entails, so she trusts he's telling the truth. When your life is necessarily based on lies, it's hard to know when anyone else is being truthful.

Arturio assures her that his visiting relatives have returned to Philadelphia, and Nadine is anxious to see her. He's out of the van and enfolded in his mother's embrace before she can maneuver the passenger side door.

"Annie Cheney!" Nadine exclaims, rushing forward to hug her. "We never thought we'd see you again."

She and Nadine have been friends since middle school, when Nadine's family moved onto the island. She is married to Burle's nephew Randall, so Annie assumes she's privy to all the dysfunction in the Cheney household. Robroy told her Nadine and Randall had always welcomed him into their home; she is grateful for this tight island community who took in her boy.

That doesn't let her off the hook; she knows it doesn't. She never once considered how these families might step forward and show kindness to her son. Her sole consideration—or rationale—was that Robert seemed genuinely fond of Robroy. She convinced herself that was enough. Funny that seeing how well Robroy turned out causes her to comprehend the inherent danger of her decision. *How could I have been so blasé about leaving him? Even if Robert wasn't abusive, what made me think he was a fit father?*

Shame washes over her as she buries her head on Nadine's shoulder. "Thank you," she whispers. "Thank you for all you did."

"Now, you never mind all that," Nadine says, pulling Annie toward the house. "Let's get out of this sun."

"Wait a second," she says, going back to the van to get the clean dish that Sloane asked her to return. "I hear your chicken and dumplings were a big hit."

"Always are," says Arturio. He takes the dish inside to Nadine's kitchen and returns with two glasses of lemonade as the women settle into the living room. He then disappears to let them catch up. "Arturio has grown into an amazing young man," Annie says. "Do you hear the band often?"

"Yes, Randall and I drive to hear them whenever they're in Charleston or Beaufort. Robroy is quite the showman."

"I've only seen videos. And they played for us last night."

Nadine looks uncomfortable, as if she'd like to ask something. She waits for it. "Annie, what brings you home? After all this time?"

"Surely you know."

"But you weren't at Millicent's funeral."

"No. No, I wasn't. I should have been. But I didn't feel safe coming back until I heard that Robert was dead. It's as simple as that."

Nadine looks at her with sympathy. "Odd, them going within a week of each other."

"Yes, it was."

"And I understand the police are investigating Millicent's death as murder?"

Annie sips the lemonade, but her throat has closed, and she chokes. After a brief coughing spell, she says, "You probably know more than I do. The kids and I have been catching up on other things."

Nadine puts her glass on a side table and leans forward. *What made me think I could visit anyone without facing the third degree?*

"Annie, I hate to hit you with this right off the bat. But have you given any thought to what you're going to do with Millicent House?"

Annie wonders who has told her she's inheriting. Probably Arturio. He's been right there in the house, overhearing everything.

"Word spreads quickly, huh?" She scrambles for time.

Nadine doesn't take her eyes off her. "It's just that it will affect all of us so deeply. If that developer gets his way, our island will never be the same."

She doesn't tell Nadine that *never being the same* strikes her as a good thing. She tries to consider Nadine's perspective—her large family has made a good living providing shrimp, scallops, oysters, and fish to restaurants and groceries along the coast. Burle's extended family and Harlan Espey's family, even Ian Cheney, are all fishermen, all good people. Robert was the outlier with his drunkenness and fighting and abuse.

The lie comes smooth and easy. "I'm sorry, Nadine, but everything has happened so fast that I haven't had time to think about it." Before she can say more, they hear the crunch of gravel and peer out the bay window to see a light green Prius pulling in next to the van. "Are you expecting someone?"

"Probably my sister, June. She drops by sometimes after finishing her shift at the hospital."

"I remember you talking about her. She didn't move to the island with your family."

"Right. She was already in college when we came, but she eventually moved to Beaufort. She was a nurse there for years and years. When Mercy's new medical director found out, she recruited her. I've really enjoyed having her closer."

A heavyset woman in blue scrubs mounts the brick steps then enters without knocking and calls, "Nadine?" She stops abruptly when she sees Annie. Her eyes flicker to her sister and back, confusion crossing her face. She visibly recovers, and Nadine introduces them.

They make small talk until Arturio joins them then listen as he chats about the band's upcoming gig. But Annie is anxious to escape June's scrutiny; the second the conversation halts, she leaps to her feet.

Nadine and June are cordial during their goodbyes, but Annie has the feeling they are waiting until she and Arturio leave to have the real conversation. She sits in the van while Arturio wraps up, then she tunes out his chatter as they drive through the sandy scrub of the back island.

Why did June look so surprised to see me? Or was I imagining it?
In all my careful calculations, have I missed something?

Chapter 32

Sloane

Eli is waiting in the kitchen, but Sloane is held captive in the study by Chief Hartwell. He leans forward in an upholstered club chair, his face showing no sign that he has dropped a grenade, courtesy of a hotel clerk in Savannah who saw her enter Ryan Carbonier's car.

"It's not what you think," she says desperately.

"So, what is it?"

She pauses, willing her panic to remain flopping in her chest rather than bursting forth into words. "I know it sounds ridiculous. But he wanted to continue the conversation."

"So where did you go? To continue this conversation?" Chief Hartwell's voice is flat, but his gaze is steely. He doesn't believe her.

"Like I said before, he thought that Aunt Millicent was truly sick, near the end. He wanted to... I guess you'd say 'shore up' my commitment to sell. I assured him I would sell the minute I inherited."

"And it took you three hours to tell him that?" Sloane hangs her head. Is it time to reveal the convoluted truth of that evening, the lies she's been forced into? Before she can decide, a voice comes from the doorway.

"No, less than thirty minutes." Her head jerks toward Eli. "Don't you remember, Sloane?" He's leaning against the door jamb, a sandwich in one hand. "He dropped you back at the hotel by six thirty, and we went out after that."

Chief Hartwell twists in his seat. "I asked you to give us some privacy, Mr. Cartwright."

"But I was there," he explains. "I know where Sloane was after she met Ryan Carbonier."

"So you know Mr. Carbonier?"

"Sure. I've interviewed him lots of times."

"And you saw him drop Miss Cheney back at the hotel at six thirty?"

"Maybe even a few minutes earlier," Eli says. He looks at her, guileless. "I know the time because I'd come to find Sloane when I saw she was speaking in Savannah, but I got hung up on a story and missed the event. I pulled in right around 6:25 or so and saw her getting out of Mr. Carbonier's car." He smiles. "We went out to dinner."

"Where?"

"Down on River Street. You know, that cobblestone street that runs past all the riverfront restaurants? I'm afraid I can't remember which one. They all look alike."

"Then what?"

"We caught up. And then I took her back to her hotel, and I drove home to Charleston. I had to work the next day."

"What time did you drop her at the hotel?"

"Around nine. That sound right, Sloane?"

She nods mutely. Chief Hartwell swivels back to face her. His jaw is rigid, and she can tell he's skeptical.

"So, you and Mr. Carbonier?" he asks her. "Where did you go?"

"Just driving around," she says then clamps her lips shut. She doesn't want to contradict Eli.

"And why didn't you mention this before? You indicated he left you in the hotel bar."

"Is that what I said? I meant to say we finished our conversation at six or six thirty. In the bar first, then his car. I... I... guess I didn't consider it important enough to make the distinction."

Chief Hartwell is no rube. He's not buying this. But he doesn't want to call them both out as liars. Not yet anyway. So far, it sounds like he's gotten his information from the hotel clerk. But what is Ryan Carbonier telling him? Dare she ask, or will she only dig this hole deeper?

Eli has no such hesitation. "So Chief Hartwell, what does Mr. Carbonier say? It's his development on the line."

The chief responds with a question. "Have you spoken to him?"

"No, I've called him every day since Millicent Roundtree's death, and he hasn't responded."

"We're having the same problem," the chief admits. "His office claims he's on a business trip to Asia, but we've been unable to contact him."

"Thought about calling Interpol?" Eli asks.

"He's not a fugitive at this point. But that's a possibility in the future." Chief Hartwell narrows his eyes. "That's all for now. I'll see myself out."

They are silent until the front door clicks shut. After realizing how easily Eli overheard her conversation with the chief, she tiptoes to the foyer to make sure he's gone. Only then does she turn to Eli.

"What the hell?" she asks.

Sloane and Eli are huddled at the kitchen table. Outside the side window, Burle is hard at work, sawing pieces of lumber and placing them one by one across a pair of rickety sawhorses. Robroy, Sean, and Derek have moved to the porch, so the two have a few minutes of privacy.

"What was that?" she hisses.

"It sounded like you needed a little help."

She stares at him. "You could get in trouble—lying to the police like that."

"As can you." He gets up and rummages in the refrigerator for a soft drink. "I guess we'll have to get married so I can't testify against you."

She bursts into laughter, the tension easing somewhat. "Smooth," she says as he slides into the seat across from her.

"Now," he says, "time to come clean. Where did you and Carbonier go last Thursday night?"

"To one of his developments outside Savannah," she responds promptly. "He said he was using it as a model for Mayberry by the Sea. But it wasn't on the coast. About a mile inland. All small town-ish, quaint. Kind of Disney-esque."

Eli's brow furrows. "Why did he want you to see it?"

"He was putting the hard sell on me, I think. I had told him I was fine with selling this property, but I expected Aunt Millicent to live another twenty years or more. I mean, she was only sixty-eight. He told me there was something he wanted me to see and drove down the interstate to that little village square. He pointed out every restaurant and bar and ice cream shop and gift store. It was one of those planned-out-the-wazoo communities, you know?"

"But he never said *why* he wanted you to see it?"

She twirls her glass. "Not expressly. But I think he was trying to convert me to the idea in general so I would lobby my aunt to go ahead and sell. Millicent could become Quaint. With a capital Q."

"Those guys are always thinking ten steps ahead," agrees Eli.

He taps the top of his aluminum can. His next question is so casual that she might not have spotted it if she weren't already on guard. "What's the name of the place he took you? The planned village?"

But she's ready. "Bluestone. Have you ever been there?"

He shakes his head. "No. But I've heard Carbonier talk about it."

As has she. Just not last Thursday.

Chapter 33

Annie

Arturio scarcely pulls into the driveway of Millicent House before Annie is out of the van and in her old Impala.

"Tell Sloane and Robroy I have some errands," she says with a wave.

She's running late for a meeting with Ryan in Beaufort. From the sound of his text messages, he's anxious to hear how things are going. *Frantic* may be more accurate. Apparently, he's avoiding the police until he can ascertain where he stands.

But before she can maneuver around Burle's truck and reach the brick posts at the driveway's entrance, a navy-blue Ford Escape pulls in, her sister-in-law Caroline at the wheel. *She was here two hours ago. What can she possibly want?*

Hopping out of the Impala, Annie trots to her sister-in-law's window, seeking to prevent her from getting out. "Caroline, I'm sorry but I'm supposed to be somewhere. I was just leaving."

Caroline's face is serious beneath her severely cropped silver hair. "Can you cancel? This is important."

Apprehension unfurls in Annie's belly. *Does she know something? Impossible.* She thinks back to this morning's reception following Robert's service. Who did Caroline talk to? She had Elliott cornered at one point. And later, Sierra, Margaret, and Sloane.

"Honestly, Annie," she says, laying a hand on her arm. "I wouldn't be here if it weren't urgent."

Annie's uneasiness springs into full-blown panic. She swallows and nods. "Give me a minute."

While Annie texts Ryan to let him know something's come up, Caroline parks and waits on the porch. She idly plucks a honeysuckle blossom that has crept into the jumble of flowering vines. "Love that smell," she murmurs.

They walk through the silent foyer and peek into the kitchen where Sloane and a young man are talking quietly. Arturio must have gone upstairs or onto the beach, so she ushers Caroline into Millicent's study and closes the door. "No one can hear us in here."

Caroline starts talking before she sits down. "It's the police, Annie. They're asking questions."

"Of course, they are. Millicent was murdered."

"No, not about that. About Robert."

Annie sits back, surprised. "Robert?"

Caroline picks at her beige slacks. She's not wearing makeup, and her face is lined from a lifetime in the sun. "Let me back up," she says. "Ian and I always felt bad that we didn't step in."

"Step in?"

"To stop Robert. I can't tell you how many times we talked about it, whether Ian should take you and the children out of the house, whether he should give Robert a taste of his own medicine. Or whether that would only make it worse for you. In the end, as you know, Ian stopped working with Robert."

"At some point, everyone stopped working with Robert."

"Well, yeah. He lost his temper when they were selling shrimp. Always thought somebody was cheating him." When Annie doesn't respond, she adds, "Anyway, we were never sure of the right thing to do. So we did nothing. I've always been ashamed of that."

Annie shrugs. "You knew I had Millicent. I didn't expect anything from the Cheneys."

"Still," she says, "we knew. We knew what was going on." She looks Annie in the eye.

"It's ancient history, Caroline." *Why did she think this conversation was urgent?*

"Well, maybe we can make up for it now."

Annie laughs. "Now? After he's dead?"

"Exactly. Now that he's dead."

Suddenly, she grows cold. "Wha... what do you mean?"

"Chief Hartwell has been out to our place twice, asking questions about Robert's drowning. Elliott told me this morning the chief had asked him about Chelsea. I was surprised the chief even knew about her, because she died long before he came here."

Annie stares at Caroline, unsure where she's going but afraid, nonetheless.

"The chief has even talked to Sierra. He's circling, Annie. I just thought you should know."

"Well, I appreciate it, but I'm not sure what it has to do with me. I've been gone for twelve years."

"Until this week."

"Yes," Annie says carefully. "Until yesterday."

Caroline looks at the floor. "But that's not quite right, is it?"

Annie starts to speak, but her throat is dry. She clears it and tries again. "What do you mean?"

"Ian saw you from his boat, Annie. On the inland waterway. On Tuesday. The day Robert died."

Seconds pass. Or maybe minutes. Annie's first instinct is to bluff. "No, Caroline. I drove to Millicent Wednesday. *After* I learned Robert was dead. After twelve years of hiding from him, why would I come back when he was still alive?"

"I can't speak to your reasoning. But Ian saw your hair. It's pretty distinctive."

Her eyes dart wildly around the study and land on Sloane's novel standing upright on Millicent's desk. Even without seeing the author's picture, she grasps at the solution it offers. "It must have been Sloane! Sloane and Robroy found Robert. That's who Ian saw."

Caroline grabs her hands. "Annie, listen. Ian saw you at dawn when he was heading out. He saw you standing in the water off Robert's yard. Don't you get it?"

Annie begins to tremble. She yanks her hands free, and her arms encircle her torso protectively. Instinctively, her body rocks in a self-soothing motion. But suddenly Caroline's initial words creep in. She started this conversation by apologizing for her failure to act earlier. Maybe she's not threatening to go to Chief Hartwell.

Caroline nods, and Annie knows she's right.

"That's what I came to tell you, Annie. We're sure as hell not going to report you. But Ian had young crew members on his boat. He doesn't know what they saw or if they knew whose property it was. Obviously, those boys don't know you, but if they see you around, they might put two and two together. Eventually."

Annie can barely take in what her sister-in-law is saying. She pictures young men shooting the breeze on a dock like Burle's, talking about the old shrimper who drowned and his place that's for sale, and "Hey, wait a minute. Is that the place we passed the other day? Where we saw that crazy woman with the wild red hair standing in the water?"

Until yesterday, it wouldn't have mattered. She'd planned to leave the island the minute she signed Millicent House over to Ryan. But twenty-four hours within these walls with Sloane, Robroy, and Margaret and her girls—well, everything has changed.

Her newborn vision of living here, of having her children and grandchildren around her once more, dissolves. Her chest aches as if her lungs are full of tears.

Again, her eyes search the lilac walls of her sister's study and this time find the portrait of Millicent House. She's spent a lifetime running from it, and now she can't return. Pain spears her ribs, and she can't draw a breath.

"Are you okay?" Caroline asks.

"Ye-yes." She's being ridiculous. Her old practicality fights to kick in. Only last week, her sights had been set on a multi-million-dollar windfall. Maybe becoming Mrs. Carbonier. More likely not. She'll simply go back to that plan. Maybe travel. Maybe buy her own bed-and-breakfast in the Florida Keys.

But the ache in her chest persists, and suddenly, she's seized by a red-hot anger liberally laced with self-pity. She doesn't mean to take it out on Caroline, but it probably comes across that way. She can hear the hiss in her voice. "Why is Chief Hartwell looking at the drowning of a stupid, violent drunk rather than at who killed my sister?"

Caroline's eyes widen. "You can't figure it out?"

What is she talking about? Caroline's earnest face irritates Annie, and she struggles not to snap at her. "No, I can't."

"The chief thinks whoever killed Millicent may also have killed Robert."

Chapter 34

Sloane

Sloane drops wearily into the kitchen nook. After her father's funeral and reception, Chief Hartwell's visit, then lunch with Eli, she'd like nothing more than to nap in the cool pink bedroom. Instead, she opens her laptop and pulls up her novel. She has the rest of Thursday afternoon and evening to delve into Elle's head, and she longs to get out of her own.

Arturio wanders into the kitchen for a soda and tells her that her mother is holed up in the study with her Aunt Caroline.

"Why?" she asks.

He shrugs. "No idea." He flips the pop-top and takes a long drink. He saunters to the kitchen window. She tries to tune out his presence, but he's in her periphery. Finally, he clears his throat. "Sloane, I think I need to warn you about something."

Her body tenses. She's not sure how many more surprises she can take.

"When we were out at Mama's, my Auntie June came by. The one who works at Mercy Hospital."

"Uh huh."

"She only moved here last year, so she didn't know Annie." He puts his drink on the counter. "But before we left, she whispered to Mama and me that she recognized your mother. She's pretty sure she saw her in the hospital last Thursday night."

Sloane freezes. "That's not possible. Mom didn't get into town until yesterday."

"I know that's her story."

"Her story! Arturio, what are you saying?"

He holds up both hands. "Sloane, I have no idea if she was at Mercy Hospital or not. But I'm telling you my auntie is going to tell Chief Hartwell she was. On the night *your* aunt was killed."

She's breathing so heavily she's nearly panting. "But you said earlier she saw Ryan Carbonier. Now she says it was Mom?"

"No, both of them. She just didn't know who Annie was before. Nobody showed her a picture like we did with Carbonier."

Sloane sits back, all thoughts of her novel edits gone. Her daydreams of reuniting with her mother splinter into dangerous shards. They hear a door open off the hallway, and Arturio motions her to be silent. Her mother ushers Aunt Caroline out the front door, then her flats slap the hardwoods.

When she enters the kitchen, her voice is artificially bright. "Is your young man gone?"

Sloane must look blank because her mother laughs. The sound is brittle. "When Caroline and I looked in earlier, you were deep in conversation with a good-looking young man."

"Oh. That was Eli." Her mother doesn't know about the most important romantic relationship of her life. "He... um... he was my college boyfriend."

"Was?"

"Yeah, we broke up after we graduated." She doesn't go into all the damage her behavior wreaked on Eli.

"And yet here he was."

"Well, he's a reporter for *The Greenbrier Herald*. The development of Millicent is a big story." She shakes her head. "But Mom, what was Aunt Caroline doing here?"

Her mother waves an arm nonchalantly, but something's not right. Her other hand, the one by her side, is trembling.

"Oh, she wanted to catch up. We didn't have time for a proper chat this morning."

Sloane looks at her, disbelieving. She can't imagine that her mother and Aunt Caroline have much in common, and she says so.

"You'd be surprised," her mother says, opening the refrigerator and selecting a diet soda. "When you and Margaret were babies, the three of us spent a lot of time at Elsie's Diner. Caroline was smitten with you two."

Arturio is studying the floor. Sloane wants to ask her mother about what his Auntie June saw, but she doesn't know how. And her mother seems so... nervous. Caroline's visit has shaken her.

"Mom, I wanted to—"

They are interrupted by the doorbell. Her mother startles. "Jeez, what's with all the visitors?"

"I'll get it," Sloane says, wondering at her mother's jumpiness.

She opens the door to a familiar figure. And while her heart sinks, she's not surprised to see Chief Hartwell. Again.

As he follows Sloane into the kitchen, her mother's face blanches. She leans against the countertop in a subtle attempt to steady herself. "I don't believe you've met my mother, Chief Hartwell. Annie Cheney. And of course, you know Arturio."

"Mrs. Cheney, it's you I need to speak to."

Sloane and Arturio exchange glances. Auntie June didn't waste any time.

Despite her nervousness, her mother's Southern manners kick in. "May I offer you tea, Chief Hartwell? We have hot or iced. Or coffee?"

He pauses, apparently calculating how to best put Annie Cheney at ease. "Yes, coffee would be great."

"Sloane keeps a pot going all day," she chatters, and again Sloane and Arturio trade quick looks. There's nothing to do but let her handle the chief's questions.

Her mother selects a china cup and saucer and busies herself pouring coffee then arranging milk and sugar on a serving tray. The police chief remains silent. When Arturio notices that Annie's hands are rattling the sugar bowl, he gently slides the tray from her. "I'll put this in the parlor," he offers.

The three of them troop after Arturio. Sloane doesn't ask if they can sit in. Chief Hartwell will have to evict them if he wants her mother alone. He eyes Sloane for a moment and chooses not to make an issue of it. "So, Mrs. Cheney, I understand you recently returned to Millicent after many years away."

"Yes, I returned yesterday."

"Twelve years away, was it? Like your daughter?"

"Yes."

"And what brought you back?"

Surely, he knows their family's history, but his open face invites her mother to give it her spin. To Sloane's surprise, she flushes scarlet. It's a trait she knows well, the bane of redheads. "It's no secret," her mother says. "My husband was a violent man. I fled from him twelve years ago and came back only after hearing he was dead. That he had drowned."

Sloane assumes the chief is simply making conversation before hitting her mother with the news about June seeing her at the hospital. But she is already squirmy.

The chief picks up on her nervousness. He plays the age-old investigative strategy of waiting, and her mother succumbs. "I had no contact with Robert all those years. None." When he still doesn't speak, she continues. "I'm not proud of leaving my children. Well, of leaving Robroy. But Robert loved Robroy, and so I told myself it was okay to leave him. Do I regret that? Yes." She stops, checks for a reaction from Chief Hartwell. "But I was deathly afraid of Robert. I would never have returned while he was alive. I didn't set foot in Millicent until Idelle Simpson called to tell me he was dead."

Sloane looks at Arturio in confusion. Why is her mother going on about her father when the chief is here to ask about Mercy Hospital? It's as if the police chief snags Sloane's thought. His gaze flicks between Sloane and her mother.

"Oka-ay," he says. "But we actually have a witness who puts you here earlier."

"No! I wasn't here earlier this week!"

"This week?" the chief asks mildly. "That's not when you were seen."

Her mother stops. A muscle in her jaw jumps. She clenches her teeth as if to keep more words from spewing forth.

The chief continues in an even tone. "Mrs. Cheney, where were you last Thursday night?"

Sloane closes her eyes. *There it is.* But her mother seems more puzzled than afraid. "Last Thursday? I was in Jacksonville. Where I live."

Sloane's head jerks up. "Jacksonville? I thought you lived in St. Pete."

Her mother waves away the comment. "Did I not mention Jacksonville? I haven't lived there long. I still think of St. Pete as home."

Apprehension grips Sloane, and she hears Margaret in her head. Their mother could hurt them, her sister said, *by pretending to be someone she's not.* Might that include pretending she's not living in Jacksonville, home of Ryan Carbonier?

But Chief Hartwell is not finished. "Jacksonville's not that far away. Maybe two hundred miles or so. Did you drive up that evening to Mercy Hospital?"

"Mercy Hospital? On the island? Of course not!"

"Your sister was ill. It would make sense for you to come and see her."

Sloane's head begins to throb. This is the same guilt trip he'd laid on her. But Arturio's Auntie June says she saw her mother at the hospital. The woman doesn't even know the Cheneys. She has no reason to lie. Is it possible her mother was there? The black coil in Sloane's belly whips its tail. *Was she there to talk to Aunt Millicent about the change to her will? Octavia said Aunt Millicent confused her with Annie. Maybe because she'd just seen her sister?*

Her mother appears near tears. "I knew she was sick," she whispers, "but I was too afraid to visit her. I was too afraid of Robert!"

She begins to cry. "I'm not proud of it," she chokes out. "But I didn't come to see my sister."

The chief coldly contemplates her mother. Then he turns his gaze on Sloane and Arturio. "Someone is not telling the truth," he says, settling in more comfortably. When that comment doesn't elicit a response, he tries another tack. "We also have a witness who saw Ryan Carbonier at the hospital the same night." He watches her mother closely. "Is that someone you know?"

Her crying halts, but she uses a tissue to hide her face for a moment. Finally, she lifts her head. "I've met him," she says. "He lives in Jacksonville, and I've run into him there."

"Are you aware that he has made multiple offers on Millicent House?"

"I know he's a big developer," she says evasively. "He has interests up and down the East coast."

"Are you aware that he is the developer that your daughter and son were prepared to sell to when they inherited?"

Her mother's eyes slide over to Sloane, and she nods slowly. "Yes, someone mentioned that. Raeford, I believe."

"Does it surprise you to hear he was at Mercy Hospital on the night Miss Roundtree was killed?"

Her mother's head starts to shake like a metronome, and her face crumples. "That is not possible. That simply cannot be true."

"How can you be so sure about someone you've only 'met' and 'run into'?"

Her mother's eyes dart around the room. The chief waits patiently for an answer that doesn't come.

His attention isn't on Sloane, and she's grateful. Because she knows that what her mother is saying is dead wrong. Ryan Carbonier *was* at the hospital that night. The question is: Does her mother know it?

Chapter 35

Annie

As soon as the chief leaves the house, Annie tells Sloane that she has to run an errand. Sloane tries to stop her, but she rushes out. Stomping on the Impala's gas pedal, she lurches onto the road outside their property before anyone else can pull into the driveway.

Forty-five minutes later, she arrives in Beaufort, a small coastal city whose charms would delight her any other time. But she is unseeing as she races toward a motel on the outskirts of town. It's far from Ryan's usual five-star accommodations, but he's ducking under the radar until he becomes the Big Man in Millicent. She pounds on his door, not caring who hears. The drive has given her time to think about the police chief's accusation and to realize she may not be the only one hiding something. Ryan flings the door open, a frown on his handsome face, and yanks her inside.

"You were at Mercy Hospital the night my sister died!" she cries. "What were you doing there?"

His face pales. "Says who?"

"Says the police chief. He has a witness who saw you."

Ryan shrugs. "Calm down, Annie. It was nothing."

"How can it be nothing? You've wanted her property forever and suddenly you're at the very place she died? The place she was murdered!"

"No, no, I swear to you. It wasn't like that. I went there to see how sick she was. You were the one who told me she was hospitalized. I've made no secret of the fact that I wanted to buy her property."

"But to go and see her when she was ill?" Her voice rises to a shriek.

"My information was that she was experiencing symptoms of dementia."

"Your information? From whom? I didn't tell you that."

He hung his head. "From Sloane."

Annie feels as if the breath has been knocked out of her. "From Sloane? My Sloane?"

Ryan's dark eyes glitter. "Remember? She was in line to inherit for years before you were. I called her once or twice a year to check in. That's all." His eyes skitter around the room, unable to meet hers.

Oh my God, is he involved with Sloane? The thought sickens her.

His tone becomes defensive. "You told me your sister was ill. I wanted to make sure whoever inherited was still ready to make the sale in case she didn't recover."

Annie drops onto the room's ugly maroon bedspread, stunned that he's known her daughter longer than he's known her. *And never mentioned it.* "'Whoever inherited?'" she echoes. "You were hedging your bet, weren't you? In case Millicent switched her beneficiary from Sloane to me?"

Her mind flashes over the span of their relationship. "How long have you known I was a Roundtree? Since long before I told you, I'm guessing. Maybe even before we met in St. Pete?"

"No, I didn't know who you were then, Annie. I thought you were a beautiful, successful entrepreneur. Which you were. And are."

"I don't believe you."

His voice rises. "You have to believe me." His face reveals the fear that all his machinations have been for naught. The young woman he groomed for years has not inherited the coveted property. The woman he courted has inherited, but if he angers her, she might simply sell to someone else. His distress is clear.

"All our plans, Annie," he pleads. "Surely you're not turning your back on all our plans."

She stares at him, this man she's slept with, this man she thought she could love. Her voice is unyielding. "Did you sleep with Sloane?"

"What? My god, no, Annie!" His panic is convincing. "Ask her! All our contact was over the phone until last week. I saw that she was speaking in Savannah and showed up to talk to her in person. She indicated that her aunt might live another fifteen or twenty years. That's why I went to the hospital. To see for myself."

"Did you kill my sister?"

If he was previously panicked, now he's explosive. "No!" he shouts. "How can you ask me that?" He paces the worn carpet between the bed and the sink, not looking at her.

"I can ask you that, Ryan, because you seem to have no boundaries." She gathers her handbag and stands. "You better prepare yourself. The Millicent police are looking for you. They have a witness who saw you at the hospital." She doesn't share that the same witness claims to have seen her.

"I know. My office told me the police chief's been calling." He looks stricken. "But Annie. What about us? You're not throwing away what we have, are you?"

"I assume you mean, what about Millicent House?" she says drily. "Yeah, that sale won't be happening."

His wheedling stops abruptly, and his face darkens. "You're going back on your word?"

"My word?" She laughs harshly. "My word? Wouldn't I have needed the truth to honestly give my word?"

"What truth?" He advances toward her. "The truth is you made promises to me."

Alarm dawns belatedly, and she inches away from him. He keeps coming.

"The truth," he whispers, "is I have invested way too much to back out now." He grasps her arm. "The truth is I love you, Annie."

She's heard those words before, spoken with similar menace. *No more. No more.*

Groping behind her, her fingers grip the doorknob. "No!" she screams with such vehemence that Ryan halts. It's all the time she needs to wrench the motel room door open and sprint to her car.

Her last glimpse is Ryan standing on the sidewalk in front of his room. He looks as surprised as Robert did when she forced his face into the salty tide.

Chapter 36

The boys are rehearsing their set for tomorrow night, and the cacophony on this floor competes with Burle's hammering above. Sloane needs a quieter place to think. Nonetheless, she watches the band for a few more minutes—Robroy beaming as Derek and Arturio take turns in the spotlight, correcting them gently when he wants a change. He's a generous leader, and she can see why these three have stuck with him while bands around them disintegrated.

But then he murmurs something to Sean, and the bass player frowns. He makes the change Robroy wants, but it's clear he doesn't agree. After a few more minutes and a few more corrections from Robroy, each a little more adamant, Sean stomps from the room.

Glad to leave the growing tension, Sloane heads out. The way Chief Hartwell was interrogating her mother earlier, she feared he was going to arrest her. But he didn't. And Annie won't stay in one place long enough for Sloane to ask about Ryan Carbonier's number in her cell phone. She raced out thirty seconds after the chief left.

Jumping into her Toyota and turning onto the main road, Sloane calls Margaret. Her sister's office is in her home, and she answers immediately. "I'm on my way to you if that's all right," Sloane says.

"I guess I have no choice if you're already on the way."

That's as close as she'll get to an invitation.

Margaret's house is a two-story brick colonial in the island's only real subdivision, Bougainvillea, home to professionals and business owners in Millicent and Beaufort. The entire neighborhood is beautifully landscaped with shade trees, dwarf palmettos, oleander, and yes, bougainvillea. But no property is lusher than Margaret and Joel's. When she pulls into their circular drive, she sees they've added wings onto each side of the house since she was last here. Sales of gas and beer must be booming.

Margaret meets her at her oversized front doors decorated with double wreathes in springtime colors. "What's up? The girls will be home from school shortly."

"I wanted to catch you up on what happened after you left the reception."

She guides Sloane into her gargantuan kitchen. "Coffee or tea?"

"I better take water. I'm overdosing on caffeine."

Margaret fills a glass and hands it to her, and they sit on high-backed stools at a marble-topped island. Everything in the kitchen is cool gray or navy.

"So," Sloane says, "Chief Hartwell was back."

Margaret's eyebrows shoot up. "Any news on Aunt Millicent?"

"Sort of. But let me start at the beginning. After everyone left, Mom and Arturio went to Nadine's. His Auntie June dropped by."

"The one who recognized Ryan Carbonier at the hospital."

"Right. But when she saw Mom, she recognized her as being there the same night."

"But that was last week. I thought Mom wasn't in town."

"Exactly."

"Wow." Margaret sits back, her mind leaping directly to where Sloane's had gone. "It's like Octavia said. Aunt Millicent thought she saw Mom." She pauses. "So, what did Mom say?"

"She denied it. Cried." Sloane fiddles with her glass. "But she also went off on a tangent, babbling on about Dad. Oh, and Aunt Caroline came over, and they were holed up in the study, all private."

Margaret makes a face. "I'm telling you, Leo, something's going on with her."

"Well, yeah, I'm starting to agree with you." She hesitates, but despite her sister's prickliness, Sloane trusts her. "And I may know what it is."

"There's more?"

"Last night, when the party was going full blast, I saw Mom's phone on a side table. She was getting a call, but it was too loud to hear it ring."

"Thanks to the Baby Stompers."

"Right. Anyway, I saw that the caller was someone she had entered as 'Babe.'"

"Whoa. Mom's got a honey?"

"But Margaret, I recognized the number. It was Ryan Carbonier."

Her sister is clearly dumbfounded. "Wait a minute. How could you possibly know that?"

"He's been calling me for years about selling the property when I inherited. I told you that."

"So Mom calls Ryan Carbonier *Babe*? That must mean... they're dating? What the hell?"

"And she let slip to Chief Hartwell that she most recently lived in Jacksonville, not St. Pete like she told us. Guess who else lives in Jacksonville."

"*Babe*, I take it." Margaret nibbles her lip. "Does this have something to do with her inheriting the house? And coming back to Millicent?"

"It has to. The question is: Did she come of her own volition? Or is Carbonier using her?"

Margaret spins her stool in a complete circle, deep in thought. Then she jerks back to face Sloane. "Did he come on to you?"

"What? No! Ew. Why would you ask that?"

"Well, that was his method with Mom."

Sloane shakes her head dismissively. "We didn't even meet in person until last week. When he showed up at my speech in Savannah." *No need to go further.*

"So you think they're in it together?" Margaret muses. "Mom and this developer hooked up and contacted Aunt Millicent to let her know Mom was alive. So Aunt Millicent changed her will. And the next thing you know, Aunt Millicent is dead. And Mom and the developer were seen at the hospital on the night she was killed. Pretty damning, wouldn't you say?"

Sloane hadn't considered the sequence of events quite so starkly, but yes, Margaret is right. Chief Hartwell doesn't know about the relationship between Mom and Ryan Carbonier. Surely the discovery will precipitate an arrest. *But this is Mom. She wouldn't kill Aunt Millicent. She couldn't. Surely Ryan Carbonier tricked her somehow.*

It's Sloane's turn to spin around, lost in thought.

Emma Sue and Sarah dash into the house noisily, excited to see Sloane, so she stays another half hour while they devour apple slices and tell her about their school day. When they rocket off for swim lessons at the neighborhood pool, she slips away.

Since tonight is the last night that Robroy, Arturio, Sean, and Derek will be at the house, she stops by the Seafood Shack to bring home some shrimp. The young men have made short shrift of the leftovers from Monday's reception, so she'll pick up baking potatoes and salad ingredients as well.

The grocery store carries the unmistakable scent of fresh seafood, which is arranged on ice under spotless glass panels. Jesse works the counter with Burle's nephew Randall, who is Arturio's father and a partner in the Shack. Burle must be unloading seafood down at the dock.

After Jesse's earlier coolness, Sloane is unsure of her welcome. But the old woman is nominally warmer as she waits on her. They chat about the quality and size of the shrimp, and she recommends how much Sloane will need for six people.

"Well, I say six," Sloane amends. "But four of them are twenty-something young men. Those boys can eat."

Jesse laughs. "Don't I remember that from when Robroy stayed with us. I always allowed double shrimp and scallops for him."

"That was so good of you and Burle," Sloane says, "letting Robroy stay with you."

Jesse's smile fades, and she busies herself wrapping the seafood. She rings up the rest of the purchases and announces the total. Sloane scrambles to recover the camaraderie of moments before, but Jesse has shifted into professional stiffness, treating her like a stranger.

"I... I've missed seeing you and Burle," Sloane says. "More than you know."

Jesse's eyes stare back, but her smile is wooden. And dismissive. Sloane turns and walks out.

As she opens her car door, she senses a presence behind her and whirls to find Randall Jenkins. His apron is pristine and white, which Jesse insists upon, even if it means changing several times during a shift.

"Hey, Sloane," he says, "we appreciate you letting the boys stay with you. I don't think our house could stand up to the band in full throttle."

She laughs. "I know what you mean. I left them practicing, and the foundation was shaking." She closes the door and leans against it. "Actually, I've enjoyed having them. Especially Arturio. He's been a big help."

"I'd have to see that to believe it." Randall smiles, and she remembers Robroy saying that he and Nadine were huge supporters of the band. "What I wanted to say to you," he says, lowering his voice and glancing back at the grocery, "is I'm sorry for the way Jesse spoke to you. She... ah... she's very protective of Robroy."

"Protective? Why?"

Randall looks uncomfortable, and she has no idea what he's talking about.

"Does she see me as a threat to him somehow?"

"No, no, nothing like that. But when you and your mother left, there were problems."

She stares at him blankly.

"Problems with your dad."

Problems between Dad and Robroy? If anything, Sloane had always been a little jealous of their relationship. Dad clearly favored him over her and Margaret. "I thought they got along great," she protests. "I'm not sure what you're telling me."

"Your father hurt the boy," Randall says bluntly. "A broken collarbone. A broken arm. Cracked ribs. Concussion." He cocks his head and frowns. "Is this news to you?"

A buzzing begins in her head. Her mouth opens and shuts, but no words emerge. Wooziness overtakes her, and she starts to slide down the car door. "Oh, no," she says. "No, no, no."

Randall grabs her arm to steady her. "Surely you knew about your dad."

"I knew he hit my mother," she whispers. "But he never hit Margaret or me. Or Robroy! We thought he loved Robroy. Took him hunting and fishing and all that stuff he never wanted to do with us. I swear to you, we thought Robroy was safe."

Randall shakes his head. "In his own way, I'm sure your daddy did love him. Loved all you kids. But when he got to drinking, whew. I reckon nobody was safe."

The world Sloane thought she knew shears off its axis. The happy island boy she'd always pictured dissolves, replaced by a skinny, solemn boy on buckling steps, bruised and shaken. "Did Margaret know? Did Raeford?"

Randall shrugs. "It's a small island."

"And so you all got together and took him in?"

"Lots of times. But then he'd want to go back to his daddy. We couldn't convince him to stay anywhere else. He'd run away. Until the next time."

Sloane bends at the waist, feeling physically ill. *How did I not know this? Did I tell myself a fiction because it was easier for me?*

"What about Margaret?" she asks again, unwilling to believe her view of things could be so distorted. "Are you sure she and Joel knew?"

"I don't know what they knew, Sloane. He did stay with them some."

Tears slip down her face, and she brushes at them angrily. A massive Range Rover creeps into the parking lot, munching gravel.

"I better see what these folks want," Randall says, awkwardly patting her shoulder. "Sorry to be the bearer of bad news."

"No, I needed to know." Even though the knowledge has carved a gaping hollow in her chest. "Th-Thank you for telling me, Randall."

The band is packing up their instruments when she walks in with her packages. "Boiled shrimp for dinner. Who's in?"

The young men cheer raucously, their earlier squabble apparently forgotten. Arturio grabs one of the bags and takes it to the kitchen. "You're the best, Sloane."

She catches Robroy out of the corner of her eye, placing his guitar into a case. She doesn't know how to broach what she's learned from Randall. Or even if she should. Robroy has never said a word about their father's abuse. In fact, he expressly denied it when telling her about his trips to Mercy Hospital. Does he assume she already knows? She doesn't know her brother well enough to guess. *How sad is that?*

Robroy looks up. "Want me to try Jesse's hushpuppy recipe? It won't be as good as hers, but I used to help her."

"Absolutely," Sean says before she can answer. "Go for it. What can I do, Sloane?"

"Okay, scrub the potatoes while I heat the oven. Then we can start chopping carrots and cucumbers for the salad. The shrimp won't go into the pot until the final few minutes."

With all of them working, they complete the prep half an hour before the potatoes are ready. She uncorks a bottle of Prosecco rosé, but predictably, the young men prefer beer. Her mother will help her drink it. *But where is she?*

"Robroy, have you heard from Mom?"

"No, she left before you and hasn't been back."

Sloane calls and gets her voicemail. "Well, if she's not going to be here to eat her share, I think I'll invite Eli."

"Fine by me," her brother says. "If you're sure you bought enough shrimp. I'd hate for ol' Eli not to get any."

She calls Eli, who responds that he's in Millicent and will be right over. "And Sloane, has anyone contacted you about the meeting tonight?"

"What meeting?"

"They will. Any minute. It's about what your family plans to do with the house."

"Why are they waiting so late to tell us?"

"It's impromptu. People were talking at the diner today and realized that both your aunt's and father's services are over, and they can approach you—without breaking the laws of Southern etiquette."

"Ha. Where and what time?"

"In the fellowship hall of Palm Road Baptist at seven thirty."

"Well, then hurry on over. We have time for dinner first."

She calls her mother again and leaves a message about the meeting. "I'm sure it's you they want to hear from," she adds. "Don't make me and Robroy face them alone."

Margaret then calls, having gotten official notice of the meeting. "I'm trying to find a sitter now," she says. "Joel will stay with the girls if I can't find one."

Eli arrives ten minutes later, and they all sit down to a feast that includes Robroy's decent facsimile of Jesse's hushpuppies.

"You were paying attention," she tells her brother after crunching into a hot morsel fresh from the fryer. "You could be her apprentice."

He dips a shrimp into cocktail sauce. "Good to know I've got a backup if the music thing doesn't work out." He points a shrimp at Eli. "So, tell us about this meeting. Will there be pitchforks?"

"Maybe," Eli responds. "As you guys know, feelings are running high. As far as I can tell, the insurance broker wants the development. And the Sandersons, who own the bank. The barber and hair salon gals want it. The coffee shop owner. Elsie from the diner is on the fence." He slathers butter on his baked potato.

"The fishermen are split about half and half. They like the idea of more local restaurants and grocery stores but fear more fishing competitors. Most farmers don't want it. I think any doctors who might once have wanted more patients have already moved their practices to Beaufort. They like coming home to the island as it is. The convenience store owners all want the development. Except for your sister's company. The Simpsons are the only chain owners who actually live here."

Robroy lifts his head. "Margaret doesn't want to sell the house? Did you know that, Sloane?"

"She never said. And I never asked." She reaches for another hushpuppy. "I don't mean to be ugly, but since she wasn't inheriting, I guess it didn't matter what she thought."

Arturio laughs. "That *is* a tad ugly."

"Actually, it doesn't matter what Robroy and I think either. Mom is inheriting the place, so she's the decider-in-chief."

"Right," adds Robroy, "and the townsfolk aren't going to get any answers if she doesn't show up. You still haven't heard from her, Sloane?"

She checks her phone again and shakes her head. The young men polish off every single shrimp and search out the remaining key lime pie left from the morning reception.

They leave the cleanup to Sean and Derek, as Sloane, Eli, Robroy, and Arturio head for Palm Road Baptist Church. Sloane calls her mother once more but gets no answer.

Chapter 37

The Impala fishtails as Annie blasts from the motel parking lot, abandoning any future with Ryan Carbonier. Her shattered emotions battle for supremacy—anger at his betrayal, disbelief at his cunning, disgust at her naïveté, exhilaration that she stood up to him.

Speeding along low-lying US Route 21 from Beaufort to St. Helena, she considers calling Chief Hartwell to tell him where he can find Ryan. He admitted to being at Mercy Hospital last Thursday night. He feared Millicent was going to live another two decades, and he couldn't face his development being stalled that long. Her stomach clenches at the thought that she introduced this man into her sister's orbit.

But wait. According to Raeford, Ryan—and other developers—had been making offers on the beach house for years. That's why Ryan was in touch with Sloane—to shore up his advantage during the time she was the beneficiary. He only turned his attention to Annie much later. *But how did he discover I had reentered the picture?*

Could Raeford have told him? No, Raeford didn't know about the new will until Sloane and Robroy called him this week.

Idelle? Or more likely, her husband, J.C. They would have had business dealings with major developers along the coast. *Possible.*

But despite her fury, can she picture Ryan sneaking into Mercy Hospital and killing a confused old woman in her bed? Injecting digoxin into her intravenous bag? This is a man she shared a bed with. A man she considered marrying.

And one more thing. If Annie reports his presence at the hospital, it will revive Chief Hartwell's interest in Auntie June's other claim—that Annie was in the hospital too. Her mind is whirring with more questions than answers. She tosses her cell phone onto the passenger seat and notices three voicemails from Sloane. She didn't hear it ring over the Impala's loud engine.

She turns onto SC 900, and the road twists and curves its watery way to Millicent. Giant oaks and cypresses crowd her, and when there's a break in them, the afternoon sun shines painfully in her eyes. She should slow down, but she's too wired. Now that she no longer has to worry about her promise to Ryan, she is free to do what she wants with the inheritance. Live here. Sell. Or both—she can live here for as long as she likes and sell in the future. Lord knows there will always be a market for beachfront property.

And if she lives here, at least for a while, it will be easier to re-connect with Margaret and Sloane and Robroy. Her heart pinches at the thought of Robroy, who somehow emerged intact from his years with Robert. She now realizes her gamble was an unforgiveable risk, though at the time, Robert's fondness for the boy made her depar-ture seem plausible. Justifiable.

Her neck and shoulder muscles constrict at the thought of her husband. For years, all she thought about was escaping him. And then hiding from him. In the months after she fled, she moved from Corpus Christi to New Orleans to Dallas to Albuquerque. She learned of the private eye Millicent and Raeford sent and dodged him by remaining on the move. That wouldn't have been possible if she'd had a ten-year-old in tow—she told herself that every night.

The Southwestern desert didn't suit her, so after Albuquerque, she moved to St. Louis, back to Corpus Christi, and only then to Florida. Marathon Key, Miami, Sarasota, then up the coast to St. Pete, as she told her children. She didn't lie to them—merely omitted a few stops.

For the last segment of that time, she was in touch with her old friend Idelle. Not only did they have a history, but Idelle was Margaret's mother-in-law, the paternal grandmother of Emma Sue and Sarah. She kept Annie up-to-date on Margaret, mostly, but also on Robroy.

To this day, she's not sure why Idelle broke down and told her the rest. Maybe because, for the hundredth time, Annie was congratulating herself on her decision to leave her son behind. It was the way she rationalized her choice. But in a phone call last December, Idelle had snapped.

"I'm sorry, Annie, but I can't listen to you excuse yourself one more time," she said.

Her words seared into Annie's brain. Every middle-of-the-night fear she'd ever faced came roaring back. "Idelle, is there something I don't know?" she asked, not really wanting an answer.

"Yes." Her breathing came hard over the phone. "It's over now. He's left home." Annie waited in dread for her next words. "But Robert did to Robroy what he did to you."

Grasping her torso with her free arm, she hugged herself tightly. All the justifications and denials fell away. Years of deceit, years of disavowal. All that remained was loathing. Loathing of herself. And loathing of the man behind all of it.

She pressed Idelle to describe every injury she'd ever witnessed, every bruise and break that had sent her boy running to Margaret or the Espeys, to Burle and Jesse or Nadine and Randall. Or, as it turns out, to Mercy Hospital's emergency room.

By the end, Annie was sobbing but would not let Idelle stop. She deserved to hear every brutal detail. "I knew he spent time with all of them, but I thought it was because Robert was out on the boat," she said. "Oh my God, Idelle, why didn't somebody tell me?"

Idelle paused then, because she was the only one who could have told her. After a long while, her response came. Coldly. "I thought you knew, Annie. How could you not?"

How could I not? That's what it came down to. *How could I not?*

Her bald tires slip off the asphalt, and she yanks the steering wheel. Fortunately, no cars are coming, and she jolts back to the center of the road. She should slow down, but memories are chasing her like voracious wolves.

For days after that phone call with Idelle, she hid in her St. Pete bed-and-breakfast, expending minimal effort on her guests. A plan began to form in her mind.

Idelle had been encouraging her to contact Millicent ever since Millicent had learned that Annie and Idelle were in touch. At first, she wrote a letter to her sister, trying to explain and apologize. But her paranoia about being found remained so strong that she made up a return address and had some guests post it from St. Louis.

Finally, in February, Annie worked up the courage and called her sister. Millicent was understandably hurt and irate that Annie had been in touch with Idelle and not her. But it didn't take Annie long to persuade her she was ready to come home, ready to return to Millicent House.

Millicent broached the subject of changing her will in March. Her reluctance—quite understandably—hinged on the fact that Annie had never divorced Robert. Neither of them wanted to risk the property falling into his hands.

Annie remained unreasonably fearful of setting foot on the island, so the sisters agreed to meet one night in their father's old office in Beaufort. That night, they both cried over their lost years. But Annie was crying over something else as well—how she'd let her foolishness at seventeen cost her her children, her birthright, her self-worth.

"If you reinstate me in the will," she promised, "I'll take care of Robert."

"How, Annie?" asked Millicent. "You were so scared of the man you ran away for twelve years."

"I still am," she admitted. "But when I learned how he treated Robroy, it cracked something open in me."

Millicent looked at her with skepticism, her eyes asking the same thing Idelle had verbalized: *How could you not know?*

No one trusted her, and Annie didn't blame them. She didn't trust herself. But something had broken inside, and the shards threatened to shred her. She had to do something to reclaim her identity. Hell, to reclaim her soul.

Ryan had been urging her to join him in Jacksonville, so she moved into an apartment there as they tested the waters of their relationship. She admitted that she was not Annmarie Crossland, as she'd told him in St. Pete, but Millicent "Annie" Roundtree Cheney. That one day she'd inherit oceanfront property on the barrier island of Millicent, South Carolina. It's embarrassing to think how she played into his hands. But the fact was, she never intended to live on the island again.

Of course, that's not what she told her sister. Her plan was to simply slip into town unnoticed and access a part of their father's estate—bank accounts, stocks, other holdings that Millicent could easily liquidate. Millicent was healthy, and Annie didn't foresee inheriting the house for decades. But once she was secreted on the island, she would hit Robert Cheney with everything she had.

The Impala squeals as Annie brakes for a squirrel darting across the road. Her heart pounds. To her right is the St. James Episcopal cemetery where her sister is buried. Her death was never part of the plan, and her heart aches in protest.

She jams the gas pedal, pain and regret swirling in her head. She lied to her sister, told her what she wanted to hear—that if she left the house to Annie, she'd not sell it. She'd not allow developers to turn Millicent into Myrtle Beach or Isle of Palms. Why did she say that? She's not even sure. All she really wanted was time to deal with Robert, time to lay low and observe his habits and decide the best way to reach him. But frankly, she was paralyzed and continued to hunker down in Jacksonville, putting off the move to Millicent House week after week as winter ended and spring arrived.

And then something happened. Her healthy sister went into Mercy Hospital for a minor UTI infection and didn't come out. Annie panicked. She hadn't managed to deal with Robert. As her legal husband, he stood to inherit half the Roundtree estate, including the iconic Millicent House. The man who had killed his sister, terrorized his wife, bullied their precious son. Annie could not allow it.

A giant oak suddenly looms in her side mirror. The car bucks, and the sickening *crack* alerts her that she clipped it. *Slow down, Annie!* But her brain and foot are not in sync.

She hadn't dared attend Millicent's funeral, though she'd crept onto the island the night before. The old shack she and Robert initially shared was abandoned, practically falling down, so she brought a sleeping bag and slept there, trembling at the memories that seeped from the very walls. The next morning, she crept on foot to watch Robert launch his boat. Then she sneaked into his sorry excuse for a house and left a bottle of bourbon. Good stuff, laced with a handful of Valium she'd saved from an old prescription. She penned a note in block letters, "Enjoy! From Robroy," trusting that Robert wouldn't know his own son's handwriting.

After hiding out all day, grieving that she couldn't properly lay her sister to rest, she returned to his shanty around midnight. From a nearby patch of scrub, she peered into his open kitchen window, getting bit by mosquitoes and chiggers and staying quiet enough to avoid notice by his two dogs.

He put on quite a show, grotesque and frightening. Robert could never pass up booze, especially free booze, and this aged version of him staggered and sang to his hound dogs and cursed her sister.

His tolerance was legendary, and by the time he passed out on the kitchen table, it was close to dawn. She shook out the numbness in her legs and sneaked into the shanty. The dogs growled, but she'd come prepared. After luring them with Slim Jims into a bedroom, she slammed the door and left them. She placed two Valium tablets inside the rusting medicine cabinet in the bathroom, wiping them carefully with toilet paper to remove her fingerprints.

Meanwhile, Robert snored heavily, unmoving. Trusting the pill-and-bourbon cocktail he'd consumed, she tipped his chair, letting his head bounce on the floor. Upon hearing the crash, the dogs howled and scratched frantically at the bedroom door. Robert's eyes jerked open, and she froze, but they closed again. The hounds continued to bark, but no one lived close enough to hear them.

This was the moment she'd been waiting for. She seized Robert's legs and, grunting and beginning to sweat, pulled him down the outdoor stairs, allowing his head to hit every step. She hoped that what the bourbon and sedative didn't do, the blows would.

She dragged him over the sandy ground around the house and down to his dock, halting every few feet to wipe stinging sweat from her eyes. He groaned a few times but didn't resist, so she tugged him into the waterway, wading in past her knees. At the last minute, his eyes opened, and he stared up at her, bewildered and sputtering from the water that splashed into his mouth. Before he could figure out what was happening, she flipped him over and held his head underwater, his neck muscles straining with the feeblest protest, his limp blond hair spreading like seaweed. His rubbery body flopped about, but she easily held him until the bubbles ceased.

She thought of Chelsea. Of Robroy. Of seventeen-year-old Annie. And she felt nothing.

Glancing upstream, she saw a shrimp boat far up the waterway, much too far for its crew to see anything in the gray morning light. Or so she thought.

She slogged back to the house and released the dogs. They ignored her and raced to the dock. Exhausted, she broke a branch off an oleander bush and swept the trail where she'd dragged Robert. Then she retrieved a full bottle of Woodford Reserve from where she'd hidden it underneath the oleander and poured the contents into the waterway. After wiping her fingerprints off the empty bottle, she waded back into the water, grabbed Robert's lifeless hand, and pressed his palm against it. She trudged to the shack, where she substituted that bottle for the nearly empty Valium-laced one. Then, taking the oleander branch, the drugged bourbon bottle, and the note with her, she trekked a half mile down the sandy road to where she'd stashed the Impala in a copse of scrub pines. She sagged into the driver's seat, wondering if she dared check into a motel in Beaufort for a hot shower and a nap. In the end, she didn't and drove the entire way back to Jacksonville.

S omehow, Annie's face is wet and her mind muddled. She tastes salt. Is it the inland tide, or tears? She fumbles in her handbag for a tissue. Another cemetery whizzes by. *Goodness, these islanders love to put their graves right up against the road, don't they?*

A Spanish-moss-laden tree leaps out of the cemetery, and she doesn't have time to swerve. This time, it's more than her side mirror that—

The last sound she hears is the scream of tortured metal. Then silence.

Chapter 38

Sloane

Palm Road Baptist Church carries a name from a more hopeful time; only a few scraggly palms currently grow along the adjacent stretch of blacktop. Instead, the redbrick building is flanked by fields of stark, dying trees whose feet have resided too long in salt water. This is one of the unlovelier parts of the island.

Fifty residents crowd into folding chairs that face a bare stage in the drab fellowship hall. Robroy whispers that members could take some design advice from the police station decorator, and Sloane hides a smile. They dare not let the neighbors think they take their concerns lightly.

The church's pastor, eager to repair the damage the sale of Camp Resurrection has caused among some townspeople, drags a single microphone to the front and encourages speakers to take turns. First up is Elsie Dennehy, who explains that she isn't taking sides, but as she plans her retirement, she needs to know if the diner will serve a sleepy beach community or a newly minted boomtown.

Raylene from Hair's the Thing is more aggressive. "Money may not matter to you Roundtrees and Cheneys,"—she points a finger at Sloane and Robroy in the front row—"but them's of us who's got mortgages and car payments and bills need the customers this development will bring."

Sloane doubts that people on vacation will want a haircut from the likes of Raylene but keeps quiet. She doesn't want her yelling about Sloane's big-city snobbery.

That charge comes from Bud Randolph, the boat-shop owner whose vehemence catches her off guard. "Millicent Sloane, we know about your high-falutin' life in Atlanta," he says loudly. "And your trashy life before that. We may live in South Carolina, but we can read, you know. And we don't want to become Atlanta."

She blushes furiously and mutters, "It was fiction." *Should I say something about his shoddy workmanship on their balcony?* Before she can decide, Margaret, sitting between Idelle and Octavia, shoots to her feet.

"Wait a minute there, Bud," she says, ignoring the microphone protocol. "I don't want development in Millicent any more than you do. But Sloane's not the enemy here. Or Robroy, for that matter."

Her gaze sweeps the room, from Burle, Randall, Nadine, and Arturio to the fishermen Espeys, the bank-owning Sandersons, and the town's small business owners. "You folks are attacking my family from both sides. Whether you're for development or against it, you're yelling at Sloane. The last we heard, it's our mother who's inheriting Millicent House. So save your kind persuasion"—she makes air quotes sarcastically—"for her."

Her words unleash a querulous buzz. Everyone knows that Annie Cheney has returned, but few have seen her.

Mack Sanderson stands and begins shouting about their mother's lack of consideration in skipping the meeting. That's when Sloane's phone rings. Grateful for the interruption, she snatches it.

When the caller gives her the excuse to grab Robroy, Margaret, and Eli and head to Mercy Hospital, she is almost relieved.

"We brought your mother here," Chief Hartwell is saying, "because it was closer, and the medics couldn't ascertain the extent of her injuries. So she may stay here or be transferred to

Beaufort." Eli puts his arm around Sloane's shoulders and holds her close.

"But what happened?" asks Margaret, taking charge. "Did someone force her off the road?" The rancor they just witnessed hangs heavily over them.

"No, as far as we could tell, it was a single-car accident. She was speeding and hit a tree near St. Mark Methodist."

"She was speeding?" Margaret is incredulous. "In that old rust bucket?"

"According to the skid marks, yes."

Robroy turns to Sloane. "Do you think she was trying to make the meeting?"

"It's possible, I guess. If she picked up my voicemails."

"She didn't," says the police chief. "We retrieved her phone from the car, and there are unanswered calls from you, Miss Cheney. Three, I believe."

"Can we see her?" Sloane asks.

The chief walks off to consult a nurse and returns. "Not yet. She's being assessed in the ER. But it won't be long."

Kent Espey rushes through the lobby doors and halts when he sees the chief. "Got your message," he says.

They must look puzzled because he explains, "I work part-time in the police department. I'll be guarding your mother's room." Sloane is not sure what surprises her more—that her old friend is a police officer or that their mother needs protection.

Margaret is the first to recover. "That's an excellent idea," she says. "Thank you, Chief."

Robroy looks confused. "I don't understand. Why would you guard Mom's room?"

"Did you not hear what we heard at that meeting?" Margaret demands. "Believe me, Robroy, I live here. People are furious on both sides of this Mayberry by the Sea nonsense."

"But no one knows what Mom's going to do," he says. "Even we don't know what Mom's going to do. Or do you?"

His sisters shake their heads.

"We haven't had time to discuss it," Sloane says.

"And there's the other thing," adds Margaret. "The obvious thing."

Robroy still appears baffled, so Margaret spells it out with a hint of exasperation. "Aunt Millicent was killed in this hospital."

He visibly deflates. "Oh, yeah, right."

A nurse comes to usher them into a waiting room, while Kent Espey and the chief consult in the corridor. As Sloane's adrenaline recedes, it is replaced by anxiety. What is going on with their mother? Sloane had longed for the stability and nurturing she'd so missed. But Annie Cheney's return has heralded nothing but chaos.

As they spread out in the chairs that line the waiting room, Robroy turns to Margaret. "Back to what you were saying about Aunt Millicent. Do you think she was killed over Mayberry by the Sea?"

Margaret shrugs. "Has to be. What else could account for killing her?"

What else, indeed. Not for the first time, Sloane ponders her sister's absence from Aunt Millicent's original will—especially now that she knows Margaret opposes the development. It seems like Margaret and her aunt would've been in lockstep over the future of the property. Margaret pulls out her phone, undoubtedly to alert Joel and Idelle to what has happened.

Eli gazes at the wall past her shoulder, and Sloane can almost see his quick mind considering and discarding theories. "What are you thinking?" she whispers.

"As soon as you make sure your mom is okay," he answers, "the four of us"—he gestures to include Margaret and Robroy—"need to sit down and talk about that meeting tonight."

"Because?"

"Because if your aunt's killer was somehow *not* Ryan Carbonier, he or she was in that room."

Chapter 39

Annie

Annie struggles to wake from a dream of driving, her foot anchored to the gas pedal, an unforgiving oak dead center in her windshield. Her heart batters against her chest, and a machine near her ear beeps in distress.

Where am I? Her panicked eyes flit around the room. Beige, beige, and more beige. She gingerly moves her head, and there's no real pain, only stiffness. But then she sees the bulge under the thin blanket. Her leg is in some sort of splint. A nurse rushes into the room, no doubt to deal with the beeping. She looks at the machine instead of Annie. Satisfied, she pushes a button to stop the noise.

"Hello, Mrs. Cheney. Do you know where you are?" Her smile is kind.

She tries to answer, but her throat is raw. The nurse offers a Styrofoam cup with a straw, and she gratefully gulps the icy water. "Easy, easy," the nurse cautions. "We've got all the time in the world."

"Hospital," Annie croaks.

"You're at Mercy Hospital on the island," the nurse affirms, her voice musical. "You were in an accident on the road into town. Do you remember?"

Annie nods.

"The first responders weren't sure how badly you were injured, but it turns out you have a broken leg. The doctor gave you some pretty strong pain meds in the ER. When they wear off, you're gonna be sore."

With the worst of her fear assuaged, she sinks into the mattress and thinks back to the wreck. She was driving too fast, she remembers that. What was her hurry? Then all the memories flood in—Ryan and the motel room in Beaufort. Robert and his dismal shack on the inland waterway. Ian's boat chugging up the creek. Caroline's guarded whispers. *Am I safe?* She honestly has no idea. And she's in no condition to run this time. Her heart starts pounding again, but she takes deep breaths, and the monitor beside the bed remains blessedly silent.

"Where... are my children?"

"In the waiting room. Are you ready to see them?"

"Oh, yes."

Seconds later, they rush in—Sloane and Robroy, then Margaret, tentative, bringing up the rear. Her older daughter is suspicious of her, that much is clear. Annie needs to win her over. A fourth person, the young man she saw earlier at their kitchen table, hugs the far wall. After she assures them she'll recover, she asks to meet Sloane's friend.

Sloane's skin flushes in a way familiar to Annie from her own mirror. "This is Eli Cartwright," she says. "We were... um... friends in college, and he's the Lowcountry bureau chief for *The Greenbrier Herald*."

"Bureau chief and sole reporter," he says with a grin. "It's nice to finally meet you, Mrs. Cheney. I've heard so much about you."

She seeks out Sloane's gaze, startled to think of her daughter telling this young man about her. Sloane has been without a mother nearly as long as she had one. And the one she had was piss poor. But Annie cannot allow her shame to bleed into every future interaction, or she'll never make amends.

"It's nice to meet you, too, Eli," she says. "I apologize for the circumstances."

"Hardly your fault." His blue-green eyes are warm, and he's a looker. She wonders why he and Sloane broke up.

Robroy comes forward and takes Annie's hand, his smile tremulous. She hopes the situation is not too upsetting for him. He's just reclaimed his mother, and now she's laid up in the hospital, the very hospital where his aunt died last week.

The thought of her sister lands like an anvil on her chest. Annie is sure this *wasn't* Millicent's room—the medical director would never allow that—but what a depressing place for her last hours. She loved beauty, loved being surrounded by the warm refinement of their historic home. To die within these bland walls must have been excruciating.

Margaret stands at the foot of her bed, frowning. Unlike Sloane and Robroy, she has stayed on this island, has interacted with Millicent and Robert and Idelle and Ian and Caroline. With Burle, Jesse, and Nadine, and perhaps even Nadine's sister, June. *Has she heard things? Does she know things?*

"What's wrong, Mother?" she asks. "Are you in pain?"

She's never called her "Mother" before. *Why so formal?*

Annie attempts her most winning smile. "No pain yet. The nurse assures me it will hit later." She squirms to sit up. Sloane and Robroy leap to help her, but Margaret remains immobile.

"Is something wrong, Margaret?"

Her daughter sighs. "We came here directly from a meeting with island residents about the development plans. But we don't want to worry you with the details until you feel better."

Well, her statement certainly planted worry. *Is that what she intended?*

"You're right. I'm too woozy to think about it right now." Annie glances around at their faces. "Do you mind if I sleep?"

Sloane and Robroy hurry to reassure her that sleep is exactly what she needs. "We'll be back in the morning," Sloane says.

Within moments, they're gone, and Annie is alone with her thoughts. She presses her call button and asks if the nurse named June can come to her room. They need to get a few things straight.

Chapter 40

Sloane

Dusk is settling in shades of purple as Sloane, Margaret, Eli, and Robroy troop from the hospital, leaving Kent Espey sitting outside their mother's door. These long spring evenings remind Sloane of school's end and the start of island summers. Had she not been on constant alert to evade her father, they would have been heavenly.

A ping alerts her to a text message from her editor.

How are edits going? Got Elle sorted?

Sheesh. She hasn't thought of the book since early morning. She doesn't intend to tell her Warner College boss John Avery that her mother was in a car wreck, but she doesn't mind playing on her editor's sympathy. She texts back:

More drama/trauma. Long lost Mom in car wreck. Will get to Elle soonest.

Which relays exactly nothing. Sloane needs to be on the road to Atlanta tomorrow for the trustees' dinner, and nothing is resolved here. Her graduation speech is no closer to being improved. The hushpuppies sit like a lump of glue in her stomach.

Robroy invites Margaret and Eli to the house to debrief from the meeting at the church. Sloane starts to object but then glimpses her brother's set jaw.

"I overheard what you suggested in the waiting room, Eli," he says. "And the band leaves for Charleston tomorrow. It'll be my last chance to sit down with you for a while."

"Yeah, I'm good," says Margaret. "Joel is with the girls."

Sloane gives in, promising one hour, maximum. Fifteen minutes later, they are seated around the dining room table, Robroy and Eli with beers, Margaret with a glass of wine, Sloane with water. She's afraid to inflict alcohol on her tortured brain or stomach.

As always, Margaret takes the lead but moves in a surprising direction. "Eli, you may see this more clearly than we do. Why don't you start?"

He has his legal pad and pen out, and Sloane sees a list of names. "What are those?"

"People who visited your aunt in the hospital."

"*What?*" Margaret and Robroy clamor at once.

"How'd you get that?" Sloane adds.

"Don't ask. Suffice it to say, we reporters can't always rely on the police to give us what we need."

"So who came to the hospital?" Margaret asks.

Eli covers his pad with a hand. "This stays among us, and you can't tell Chief Hartwell where you saw it, right?" He waits until each of them promises.

Then he spins the pad for them to view. Raeford Carlisle. Octavia Hargrove. Jesse Jenkins. Burle Jenkins. Margaret Simpson. Idelle Simpson. Elsie Dennehy. Robroy Cheney. Mack Sanderson. Ryan Carbonier. Annie Cheney.

"Good Lord! How were this many people in a single hospital room?" Margaret asks.

"Well, she was there four days," Eli says. "This includes all her visitors."

"From a sign-in book?"

"And from police interviews with hospital staff."

Robroy looks stunned. "Wait a minute. Mom was there? I thought she wasn't in town until yesterday."

Sloane and Margaret trade glances. "Yeah, Arturio's Auntie June recognized Mom when she visited Nadine's house earlier today," Margaret says. "June is a nurse at Mercy. Arturio didn't tell you?"

He shakes his head numbly.

"Sorry, we should've mentioned it, but things have been so crazy," Sloane adds.

"We think," says Margaret, "that she may have been there with Ryan Carbonier. They are... ah... dating."

Robroy looks from one sister to another with disgust. "That's insane, Margaret. Where did you get such a stupid idea?"

She gestures at Sloane. "Tell him what you saw."

"Are we off the record, Eli?"

Eli looks as bewildered as Robroy, but he agrees, and Sloane plows ahead.

"Ryan's phone number is in Mom's contact list. Under the name *Babe*."

Robroy shakes his head. "I'm not sure I believe that." He holds up his hands in a placating gesture. "Or that it means what you think it means. But the fact that Ryan Carbonier's name is on the hospital list seems pretty conclusive, don't you think? I mean how long has this guy been after the house? And he thinks it's okay to visit Aunt Millicent? In the hospital?"

Robroy has a point, but Sloane looks hopefully at the other names on Eli's purloined list. Because if Ryan Carbonier did slip a deadly drug into her aunt's intravenous bag, she'll never forgive herself.

"So Robroy, when were you in town?" asks Margaret, pointing at his name on Eli's list. "And why didn't you stay with us?"

"I came as soon as Raeford called, but only for a couple of hours. Monday, maybe? I didn't spend the night." He gets up to grab more beers for him and Eli.

"Do you notice anything about the list?" Eli asks when Robroy sits back down. "About where people stand on the development?"

"Most are against it," Margaret says, running her finger down Eli's handwritten page. "The only ones for it are Mack Sanderson and Ryan Carbonier. Elsie is neutral. I don't know about Raeford and Mom. Or you, Robroy."

He shrugs. "I don't live here. Don't have a dog in the fight."

"But you agreed to the sale to Ryan Carbonier before Raeford pulled it back, didn't you?"

"Yeah, but only because Sloane already had it lined up. I literally found out I was in the will when Raeford called this past weekend. And we signed the sales agreement on Monday. I didn't have time to give it much thought."

Sloane returns to Eli's question. "It makes sense that Aunt Millicent's closest friends thought like she did. Anti-development. And that's who visited her in the hospital."

"But you'd think someone who *supported* the development would be the one to want your aunt out of the way," Eli muses. He taps his pen against his pad and shoves his chair back. "But we're not going to get anywhere until the police locate Ryan Carbonier. And the fact that they can't find him doesn't look good for him. I'm heading down to Jacksonville tomorrow to nose around his office."

He stands. "Thanks for sharing your thoughts, Cheneys."

Sloane walks him to the door and releases him with a quick hug. But her mind is elsewhere.

When she returns to the dining room, Margaret is stepping into the pumps she kicked off. "Ten more minutes?" Sloane asks her.

"You were the one who gave us an hour deadline."

"I know, but there's something else I want to know. I hope it's okay to talk about it in front of Robroy."

Both of them look at her curiously but sit back down.

"It's about you and Aunt Millicent. I can't understand why you weren't in the will when you and she were in total agreement about not selling the house. And Robroy and I were totally going to sell."

"So you don't think it was because I was already 'taken care of'?" Margaret makes her air quotes again. "Or that she was mad at my mother-in-law?"

"No, I don't."

Margaret draws a deep breath. "Understand that nothing was ever spoken. In that vaunted way of Southern matriarchs, Aunt Millicent never deigned to come right out and tell me. But I always suspected it had to do with something I said about Mom."

Whatever Sloane was expecting, this wasn't it. "Mom?"

Margaret sighs. "The night Mom left, she stopped by my house. You were at your high school graduation party. Dad was out on his boat overnight, and she left Robroy alone." Margaret cuts her eyes at their brother. "She and I got into a screaming match."

This is hard for Sloane to picture. "A screaming match about what?"

Robroy is staring at Margaret. "About me?"

"Yeah. I couldn't believe she was leaving you. She called me a know-it-all and said I could never understand because my husband was good to me. I said some pretty ugly things like, 'I had the good sense *not* to choose someone like Dad.' And so on. It was a horrible way to end things, and I've regretted it more times than you can know."

She raises her head, and Sloane can see their aunt's steeliness in her. "Then," she says, "I compounded things by being honest with Aunt Millicent. I told her Mom was being immature and self-centered and was taking a huge risk in leaving Robroy with Dad."

A look Sloane cannot fathom passes between her brother and sister. Or maybe she can. She hears Randall once more: *Your father hurt the boy.*

Margaret continues, and Sloane snaps her attention back to her sister. "Aunt Millicent didn't want to hear a word against Mom. She did that thing of drawing up and looking down her nose at me. You remember that move?" Margaret throws her hands out in supplication. "And that was it as far as we were concerned. She never said anything directly, but I understood I had crossed some sort of loyalty line."

Robroy finishes his beer and stands. "Heard enough?" he asks Sloane, running a hand through his hair. His back is stiff as he heads through the kitchen to join his buddies on the porch. Margaret collects her shoes and purse, not meeting Sloane's eyes.

"Margaret," she says. "There's more, isn't there?"

She stops, her back to Sloane. Sloane expects her to turn around, then she realizes her sister is trying to pull herself together. Finally, she drops into a chair, running her fingers under her eyes to remove smeared mascara.

"Now that Robroy's gone, can you tell me?" Sloane asks softly.

Margaret rises wearily and motions Sloane into the study, where she closes the door.

"I don't want Robroy to hear this," she says. "He'll feel awful."

"Okay."

"As you know, I had just turned fifteen when he was born. The same age Aunt Millicent was when she took over raising Mom. So when Mom left, and Joel and I were settled into our house, Aunt Millicent thought I should adopt Robroy." She raises a tear-stained face. "And Sloane, I tried. I honestly did. But Robroy would *not* leave Dad for more than a few nights at a time. I talked to him. Joel talked to him. J.C. talked to him. No one could get him to leave Dad, no matter how many times Dad hurt him."

She starts to cry but does her best to keep talking. "I couldn't make Aunt Millicent understand. She was just so mad at me. So disappointed."

Sloane is flummoxed by the currents that have buffeted her family in her absence. "Margaret, that is so unfair. I'm surprised she did that, but I'm also surprised you let her lay that on you."

Margaret throws Sloane a look that is half smile, half scowl. "I probably wouldn't have, except for one thing: I agreed with her."

"Oh no, Margaret, no. That's not right." Sloane can scarcely believe how her father's damage continues to infect their lives—and probably will for years, if not generations, to come.

"You haven't heard it all," Margaret says. She sighs, wiping her eyes, and inhales deeply.

Sloane braces.

"Did you notice that the Espeys weren't at Aunt Millicent's funeral or reception?"

"Yeah. Kent told me Robroy and Scotty had a falling out."

"He didn't tell you why?"

"No, but Robroy said it was over a girl."

Margaret laughs drily. "Hardly. When the boys were sixteen, Robroy was staying with them after one of Dad's rampages. He had a huge black eye—the bruise covered like half his face." Margaret glances sideways at her sister. "You know about all that, right?"

Sloane grimaces. "Actually, I only found out this afternoon. From Randall."

"I figured you knew and just didn't want to talk about it," Margaret says. "Anyway, he stole around fifteen hundred dollars that Harlan Espey had in the house."

Sloane stares. "Robroy? No way."

"They knew it was him because he suddenly had all this new music equipment. Not exactly a criminal mastermind."

Sloane can't believe what her sister is saying. "Margaret, are you sure?"

"Oh, yeah. He finally admitted it to me and Joel, just not to the Espeys. Never apologized to them. We paid them back to keep them from reporting it to the police. And you know, they were sympathetic, to a point. But they never had him in their house again."

Sloane takes a moment to process this new facet of their brother. *But Robroy was only sixteen, immature and reeling from a broken family and an abusive father.* "Wait." She sits up straighter. "Did he ever steal from you? Or Aunt Millicent?"

Margaret waggles a hand to indicate *maybe*. "Nothing of consequence. We were careful never to leave more than a few dollars lying out. And it wasn't much more than a year later that he left home and went on the road with the band." Her voice rises with the slightest hint of hope. "He seems to have grown up a lot. Don't you think?"

"Yeah, I guess." Sloane shrugs. "Not that I'd really know." Once more, she is reminded of how much she has missed, how much family strife she has avoided. Margaret may blame herself for failing Robroy, but he had more than one sister.

After Margaret's departure, Sloane can't face any more coffee, so she makes a cup of hot chocolate. She sits in the kitchen nook with her laptop, the voices of Robroy and his friends a low murmur from the nearby porch, occasionally spiking into laughter.

The graduation speech is thirty-six hours away, so it's do-or-die time. Scrolling idly through the manuscript, her mind wanders to the book club speeches she's given all over Georgia. A good anecdote inevitably gets her started. Whether funny or sad or thought-provoking, a personal story draws an audience in, invites them into her world. From there, they follow her into the *Girl, Lost* world of Murphy.

The Warner College speech is directed at graduating seniors. *If I could tell twenty-two-year-old Sloane anything, what would it be?* She turns off the kitchen light and slips to the open window, where she peers at the moonlight glittering on the ocean. Above the boys' muffled voices is the roar of high tide, the soundtrack of her childhood. *I'd tell her not to be so quick to toss aside her home, her history, her family.*

The idea dawns sharp and clear: *Tell them the story of the past week. Tell them of poor decisions and loss, of relationships that endure recklessness, of family that sustains.*

She slides along the bench into the nook and begins to write the story of Millicent House and her escape from it, how refusing to make decisions became decisions, how things were wrung from her control by time. And death.

She includes funny bits about Aunt Millicent—her fabulous hats, her pearls worn with capris, her tea lessons, her fire-red lipstick, her sharp tongue at Town Council meetings. Her mother is a minor character, included only to explain why Sloane spent so much time with her aunt.

Mostly, it's a cautionary tale about how she always thought there would be more time. How she concentrated on her book, her book, and solely her book, and while some people might find that admirable, she'd lost something fundamental. Something crucial. Something she can never regain.

An hour passes in a blur, and the speech now has three pages of memoir to kickstart it. It's good—that is, if she can deliver it without crying. She scrolls to the end and adds another half page about Margaret and Robroy, Emma Sue and Sarah, Jesse and Burle, about her intention to reclaim her relationships. To repair and restore. To reach for redemption.

She leans against the wall, relieved and elated. After taking a break to stretch and maybe walk on the beach, she'll blend the new text into what she already had, splicing more personal tidbits into the center of the speech. *This will work.* She pours a celebratory glass of pinot noir and shoves open the screen door, expecting to find all four Baby Stompers. Instead, her brother is alone in a rocking chair. When he sees her, he hastily wipes his eyes.

"Robroy, are you crying?" She's never seen her siblings cry until this week, and she's too surprised to be tactful.

"No." He lies like a kid caught red-handed.

She attempts a joke. "You songwriters are such a sensitive bunch."

"Very funny."

"Seriously, what's wrong?"

"Well, let's see. We've lost our aunt and our dad in a single week. We were rich but now we're not. Half the neighbors hate us. Oh, and our mother is in the hospital. A better question might be 'What's right?'"

"Duly noted." She sinks into the rocker beside him. "Want to walk?"

He gazes down the beach to where Shark Island is dimly lit across the dangerous inlet the locals call Dead Man's Creek. Currents swirl through it, changing with the tide, sweeping unvigilant boaters out to sea. "Sure," he says, getting to his feet.

They strip off their shoes and cross the belt of fragrant grass Burle must have recently cut. They reach the sand and turn right toward Camp Resurrection, the surf curling at their feet as it dances in and out. The absence of electric lights makes this stretch a turtle sanctuary, but the moon on the swelling water is surprisingly bright.

They chat about what this beach will look like if their mother sells and what may happen if she doesn't. He tells her about upcoming band dates and a recording planned for later in the summer. She listens with half an ear, wondering if she should bring up Randall's confidences—or Margaret's.

As they approach the curve where the westerly inlet has pushed a sandbar into its distinguishing J shape, she halts and faces her brother. "When I was getting shrimp at the Seafood Shack, I talked to Randall." In the moonlight, Robroy's face creases into a smile.

"Oh, yeah?"

"He followed me to my car to explain why Jesse was so cold to me. He said she is mad at Mom—and me, to some extent—for abandoning you. He said..." The words stick like glass slivers in her throat, and she swallows painfully. "He said Dad beat you. Like he did Mom."

Robroy's smile fades, and he ducks so his face is in shadow. "Randall is exaggerating. It wasn't that bad."

"He said you had broken bones. And they weren't from falling out of trees or playing baseball."

"Some of both, I guess."

"I am so sorry, Robroy. I honestly thought you were safe. Why didn't you tell me?"

He kicks sand in the direction of the ocean. "What could you do? You were a college student, hundreds of miles away."

"But Randall said when people tried to get you to stay with them, you'd run away. Back to Dad."

Robroy turns to face her. "I don't know why, Sloane, okay?" he says, raising his voice. "I was a little kid. Dad was good when he was sober, and he needed someone to take care of him when he wasn't. Most of the time, I could time it right. A few times, I couldn't."

Her heart is breaking, picturing skinny little Robroy dodging blows and running from that splintered shack on the tidal canal. "I am so sorry. I don't know what to say."

Now that he's talking, he can't seem to stop. "Also, and I know this sounds crazy, we always had dogs. I was afraid if Dad was on a bender, he wouldn't feed them or let them out."

"And you didn't want to live with Margaret? Or Aunt Millicent? They were family. They would have taken in you and your dogs." She thinks about the peculiar vibrations she's noticed between him and Margaret. "Did they know?"

"They knew," he says flatly. "Everybody knew. And Sloane, you may not understand this, but by the time I was fourteen, I didn't want to take any more charity. I mean Burle and Jesse, Nadine and Randall, Scotty's parents, they'd fed me and washed my clothes and had me spend night after night after night. Margaret bought my school clothes, and I guess Aunt Millicent covered my hospital bills. And who knows what else I never even knew about?"

Again, he kicks sand. "There comes a point when it's too embarrassing. I was so tired of relying on everybody. I said I didn't want a class ring, a tux for the prom, a robe for graduation. I just didn't want anybody paying for me anymore, you know?" He hangs his head. "I was so damned tired of being poor."

Margaret's words from earlier in the evening resurface. "Is that why you and Scotty Espey aren't friends anymore? Embarrassment?"

He's silent for a moment. "No, I told you. We both wanted to date the same girl. Just normal teenage stuff."

So he's not going to tell her the truth. Sloane wonders whether to press him and decides to leave it. *For now.* "But you never made up? Not even after you'd moved on from... the girl?"

"No, we didn't." He is clearly aggravated by her questions. "Man, I wouldn't have agreed to walk with you if I knew you were going to give me the third degree."

She laughs sadly. "I needed to know. I've spent so much time feeling sorry for myself, and I'm the one who got off scot-free."

She places a hand on his back as they walk in silence back to the house. She's hardly in a position to call him out for lying.

Chapter 41

Annie

Nadine's sister, June, stands by Annie's hospital bed, teddy bears frolicking on her green scrubs. "You must have been a pediatric nurse at some point," says Annie, unsure what tack to take.

"Pediatrics, geriatrics, operating room, you name it." June's smile is hesitant.

Annie decides to dive in. "I understand you think you saw me here last Thursday, the night my sister was killed. I wasn't on the island, so I'm wondering what you actually saw."

June narrows her eyes. "It was you." Her voice is not unkind but firm. "You were with that developer fellow."

"Can you tell me where I was? In Millicent's room?"

"No, I saw you down the corridor."

"And how far away were you?" Does she sound like some demented Columbo?

"I was at the nurses' station, so maybe twenty feet."

"And you're sure it was me? Was I turned toward you or away from you?"

"Kind of sideways, so I could see your profile. And your hair, of course. It's pretty distinctive."

"Yes, I suppose it is." It will do her no good to argue with this woman. She comes across as reasonable, competent. "Thank you, June. Please tell Nadine and Randall I said hello."

June slips from the room, thankful, no doubt, that she's not Annie's regular nurse. Annie's mind flips like a Rolodex through rea-

235

sons the woman may have for lying. The most obvious connection is Nadine and Randall, who provided refuge for Robroy when he'd been hurt by Robert. Could they harbor such animosity that they'd wrongly accuse Annie of harming her sister?

Or could the link be June's nephew, Arturio, who's been ensconced at Millicent House all week? Has he seen something that he shared with her?

Thinking back to the stout woman in scrubs, Annie realizes she's being absurd. June told the police chief she'd seen Annie because… she thought she'd seen her. But she hadn't. So who did she see?

Oh.

Of course. Her mind whirs, slotting new information into old conversations—exchanges she'd had directly with her children and chatter she'd overheard.

They'd had a dinner date scheduled last Thursday, Annie and Ryan. But he'd cancelled because of a sudden business trip to Savannah.

Where Sloane was speaking.

Midnight comes and goes, and sleep eludes her. Kent Espey, whom she remembers as a polite kid who had a crush on Sloane, sticks his head in the door occasionally. Apparently, the police chief thinks she needs protection. *Is that possible?* Does the animosity surrounding Millicent House really extend to her?

Her head is throbbing along with her leg, and the promised ache is settling all over. But

she's unwilling to ask for more drugs until she figures out why Sloane was at Mercy Hospital the night Millicent died. And why she hasn't admitted it.

Reluctantly, she keeps returning to one fact: Sloane thought she was inheriting the valuable property. Could all her flouncing around about graduation speeches and book edits and getting back to At-lanta be an act? Could she have orchestrated Millicent's death?

Annie's body shudders at the vile thought. If her daughter could do such a thing, Annie is to blame. *She's a Mini-Me. Tree and apple.*

The nurse hears her groan, and Annie finally accepts the offered medication. Even if it weren't for the physical pain, she's ready for a mental release. She clenches her teeth until a fog mercifully shrouds her brain and limbs. She drifts into an uneasy dream of drowning, but instead of holding Robert's head underwater, she is the one in the canal, red curls bobbing on the tide. Water splashes into her mouth, and when she startles, Sloane's smiling face hovers above her.

Chapter 42

Sloane

Robroy and his bandmates are asleep, and the house is quiet—quieter than it's been since Sloane arrived on Monday. She should be in bed too; she's got a five-hour drive to Atlanta tomorrow. But after speaking with Robroy on the beach, she's edgy. To take her mind off images of him at ten—images that feel like punches to her lungs—she tackles the speech once more, editing and polishing until she's satisfied.

She carries the laptop to the study and attaches it by cable to the printer. As the pages churn forth, she recalls the police search on Tuesday. It doesn't matter now, but they never found the letter that her mother supposedly wrote to Aunt Millicent.

Surely, the officers went through every desk drawer, file drawer, and book. *What could be left?*

From Aunt Millicent's desk chair, Sloane surveys the room. Lamplight glows against the lilac walls, creating warmth and coziness. A museum-style light fixture is attached to the top of the house portrait so that it dominates the study at night as fully as it does during the day. Coral shutters gleam against white siding, and glossy foliage and peach-colored flowers shade the deep front porch. Her grandfather commissioned the portrait in the 1940s, her aunt told her countless times. While all homes are important to the families who live in them, this house *was* Aunt Millicent's life.

Her life. Sloane stands and crosses to the painting, kneeling on the sofa cushions beneath it. Carefully, she lifts the heavy frame off its hooks and rests the canvas face down. An envelope is taped to the back.

It strikes her that she doesn't know her own mother's handwriting. But the return address is St. Louis—as Chief Hartwell had said. With trembling hands, she opens the envelope and removes the single sheet of paper inside.

December 26

Dear Mills,

I have started this letter a hundred times and never had the nerve to mail it. But as I believe you have heard from Idelle, I am alive and occasionally well.

First, I must apologize for not sticking to the plan twelve years ago. I tried, Mills. Honestly, I did. But he found the hole before he got far enough outside the waterway and was able to make it back to the dock. Fortunately, he assumed Clive Barnstable had done it. They'd had a blowup two nights earlier. I knew it was only a matter of time before he figured out it was me. So God help me, I ran.

If there was one belief I clung to all this time, it was that Robroy was safe. But I have recently learned that was not the case. Whether I truly believed it in my deepest, darkest nights, in my heart of hearts, I'm not sure, and I won't ask you to believe me. Idelle doesn't. Now I must face what I have done. What I have let happen.

Part of me wants to come home to Millicent House—and to you. But part of me feels like that scared teenager who got in over her head 35 years ago. I tried to wait until I could decide what to do before mailing you a letter. But Idelle insisted I get in touch.

I'm so sorry for the pain I have caused. My heart aches to see you, Mills, along with Margaret, Sloane, Robroy, and the granddaughters I have never met. Please don't be angry with Idelle. Or with me.

Your loving sister,

Annie

Sloane reads the letter five times. *Hole? Waterway?* Did her mother punch a hole in her father's boat? What happened to the woman who cringed when she heard his boots mount the porch steps? *Where did she get the courage to do such a thing?*

She shakes her head in astonishment. At least it explains why Aunt Millicent didn't give the letter to Chief Hartwell. Her mother might have gone from runaway to fugitive. But she can also see why her aunt asked the chief to find Annie. The letter doesn't indicate that she's coming home.

Flopping onto the couch beside the painting, Sloane considers the timing. Her mother mailed this letter five months ago. Did she ever see Aunt Millicent again? Her mother says no, that she showed up on the island only yesterday. But Arturio's aunt claims that Annie was in Mercy Hospital a week earlier; Sloane would love to believe the Roundtree sisters did reunite.

But another part of the timeline tickles the back of her brain. Her mother says she returned to the island yesterday, the day *after* her father died, which makes sense. Cause and effect. Her father was dead, so her mother no longer feared being on the island.

But could it be the other way around? Could her mother have returned to Millicent, and then her father died? If Sloane is reading this letter correctly, a younger Annie tried to kill him once before. *Could she have found the mettle to try again?*

Something else about the letter is scrabbling for her attention. She rereads it. There it is: Her father thought a man named Clive Barnstable sabotaged his boat. *Barnstable.* It's an unusual name. The same name as Robroy's bass player. Sean Barnstable.

She plops into the desk chair and keys Clive Barnstable's name into her laptop. The first mention is an obituary, and her heart seizes. But when she clicks through, she finds that Mr. Barnstable died of cancer two years ago. Her father may have blamed him for a hole in his boat, but at least the man survived any altercation that ensued.

She scrolls down to the last few paragraphs. He was survived by one son. Sean.

She leans back in the chair, staring at the ceiling. She'd never heard of the Barnstables when she lived here, and she didn't realize Sean was from the island. But if he's Robroy's age, she wouldn't have noticed him. *Did the family harbor bad feelings toward Dad that extended to Aunt Millicent?* It was a stretch. But Sean has been in this house all week, and possibly before, if he's tagged along with Robroy. She pictures the balcony railing, ostensibly shiny and new but treacherously awaiting the slightest weight.

It's past three in the morning, but she's too twitchy to sleep. Thrusting the thought of Sean aside, her mind mires in a loop of her mother's movements. Arturio's Auntie June said Annie was at Mercy Hospital last Thursday night. She said Ryan Carbonier was there the same night. Sloane knows that part is true because... *Oh, my God.* She jerks upright. She was so sure no one saw her.

Now June's statement makes sense. *Of course.* Sloane assumed June saw Ryan and her mother at separate times during the evening. But if she saw them *together*, the scenario becomes clear: It wasn't her mother June saw. It was Sloane. Their builds, their hair, their skin color, so eerily alike. From a distance, they could easily be mixed up, and Sloane knows for a fact that June wasn't anywhere near her.

Her breathing becomes labored as she considers the lies that threaten to engulf her. She is most frightened of the one she told Eli about driving with Ryan Carbonier to Bluestone, because Eli is a stickler for truth. He will be livid if he finds out.

In her defense, she was as honest as she felt she could be. Ryan Carbonier *did* attend her speech in Savannah. He *did* invite her for a drink. She *did* leave him in the bar at a quarter of six, assuring him she would sell Millicent House when her aunt died—but that it would likely be fifteen or twenty years away.

What she didn't tell Chief Hartwell or Eli was that, minutes later, Ryan knocked on her hotel room door. She was startled because she hadn't gotten a sexual vibe from him. But that's not what he was after.

"I've had a minute to think over what you said, and I think we need to drive to Millicent and see for ourselves how sick your aunt is."

She laughed. "That's crazy. I'm not doing that."

"It's only an hour away," he said. "I'll have you back before you know it."

She kept shaking her head, but he didn't give up.

"Don't you feel you need to see your aunt? What if she's worse than you think?"

"How is that your business?"

"I need to know one way or the other. If we are truly talking twenty years, I need to revise my plans for Camp Resurrection."

"You don't understand," she told him. "I haven't set foot in Millicent for twelve years and don't intend to."

She tried to shut the door, but he pushed against it. He looked at her steadily, and his tone changed. "No, Miss Cheney, I'm afraid it's you who don't understand."

Sloane blinked and began to get angry. "What is your problem?" Her voice involuntarily rose an octave. "I'm not going anywhere with you."

"Would you rather I called my friend Travis Kildaire?"

She stiffened at mention of the chairman of Warner College's board of trustees. "Why would I care if you called him?"

"Well, he might be interested in the episode in your novel that took place in Columbia. Where Murphy stole a man's wallet?"

Her stomach spasmed, but he continued conversationally. "Because oddly enough, the Columbia police report doesn't say *Murphy*. It says *Sloane Cheney*."

She closed her eyes. Her attorney had assured her the file was expunged, but she recalls from her days on the *Herald* that *expunged* isn't literal where police files are concerned. If you have an inside track, you can sneak a look. Obviously, Ryan had—and had been holding onto its contents for use on just such an occasion.

Suddenly, he was all business. He clapped his hands. "So, if you don't want your employers to know that you are a thief, let's get in the car and go see Aunt Millicent, hmm?"

Fear can bloom in odd ways. Sloane's mind flashed to a vision of herself in a graduation robe speaking in the Warner stadium and Chairman Kildaire rising from the front row to haul her off the stage. Bile rose in her throat.

Wordlessly, she grabbed her purse and accompanied Ryan through the hotel atrium to his BMW sedan. They didn't go to Bluestone Village, as she'd told Eli, but to Mercy Hospital. Setting foot on the island—even the hospital parking lot—caused her body to react viscerally; as she exited the car, her legs were rubbery, her breathing shallow. She stumbled after him through the hospital's empty lobby and down the corridor. They reached the room where the changeable nameplate read *Millicent Roundtree*. Something hitched inside Sloane's chest at seeing the name. Voices from the nurses' station around the curve reached them, but they could see no one.

Shame overwhelmed her—she wasn't there to visit her aunt, as she should have been. She was there to accompany the man who was waiting, vulturelike, for her property. For her death.

Sloane approached the slight figure in the bed. Aunt Millicent had always been a robust woman, a hearty eater. "Ain't nothing uglier than a skinny old woman," she'd told Sloane more than once. But now she *was* skinny. And frail. *When did this happen?* Convinced that her face reflected her distress, Sloane was glad when her aunt didn't recognize her.

"Talk to her," Ryan ordered.

She turned her back on him, overwhelmed at the sight of this woman who'd been such an important part of her childhood. Memories flooded in: Aunt Millicent reading *How the Grinch Stole Christmas* as Sloane snuggled beneath a pink comforter, safe and oblivious to what was happening at her creek-side home. Her aunt's boisterous laughter in the kitchen with Jesse. Her quiet pleas for Sloane's mother to join them, to leave her father, *to take a stand for these children, Annie.*

Sloane's chest swelled, and she could barely speak. "Aunt Millicent, it's Sloane," she whispered. "I was in Savannah and heard you were ill."

Her aunt was quiet for a moment, as if listening to a voice that wasn't there. Then she spoke. "Octavia, tell the nurse I'm ready to go home. I want to wear the yellow suit with the matching hat and the tan pumps. And we need to check those flowers before we go."

Sloane's tears splashed onto the wrinkled hand that lay outside the blanket, and she gently rubbed them away. "We need you to get well," she told her aunt. "Those hydrangeas won't cut themselves."

"You can cut a hydrangea, Octavia! Use my blue-and-white vase."

Sloane turned to Ryan. "Are you happy? She thinks I'm her best friend."

Ryan's face was dour, but he nodded. "She seems pretty bad to me."

"You don't talk like that in front of a patient," Sloane snapped. She turned again to her aunt, anxious to get this man away from her. "We have to go, Aunt Millicent. But I'll try to get back to see you next week after I finish my semester."

"The lilacs should be peaking. Tell that nice gardener we'll need some for our luncheon."

"I love you, Aunt Millicent."

The corridor was vacant as they left, the croon of unseen nurses' voices the only sound. When they reached the lobby, Ryan said he needed a bathroom. Sloane hurried to the car, eager to escape the surreal charade.

He joined her minutes later, and they drove to Savannah without speaking. "I upheld my part of the bargain," she said as they reached the city limits.

"Yes, you did. Travis won't hear about your indiscretion from me."

"Good to know." She slammed the car door and ran into her hotel, cursing her youthful stupidity for opening her up to blackmail. She remained in a fury all the way to Atlanta the following day, only gradually concluding that no real harm had been done.

Until Octavia stood up at her aunt's funeral and announced that she'd been murdered.

It's four in the morning, and Sloane is no closer to sleep. Has she been stupid to lie to Chief Hartwell—and Eli—about going to Mercy Hospital in order to keep her theft arrest hidden? She's never told a soul, outside her lawyer, about the incident, and certainly didn't admit it on her job application to Warner. If word got out, she would be fired immediately. And the academic world is small. She'd likely be blackballed from any other university position. No, she's right. The risk is too great.

Her laptop is still open, so she idly pulls up the manuscript for her novel. Elle has a close relationship with her feisty grandmother—the one in the nursing home—but Elle's mother is not a well-developed character. Sloane scrolls to the edits she made—was it only yesterday?—and notices something odd. She'd added passages about Elle's mother, but in them, she becomes the naysayer, the critic. She discourages Elle's quest for the truth about the 1940s murder. She hides a connection between Elle's family and the murder victim. *Why did I make those changes?*

She'd wanted to create a warm and supportive family for Elle, but these edits veer into hostility. Was she trying to make it more realistic? Or was she letting suspicions about her own mother slip in? Because the fact is, Annie Cheney is in bed—pun intended—with the man who wants their homeplace.

The man who blackmailed Sloane to gain information about her aunt's health.

The man who killed her.

Sloane's head is too full of Aunt Millicent and this house and her mother's subterfuge to enter the fictional world she's created. The former is bleeding into the latter, and it may well ruin her book. She has to tell her editor that the final draft won't be ready this month. She'll regret it for the rest of her life if she doesn't take the time to finish it properly.

A weight lifts at the decision, and she switches over to email her editor and agent.

Now she's tired and gritty-eyed, and she mounts the grand staircase to go to bed.

Chapter 43

Friday
Annie

Aslight graying at the edge of the window shade tells Annie that dawn is breaking. The medication bought her five hours of sleep, which is better than nothing. She shifts in the hospital bed, every muscle moaning. She buzzes for a nurse, hoping to get a sponge bath before Sloane and Robroy arrive. They promised to stop by before hitting the road.

Kent stands at the threshold to her room. "Everything all right, Mrs. Cheney?"

"Yes, Kent, thank you. Why don't you go home? Nothing's going to happen during the day, surely."

"I can't leave until the chief says so, but I won't bother you." He ducks back into the hallway.

A young nurse arrives and, after checking Annie's vital signs, agrees to give her a sponge bath and a clean gown. The nurse holds a mirror while Annie applies mascara and lip gloss and pulls her hair into a messy topknot. Afterward, her arms ache from the effort, but she feels a little more human.

Another employee brings a breakfast of scrambled eggs, French toast, fruit, and coffee, and Annie wonders how much Millicent had to do with the menus her hospital serves. Annie will always think of Mercy this way, as *her sister's* hospital.

Finally, she hears familiar voices greeting Kent, then Sloane and Robroy burst into the room. "We ran into Chief Hartwell on the way in," Sloane says breathlessly. "He'll be in after he finishes with Kent."

Robroy holds her hand and asks how her night was. Her heart twists at his thoughtfulness, and she wonders if this painful guilt will plague every conversation with her son.

Moments later, the spit-polished police chief enters her room, his black eyes raking over the three of them. "Is your other daughter on the way?" he asks.

"She's dropping her daughters at school first." As if on cue, they hear Margaret greeting nurses in the hallway. She steps into the room then stops short. The chief ushers her to Robroy's side, apparently lining them up so he can see all their faces.

"I wanted you all together to hear something," he says. "The Beaufort County Sheriff's Office got a tip on Ryan Carbonier's whereabouts. He was holed up in a motel on the outskirts of Beaufort. A young man delivering pizza recognized him from his picture in the law enforcement center and called it in."

"That's fantastic!" Robroy says.

The chief remains stone-faced. "Well, yes and no. When deputies arrived, Mr. Carbonier was dead." He allows the sentence to hang in the air, and they stare at him without speaking. As one, her children turn their gazes to her. *What do they know?*

The chief leans against the wardrobe that holds the clothes shredded in her accident. "I think it's time everyone tells me exactly what his or her relationship was to Ryan Carbonier."

Sloane's face shows the same shock as hers must, her mouth tight. "I'll start," Robroy volunteers. "About two hours after Raeford let me know I was inheriting half the house, I got a call from Mr. Carbonier. But I never laid eyes on him."

"What did he want?"

"What else? To buy the house."

"And when was this?"

"Last Saturday. We were doing a sound check before a show in Columbia."

"And how did he hear so quickly about your inheritance?"

"Who knows?" Robroy throws his palms out. "Raeford, maybe?"

"What did you tell him?"

"That I hadn't had time to think about it, and I'd go along with whatever Sloane wanted to do. I knew she'd had years to consider it."

The chief appears satisfied. "And you, Mrs. Cheney?" Before she can answer, Margaret interrupts. "Wait a minute, Chief. How did he die?"

The chief studies Annie's older daughter. "A syringe was lying on the bed, and his leg showed signs of an injection. We can't say for certain yet, but I suspect we'll find it was digoxin."

Annie can't contain her surprise. "He killed himself?"

"Possibly." After a beat, he resumes. "Your relationship, Mrs. Cheney?"

The whole debacle with Ryan is humiliating. But now that he's dead, she has no reason to hold back—as long as she can keep the strands of her narrative separated. Meaning, she can't allow a whisper of Robert's drowning to enter the chief's mind.

"It's a long story," she warns. "Basically, Ryan and I met in St. Pete, where I was managing a bed-and-breakfast. I was going by the name Annmarie Crossland, and we started dating. Shortly afterward—and completely unrelated—I wrote to Millicent about how tired I was of living on the run and how much I missed home." *Careful, careful.* She invents this next part. "The B-and-B owners returned to St. Pete, and I wasn't really needed. So I moved to Jacksonville and told Ryan my real name."

She makes a show of getting more comfortable in the bed, but it's actually to give herself time to redact her story. She resumes, closer to the truth. "In retrospect, I realize he knew all along who I was.

It's embarrassing to admit, but I think all he wanted was an 'in' to obtaining Millicent House."

"So he knew you had been reinstated as beneficiary?"

"By April, he did. Not before because I didn't know what Millicent was planning until then." She's not sure how much further to go, but someone at Ryan's motel may have seen or heard her, so she plunges ahead. "I didn't put it together until yesterday when you visited, Chief Hartwell, and told me that Ryan was here in the hospital on the night my sister was killed. When you left, I rushed to confront him in his motel room, and we had it out. He denied killing her, but I wasn't entirely convinced. I stormed out, telling him I would *not* sell the house to him. I was very upset, which undoubtedly caused me to wreck on the way home."

The chief watches her closely.

"Wait a minute," she adds. "Do you think Ryan killed himself because he thought I would turn him in?"

"It's possible," the chief says. "He certainly knew he could be arrested."

He casually crosses one sharply creased pants leg over the other and turns his attention to Margaret. "Mrs. Simpson?"

"The only time I've seen Ryan Carbonier was at zoning hearings when we were building our gas stations in Georgia. I've never had a conversation with him."

"But your in-laws knew him?"

She looks puzzled. "My father-in-law knows everyone, so yeah, I imagine so. We never talked about it."

The chief raises an eyebrow. "With all that's going on in Millicent, you never talked about it?" The chief's body language doesn't change, but Annie senses his interest sharpening. She thought Sloane was the one who needed protection, but was Margaret somehow involved with Ryan as well? *My God, the man's tentacles were everywhere.*

Margaret looks peevish at being challenged. "Well, sure, J.C. talked about him in the context of developing Camp Resurrection and possibly Millicent House, but I never got the sense they were friends or anything."

Chief Hartwell is silent for a moment, then he addresses Sloane. "Miss Cheney, could I speak to you privately?"

Sloane looks surprised but starts for the door.

"Oh, and one more thing that gives us pause," the chief says conversationally. "Mr. Carbonier's room was wiped clean of fingerprints. Why does a man who's about to kill himself do that?"

Chapter 44

S loane halts at the door to her mother's room, her mind boomeranging wildly. Apparently, Ryan Carbonier killed himself because he thought sheriff's deputies were closing in on him. *That's an admission that he murdered Aunt Millicent, right? But wait. What is Chief Hartwell saying about fingerprints?*

She tries to swallow, but her throat is too dry. "Wh-What do you mean when you say fingerprints were wiped clean?"

"Some things in the room," the chief explains, "had Mr. Carbonier's fingerprints—the alarm clock, the bedside phone, the toilet handle, the shower fixture. But the doorknobs, the sink tap, and the syringe did not. They had no prints at all. Strange, huh?"

"I don't know what that means."

"It means that someone else could have stuck that syringe into Mr. Carbonier's leg then cleaned any surface in the room that they had touched."

Before the four of them can express their shock, a rap on the door makes them jump. "Are we interrupting?" asks Raeford's deep baritone as Octavia clomps in. Sloane has never been so glad to see anyone. Maybe their presence will give her a reprieve from further questioning about her relationship with Ryan.

Her mother's face is bone pale, but she attempts to greet her old friends.

"It's all over the news," Octavia says. "That developer fella was found dead in Beaufort." The Cheneys leave the response to Chief

Hartwell, who appears unruffled. Octavia doesn't register the tension in the room. "The big question, I suppose, is what this means for 'Mayberry by the Sea.'" Her tone mocks the name of the proposed resort. "Ryan Carbonier may be dead, but I reckon there are a slew of developers lined up behind him."

"Can you tell us anything more, Chief?" Raeford asks.

"Sorry, Mr. Carlisle," he says brusquely. "I can't right now." Turning to Sloane, he repeats, "Miss Cheney? In private?"

Her mother looks stricken. Robroy interrupts, "My friends are waiting in the van. Is it okay if we get on the road?"

"Yes, Mr. Cheney," the chief answers. "I have your phone number and will call if I need you."

Sloane trails the chief from the room, her heart already racing.

"May I call Eli and let him know there's no need to drive to Jacksonville?" she asks as they take seats in an office that has been loaned to the chief.

"I'm sure that's not necessary. Those reporters know police business almost before we do." His face is as serious as she's seen it, but the anger is temporarily at bay. "Miss Cheney," he says, "I know you haven't been honest with me. I'm about to give you one last chance before I cite you for obstruction of a police investigation. Do you understand?"

She nods wordlessly.

"The reason I'm not angrier is because I sense you are clumsily trying to protect your mother. A mother you haven't seen for twelve years."

She bows her head. *Not exactly.*

"I know that you and Eli Cartwright concocted that silly story about going out to dinner in Savannah last Thursday. So I'd like to circle around and give you the opportunity to tell me the truth about you and Ryan Carbonier. A witness saw him and allegedly your mother here at the hospital within ninety minutes after you left

Savannah in his car. But I suspect it may have been *you*, not your mother. Is that correct? Don't even think about lying to me again."

Her nose is stuffy and her eyes full, but she blinks the tears away.

"You're right," she admits. "I left him in the hotel bar like I told you. But then he came to my room, wanting me to come to the hospital with him so he could see for himself how sick Aunt Millicent was. I told him no; I was absolutely not going to the island. But he threatened to—" She breaks into violent hiccups and can't go on.

The chief waits patiently. "Take your time."

When she catches her breath, she closes her eyes and continues. "He threatened to tell my college about my arrest for petit larceny years ago in Columbia."

He raises his eyebrows, genuinely surprised. "Petit larceny? What did you steal?"

"A wallet. From a man."

"So he must have been—what? In a bar? In a hotel room?—for it not to have been a robbery charge?"

She nods miserably. "Lying on a table in a bar. And it held only eight hundred dollars. So not grand larceny."

The chief leans back in the office chair. "Did not see that coming," he says, trying to hide a smile. "So you agreed to come to the hospital with Ryan Carbonier in exchange for his silence?"

"Right. We visited Aunt Millicent's room, but she didn't know me. She thought I was Octavia."

"And when Octavia visited, your aunt thought she was your mother."

"Yeah. Who's on first?"

For the first time in Sloane's presence, the chief laughs. He must be confident that Ryan Carbonier is her aunt's killer and he can get back to pursuing illegal dumpers and out-of-season hunters. "I'm sorry you didn't feel you could be honest with me. I honestly have zero interest in your old police record."

Her shoulders slump. "It's just that I had a very ugly time in my early twenties, and I've spent the past few years trying to reinvent myself. I don't want the old Sloane rearing her head and getting me fired."

"Understood. And your actions finally make sense." His face grows thoughtful. "I'd be tempted to close this case if it weren't for one pesky little thing."

Her stomach cramps, for she knows what's coming.

"Those missing fingerprints."

Chapter 45

Annie

Every muscle in Annie's body simultaneously aches and cries to get out of this bed. She is accustomed to running, disappearing, hiding. It's frightening to think she must stay and face whatever comes, immobile, defenseless.

Robroy and his bandmates have departed for Charleston, and Chief Hartwell has escorted Sloane to another room. Only Margaret remains, glowering, alongside Octavia and Raeford. She hopes they won't leave her alone with her daughter.

"So," she says brightly to her friends, "pull up some chairs and fill me on island gossip. Gossip that the Roundtrees are *not* part of."

Octavia cackles appreciatively, and even Raeford smiles. Margaret's face remains impassive. *Why is she so suspicious?* Sloane and Robroy seem close to forgiving her long absence. *Does Margaret suspect something about Robert? If she did, would she care?*

It's hard to keep up with the conversation as these questions tumble through her brain, but Annie makes an effort. Raeford asks about her plans for the house, politely not adding "now that Ryan Carbonier is dead."

She tells him honestly that she hasn't decided. Looking at Margaret, she adds, "But the chance to get to know my grandchildren is awfully tempting. It's what Millicent wanted for me, and suddenly it sounds wonderful."

Margaret's voice cuts through the room like a scythe. "May I speak to my mother alone?"

Raeford stands immediately and helps Octavia to her feet. "I'll be in touch when Chief Hartwell releases the estate for probate," he says. "Don't worry, Annie. We'll figure it out."

Alone with her older daughter, Annie braces for what's to come. She doesn't know which of her transgressions Margaret is angriest about. So she waits.

"How could you?" Margaret's voice is low, venomous. "You must have lied to Aunt Millicent about your intentions for the house. And you brought that slimeball Ryan Carbonier into her life."

"You think I'm not beating myself up about that?"

"What did you do?" she presses. "Did she switch beneficiaries because you promised you'd keep the house from developers? Is that how you did it?"

Margaret is right, but not for the reason she thinks. Her daughter assumes she was after the money. She can't find out that Annie could see no further than Robert's demise.

"Regardless of my initial objective," Annie pleads, "I decided along the way *not* to sell to Ryan. Or to anyone, for that matter. I was truthful about wanting to repair my relationship with you and your brother and sister. And to get to know Emma Sue and Sarah."

"But, Mom, he killed her! Do you not get that?" Margaret's voice is filled with self-righteous anger. "*Yay* that you want to play lady of the manor now. But Aunt Millicent *died.*"

Annie's gaze escapes to the window and the magnificent display of lilacs, hydrangeas, and lilies nurtured by her sister. Ryan was stupefied when she accused him of the same thing. Steel returns to her voice. "You know, Margaret, I'm not so sure about that."

Her daughter eyes her skeptically. "No? You don't think your *babe* had it in him?" *Goodness, where did this hatefulness come from?*

"Margaret, this won't mean anything to you, but I knew Ryan fairly well. Yes, he tricked me. Yes, he wanted Millicent House. But if you could've seen him when I accused him of killing Millicent…" She meets her daughter's eyes. "He honestly was caught off guard."

Margaret snorts in disgust.

"And could he have gotten past Millicent to tamper with her balcony?" Annie continues. "That would've taken some chutzpah." She grabs an extra pillow from the chair beside her bed and struggles to place it behind her back. Margaret doesn't move to help. "But something else I've been wondering, something that makes no sense. If you and Millicent agreed on the house—that it shouldn't be sold—why did she leave it to Sloane, who was clear about her intention to sell?"

"And to Robroy," Margaret mutters.

"Well, yes, him at the last minute."

"Do you really want to know, Mom?" Margaret steps closer to the bed, grabbing the pillow Annie has placed behind her. *But is she plumping it, or is she pulling it out?*

"Yes," Annie says, though her voice wavers. "I do."

Suddenly, Margaret's face is not the beloved face she knows but one filled with rage. She yanks the pillow away and Annie sinks onto the mattress, her rib muscles howling in protest. Suddenly, this woman is someone she doesn't know. Like the murderous Sloane of her dreams, Margaret no longer seems to share Annie's blood.

"And how are we this morning?" a nurse calls out, crossing the threshold into the room. Margaret thrusts the pillow at her mother and whirls for the door.

"We'll talk later," she says, waving a wordless goodbye to the nurse.

Chapter 46

Sloane

Sloane is on the road by ten in the morning, which should allow her time to reach Atlanta by midafternoon, shower, and join the trustees in their fancy dining room for Friday night dinner. Her mind is so full of questions that she snaps the radio off in annoyance.

First up: *Did Ryan Carbonier kill my aunt?* It certainly looks like it. He's been hiding from the police, and he was found with digoxin. But the lack of fingerprints? Did he have an accomplice who turned on him?

That's where her questions get uncomfortable. Her mother admits she was in Ryan's motel room yesterday. Clearly, they had a relationship that included a plan to turn Millicent House into Mayberry by the Sea. Her mother swears their plan *didn't* include killing Aunt Millicent. But can her children trust her? From the look on Margaret's face when they parted at the hospital, that's a flat no.

And the letter Sloane found last night: *Did my mother really try to sink my father's boat twelve years ago?* If so, it adds a whole new dimension to her disappearance. There's no way she could have stayed, fearing every minute that he'd figure out it was her, not Clive Barnstable.

The questions keep coming, roiling through her head faster than she can finish a thought. The porch railing. Sam and Robroy said a post and a top rail were sawn cleanly through, and the spindles weren't glued or screwed to lend further support. *Was it a clumsy attempt to kill Aunt Millicent long before she entered the hospital? Or was it intended for later occupants of the house—me, Robroy, my mother?* And how reckless someone was. Think of the innocent people who could've died—Sam, Arturio, Derek, Sean. Unless, of course, Sean Barnstable *was* the culprit. So many people have been coming and going in the house, and there's no way to know when the trap was laid.

A thought occurs to her, and she veers abruptly onto the next exit off I-20 West, pulling into the first gas station she finds. Locating Bud Randolph's Boat Repair on her phone's map app, she calls. She's not anxious to speak to the grumpy old man who said such nasty things at the church meeting, but as soon as she introduces herself, his voice grows subdued.

"Sloane, my wife says I owe you an apology for what I said at the church." He rushes into an explanation before she can pose her question. "She may be right. But Chief Hartwell was by my shop, questioning my work on your aunt's house. I swear to you what I told him: That balcony rail was solid when I left."

"But the balusters. Did you plan to come back later and secure them?"

"No!" his voice grows louder. "They were glued down with industrial-strength wood glue. Miss Millicent, she came out and shook them hard after they'd dried. Them spindles weren't going anywhere."

"So what happened?"

"From what the chief showed me, the glue had been cut clean through just like the post and top rail. Six of them spindles. Then they were slid back in. It wouldn'a taken much weight on that rail to send them flying."

"When did you do the work?"

"Third week of April."

She considers the timeline. Right around the time Aunt Millicent wrote the new will, making Sloane's mother the sole beneficiary. "I know Burle did most of my aunt's maintenance work. Had you ever been out there before?"

"Oh, sure. When Burle was fishing or busy with the store, I'd come out to cut down tree limbs or repair her dishwasher. Painted some shelves one time. Fixed a leak on the roof. That was a project, I tell you."

When she doesn't respond, he continues, "Whether you believe it or not, me and Miss Millicent were friends. We went way, way back, all the way to grade school. She and I were both big supporters of the turtle ladies who are helping those mama turtles down on the beach. I wouldn'a hurt Miss Millicent for anything in this whole wide world, and that's a fact."

A sigh escapes her lips. "I believe you, Mr. Randolph. And I take it you and Aunt Millicent were in agreement about this development business."

"Yes, we were, Sloane. And that's why, for the life of me, I couldn't figure out why she wanted to leave that house to you, knowing you were going to turn around and let some developer get his hands on it."

"Yeah, well, that's all up in the air right now."

"Is it?" His voice sounds hopeful. "I heard about that developer feller dying, but I figure there are more where he came from. And your mama..."

She doesn't want to discuss her mother with Bud Randolph, so she tells him she has to go.

As long as she's stopped, she enters the station's convenience store for coffee. Eli calls as she's paying, his voice excited.

"Sloane, where are you?"

"About fifteen miles past Augusta."

"I've heard some pretty big news. The Beaufort County Sheriff's Office put out a four-state alert, asking pharmacies if they were missing digoxin. They just got a hit."

"Where?"

"An independent pharmacist called from Augusta. She works for a mom-and-pop store, Kramer Drugs, that's been there for decades. And get this, she told the detectives she's originally from Millicent."

Sloane climbs into her SUV, stunned. "What's her name?"

"Jayroe Martin."

Jayroe. She's heard that name recently. Then it clicks, and she sets her coffee into the cupholder with a thump. Hot coffee splashes over her hand, making her cringe. "Eli, she's the sister of Mercy Hospital's medical director."

"No way."

"When Margaret and I visited the hospital, Dr. Rasmussen mentioned that her sister is a pharmacist. Margaret knew her."

Eli goes silent. "Eli? What is it?"

"When you made the hospital link, I was thinking... well, a hospital link. As in staff."

"Yeah?"

He hesitates, and Sloane wonders what he's getting at.

"But what if the link is Margaret?"

Sloane sits, unmoving, in the busy parking lot of the gas station in Georgia. The afternoon sun beats on her Toyota, so she cranks it to get the air conditioner working. She chews her lip, thinking furiously.

Margaret and Joel build their Gas 'N' Such outlets along the coastal roads, not as far inland as Augusta. It makes far more sense that the connection with Jayroe would be her own sister at Mercy Hospital, not Margaret. *But can I be sure?* She recalls how quiet Margaret became after Dr. Rasmussen explained that the hospital wasn't missing any digoxin.

Sloane grabs her phone, types in Kramer Drugs, and gets an address near a turn-off she passed sixteen miles ago. She glances at her watch, calculating what a turnaround will cost her. She's cutting it too close. Nevertheless, she wrenches the wheel toward the exit for eastbound I-20 and heads back the way she came. "On my way," she says aloud.

Kramer Drugs is located in an aging strip center two miles off the interstate, surrounded by more recently constructed fast-food restaurants. She pulls into a spot directly in front of windows displaying Christmas villages, plastic pool toys, and Russell candies.

A bell hanging from the door handle announces her entrance, and a woman at the cash register smiles in greeting. Sloane points to the rear and mouths "pharmacy," and the woman nods.

A young man with a child in a stroller stands in line. In a moment, a striking Black woman, her hair pulled into a neat bun, emerges from the back, a prescription bottle in her hand. *This has to be Jayroe.* She bags the bottle, rings up the man with polite conversation, then turns to Sloane.

"Whoa," she says, her eyes widening. "You have got to be related to a woman from my hometown. Annie Cheney. Am I right?"

"Guilty. I'm her daughter, Sloane." She grins. "Margaret's much younger sister."

Jayroe laughs. "I met your mom a few times at the high school. Before your time there, I'm sure. So how can I help you, Sloane?"

She starts out with a white lie. "I was talking to Millicent's police chief, Dan Hartwell, and he told me that you answered an alert for some missing digoxin."

"Wow. Word gets around fast."

"Well, I've been meeting with him almost every day." Not wanting to give Jayroe time to wonder why she's meeting with the police chief, she hurries on. "So it was stolen from your pharmacy?" A flick of her head indicates the shelves of medication behind Jayroe.

"Yes, and we have no idea how. But when I went to fill an order, I saw we were short a box of six ampoules."

"When was this?" Sloane expects Jayroe to ask why she wants to know, but she seems surprisingly uncurious.

"I noticed it on Monday. So four days ago. I know because I had to look up my records for the sheriff's office in Beaufort."

There's something else Sloane needs to ask, but she doesn't want Jayroe to connect the two. Broaching it as casually as possible, she says, "By the way, Margaret and I visited your sister at Mercy Hospital this week."

Her face splits into a wide smile. "So you know Erin?"

"Yes, and Margaret was asking her about you." She strains for nonchalance. "When was the last time you saw Margaret, anyway?"

"Oh, recently. She stopped by a week or so ago when she was passing through Augusta. But we've kept up through high school reunions too."

Sloane keeps smiling, but her face feels like it's about to crack. Jayroe doesn't appear to correlate Margaret's visit with the missing digoxin. *But why would she?* Margaret would've been standing right where Sloane is standing now. *Could she have gotten around Jayroe somehow?* Sloane starts to back away.

"Well, it was so nice to meet you, Jayroe. I'm heading home to Atlanta and was stopping for gas when I recognized the name of your drugstore. From your sister. Thanks so much."

She exercises all her willpower not to sprint from the store.

Sitting in the Toyota once more, heart thundering and sweat gathering on her forehead, she makes a decision. Probably not the best one.

She looks up Kildaire Chrysler Buick in Atlanta and, within five minutes, has Travis Kildaire on the phone. "Mr. Kildaire," she addresses the trustee chairman, "this is Sloane Cheney. I was literally on my way to Atlanta to have dinner with you and the other trustees this evening. But I've just received word of a family emergency back in South Carolina. I am so very sorry."

"Nonsense, Miss Cheney. You take care of family first. Always." He pauses. "Will this keep you from speaking at graduation tomorrow evening?"

"Oh, no. I'll be there in time for graduation. I just need another twenty-four hours."

"Very well. And if there's anything we can do to help, please let us know."

"I will. Thank you, sir."

She sits outside Kramer Drugs for a few more minutes, trembling, arguing with herself, screaming at Margaret. Then she pulls out of the lot and follows the inexorable tug of Millicent.

Chapter 47

Annie

Annie refuses to fear her own daughter. Whatever the cause of Margaret's anger—and she acknowledges that her twelve-year absence is sufficient cause—Margaret would never harm her. Of course not—nor would she harm Millicent.

She closes her eyes and remembers the argument she had with her eldest daughter on the night she fled the island. Margaret wasn't even a mother then, but she had plenty to say about Annie's mothering abilities. Or lack thereof.

Her pale blue sundress stuck to her back from the exertion of hauling two suitcases down their house's wobbly steps. She'd thought about taking Robert's newer truck but realized that would make him more determined to find her. Not to mention, easier. So she took their old station wagon, knowing she'd trade it the first chance she got.

Her last stop was Margaret's fabulous house in Bougainvillea, which Idelle and J.C. had helped finance. Honestly, maybe that house was part of her rancor. Her daughter was twenty-four years old and living in a home that rivaled Millicent House. Not in history or location, maybe, but in luxury.

Margaret opened her front door in surprise, barefoot, already dressed for bed in a tank top and pajama bottoms. She ushered Annie into her gleaming kitchen, offered decaf coffee—the perfect hostess. Until Annie told her she was leaving.

Margaret spun from her elaborate coffeemaker. "You're leaving Robroy? And Sloane?"

"Margaret," she said quietly. "You don't know what your father's done to me."

Her daughter's voice rose. "I don't? *I don't?* How exactly do you figure that?"

"Well, then, if you do, you should understand why I'm leaving."

"That's fine, Mom. I've wondered why you stayed this long. And Sloane will be gone at the end of the summer. But Robroy? You can't leave Robroy with him."

"He likes Robroy," Annie said, and her words sounded inane even to her own ears.

"Yeah, and he liked you at some point."

She recoiled at her daughter's tone. "It's easy for you to be all high and mighty. Your husband is good to you."

Margaret's face darkened, and she lashed out. "Well, I had the good sense not to marry someone like Dad. Not to subject my children to someone like him."

A devastating silence descended. Annie had intended to tell her about her failed attempt to sink Robert's boat on the open ocean. *How long before Clive Barnstable convinces Robert it wasn't him who drilled the hole?* She had no choice but to run. But given Margaret's anger, her daughter might march right into the police station if she knew.

So Annie gathered her purse and, without a word, walked out the front door.

Now the nurse is finished with her bustling check of Annie's vitals. All this time, she's worried about what she'd done to Robroy, and to a lesser degree, to Sloane. But was it her oldest child who was most upset by her disappearance? The one who was already safely ensconced away from Robert?

"Will you be going home with your daughter when you're released?" the nurse asks.

"No," she answers quickly. "No."

Chapter 48

Sloane

Recalling her mother's wreck, Sloane tries to stay under the speed limit. But her anxiety amps up, her foot slams down, and she races from Augusta back to the island.

Where am I going? Millicent House? Mercy Hospital? Bougainvillea?

She doesn't want to confront Margaret in front of their mother, so she chooses the subdivision, hoping her sister is working from home. Sloane swerves too fast into Margaret's driveway, earning a scowl from the next-door neighbor, who is watering newly planted petunias against a lawn so green it could be AstroTurf. But such gauche landscaping would never be tolerated in this neighborhood.

She scurries to Margaret's door and rings the doorbell. Her sister doesn't seem surprised to see her and grabs her arm, tugging Sloane inside.

"Now do you see what I mean about Mom?" Margaret demands.

Sloane's head is so filled with questions about Margaret's visit to Kramer Drugs that she is stumped by the greeting. "What about her?"

Margaret looks at her in disbelief. Her mind is clearly still at the hospital, where they saw their mother this morning. "Sloane! She was involved up to her eyeballs with Ryan Carbonier. Who, you may remember, killed Aunt Millicent. The only question is: Was Mom a willing participant? Or just stupid?" She looks at Sloane quizzically and interrupts herself. "Wait a minute. I thought you were going to Atlanta."

"I was. But I stopped in Augusta. At Kramer Drugs."

Margaret goes still. She turns on her heel and heads to the kitchen. "Tea?" she asks. She reaches into the refrigerator and takes out a pitcher of tea then fills two glasses with crushed ice. She takes her time pouring then hands Sloane a glass. Not a word passes between them for a full minute.

"Kramer Drugs," Sloane repeats. "Ring a bell?"

Margaret takes her time answering. "Yes, that's where Jayroe Martin works. Dr. Rasmussen told us, didn't she?"

"Actually, no. She didn't mention the drugstore."

"Oh, I thought she did." She slides onto one of her high stools and twirls her glass on the island countertop.

"Margaret, what the hell?"

"What do you mean?"

"Jayroe's pharmacy had digoxin go missing."

She looks startled. "How do you know that?"

"The Beaufort County Sheriff's detectives traced it."

Margaret is keeping her game face on; Sloane will give her that. But she can't control the color, and it drains away.

"So?" Sloane presses. "The digoxin went missing in a drugstore you recently visited."

"Sloane, it's not what you think."

"How do you know what I'm thinking?"

"Obviously, that I got hold of that drug and killed Aunt Millicent."

Sloane supposes that is what she's thinking, but hearing it expressed so baldly shocks her. *Do I really believe that my sister killed our aunt?*

"Honestly, Margaret? I don't know what to think."

Her sister takes a deep breath and leans toward her. "Sloane, I can't explain how Ryan Carbonier got hold of digoxin in Augusta. Or if he got it in Florida, and it was a coincidence that Jayroe's stock was pilfered. I can tell you only two things."

Sloane looks up and, for the first time in her life, can't tell if her sister is lying.

"One," Margaret says, "I didn't steal any drug, from Jayroe or anyone else. And two..." She reaches out and touches Sloane's arm. "It's Mom who is not telling us the truth."

Sloane sits back, trying to order her thoughts. She came here to find out about Margaret's visit to the Augusta drugstore. But her sister is shutting that discussion down.

"Okay." She relents. "Mom is not telling the truth about what?"

"About how close she was to Ryan Carbonier! About the extent of their plan to get Millicent House." She looks at Sloane with pleading eyes and lowers her voice. "And Sloane, she admits she was *in his motel room*. What if they killed Aunt Millicent then fell out, and she killed him?"

She might as well have punched Sloane in the chest. "No, Margaret, no. I mean, this is Mom we're talking about."

But Margaret is not finished. "Or maybe he wasn't supposed to kill Aunt Millicent, and Mom got angry when he did. And killed him with his own syringe."

Sloane stops to consider this scenario. *It's not as bad as Mom coldbloodedly killing Aunt Millicent.* Then she stops herself. "No, this is craziness. There has to be another answer. Maybe Ryan had a business partner in the background. Or someone in town with proximity to Aunt Millicent—someone who could get onto her balcony without raising suspicion."

Margaret shrugs. "I think you're making excuses. Let's go talk to her. Together."

Sloane nods miserably and grabs her purse.

Chapter 49

Annie

Midafternoon on Friday, Margaret and Sloane enter Annie's hospital room. One look at their faces tells her she's in for more questions. She doesn't know who's worse—the police chief or her daughters.

"I thought you had dinner with your college trustees tonight," she begins.

"I cancelled it," Sloane answers. "I'll head up tomorrow morning for graduation." She glances at her mother's leg, bulky in a new cast under the blanket. "How do you feel? Are you hurting?"

Annie wags her hand to indicate *so-so*. "They've already got me working with crutches so I can go home on Sunday."

Sloane looks eager. "That'll work out well. I'll drive back from Atlanta that day, and we'll get you set up downstairs."

Margaret gives her sister a withering look and, as usual, gets right to the point. "We want to ask you about Ryan. Without the police chief around."

"All right." Automatically, Annie goes on alert. Her relationship with Ryan was secondary to her resolve to remove Robert from the Roundtree inheritance, but with the messy web she's created, it's hard to separate one from the other.

"You never answered what I asked you this morning," Margaret continues. "What did you tell Aunt Millicent to make her switch beneficiaries from Sloane and Robroy to you?"

Well, she's not mincing words, is she? "Margaret, you frame it as if I took something from Sloane and Robroy, but it wasn't like that. All my life Millicent said the beachfront property belonged to both of us. The only reason Father didn't name me in his will was because he didn't want Robert to get his hands on the house. He and Millicent were transparent about that."

Margaret retains a bulldog expression. "Fine. But Aunt Millicent had designated Sloane and Robroy as her heirs. What did you say to change her mind?"

"That I was alive and ready to come home," she says simply.

Her older daughter looks skeptical. "And not that you'd keep the house from being sold?"

"Margaret, I wasn't thinking that far ahead." *Not exactly true, but close enough.* "Millicent was sixty-eight. I thought she'd live for years and years. Yes, practically speaking, I might have sold in the future. But I wasn't looking to do anything as long as my sister was alive."

Annie hears her mistake as soon as she voices it. She has handed her daughters the motive they seek. Margaret looks satisfied. Sloane looks stricken.

Her next words are deliberate. And true. "In retrospect, I confess that my plan to return, my relationship with Ryan, almost certainly led to Millicent's death. I am guilty in every way except physically tampering with her intravenous bag."

Sloane leaps to her defense. "You couldn't have known, Mom. Ryan was a really slick operator. I found that out myself."

Annie recalls her midnight realization that Arturio's Auntie June likely saw Sloane, not her, on the night of Millicent's murder.

Margaret turns to her sister. "What do you mean?" she asks. "How did you find out Ryan was a 'slick operator'?"

Sloane looks like she wants to haul her words back. She slumps into a chair. "I told Chief Hartwell this morning, so I might as well tell you. Brace yourselves. It's ugly."

Margaret's face is stony as Sloane begins.

"After Ryan left my hotel in Savannah last Thursday, he turned right around and showed up at my room. He wanted me to drive here with him to see how sick Aunt Millicent really was. I said, 'No way.' And he... he blackmailed me." She hangs her head.

Annie's previous suspicion of her younger daughter returns, causing her to quiver with anxiety.

Margaret's voice is sharp. "Blackmailed you? What the hell, Sloane?"

"He threatened to tell the chair of Warner's board of trustees that I'd been arrested for petit larceny years ago. To keep him from calling the trustee, I came here with him." Sloane's voice grows fainter and fainter. "To Mercy. To see Aunt Millicent."

Margaret's voice fires like a rifle shot against Sloane's whisper. "You were *here*? The night Aunt Millicent was murdered? In her room?" Her last words rise to a howl.

A nurse steps in from the hallway, her eyes darting nervously. "Everything all right?"

"Yes," Annie assures her. "We're fine. Thank you."

After the nurse leaves, Sloane's next words come out in a rapid stream, as if she's vomiting them before they can choke her. "I talked to Aunt Millicent, but she thought I was Octavia. When I left, she was fine. Confused, but I swear she was fine. But then..." She gags on a sob. "Then I ran out to the car, and Ryan stayed behind. 'To go to the bathroom,' he said. That's when he must have done it." Sloane covers her face with her hands, tears slipping through her fingers, shoulders heaving.

Annie hands her a tissue from the box beside her bed.

"And you told Chief Hartwell all that?" Margaret asks, a little calmer.

"Y-yes."

Margaret sighs and turns her gaze out the window. "Well, I guess that's the end of it, then."

Annie shifts her good leg to get more comfortable. *But is it the end? Sloane lied for an awfully long time about seeing Millicent that night. She's only confessed now that Ryan isn't around to refute her. And Margaret? She harbors such a deep animosity toward me.*

Yet, her daughters aren't the only ones concealing secrets. Annie recalls her furtive trip to the island two days before her announced arrival. She recalls Caroline's warning that the young crew on Ian's boat might someday realize what they saw in the waterway. That possibility strikes her as slim, something she can bluff her way out of. But she's unsure if she and her daughters can ever be in a room together without doubts creeping over them, slithering among them, choking off the possibility of joy.

Annie watches Sloane raise her head and stare at her sister. When Sloane twists to give her mother a tremulous smile, Margaret reflects an identically severe gaze upon Sloane. Clearly, her girls haven't dismissed their suspicions about each other.

Or about me.

Chapter 50

Sloane

Sloane regrets her hasty decision to drive back to the island. She is no closer to discerning what her sister has done than she was while sitting outside Kramer Drugs in Augusta.

"I hate that you're missing your trustees' dinner," Margaret says as they head out of the hospital.

Will this be our lives from now on? Surface-level conversations hiding deeper, treacherous currents?

There is no choice but to play along. "Yeah, me, too. It was stupid. Now I have to repeat that three-hour drive, plus two hours more." Not to mention, she's operating on four hours' sleep.

Surely, Margaret is going to press her on why she did it, press her on the questions raised about Jayroe Martin's pharmacy. *Or maybe she already knows.* So much remains unspoken between them.

"You doing anything tonight?" Sloane asks as Margaret climbs into her BMW.

For the first time, her sister's face brightens, and she looks at her watch. "Yes, and I'm running late. Joel and I are going to Charleston with Nadine and Randall to hear the band. You wanna come?"

"No way I'm getting back on the road again. But I'm glad you're going. Have fun."

Margaret drives off with a flutter of her hand, and Sloane climbs into her RAV4. After sharing the house all week with Robroy, his bandmates, Sam, and her mother, she will suddenly be alone. Maybe she should go to Elsie's for dinner. But nothing is resolved about the sale of the house, so inquisitive neighbors will be swarming. She discards the idea.

A few minutes later, she pulls into the deserted driveway of Millicent House. Rich-purple wisteria has blossomed during the week, and its dripping fronds are lovely, old-fashioned. They bring on a wave of nostalgia. Her phone rings, and she's thrilled to see it's Eli.

"Are you in Atlanta?" he asks.

"No, I'm back in Millicent. All alone in the house. Want to join me for dinner?"

"Sure. But why aren't you at the college?"

"Long story. I'll tell you when you get here."

"You must have turned around right after I caught you," he persists. The man can't let anything go. "Anyway, I can't wait to hear. I've got another hour of work, then I'm driving from Fripp. So I'll be there in, say, two hours."

"Perfect. That'll give me time to come up with something to cook. Or reheat."

"Anything's fine. See you soon."

She hops out of the SUV, far more cheerful than she was minutes before.

Half an hour later, Sloane is showered and dressed in billowy white pants and a sleeveless lime tunic—beachy designs that Margaret brought over when she saw how little she'd packed. She dons flat sandals and runs her fingers through her freshly washed curls, allowing them to air dry—which will take another ninety minutes. Mascara, lip gloss, and light eye shadow finish her primping, then she crosses the upper floor landing to the small reading room. Through the glass doors, she can see that Burle has rebuilt the railing but left it unpainted for the wood to cure.

Venturing onto the balcony, she inches to the edge, her stomach somersaulting. The beach is empty and the ocean calm, in shades of aquamarine up close, blue and navy in the distance. The sun is above the horizon but already taking on a fiery red glow.

Standing well away from the rail, she reaches out to shake it. It's solid. She pokes at the balusters. Solid, too. Forcing herself to the brink, she peers into the yard below. Something red lies tucked between the porch and the shrubs. Trash, maybe. Or a T-shirt.

She spins and hurries downstairs, slams through the screen door, and hurtles down the porch steps. Behind a glossy evergreen shrub, she spots it, wedged tightly in the prickly leaves: a red-and-black Georgia Bulldogs cap. She gazes up at the balcony. So many people have been on this property, swimming, throwing Frisbees, cutting grass, repairing rails. Sean wore a green John Deere cap, Derek a navy-and-red one from the Atlanta Braves, Robroy a crazy plaid from the House of Blues. So not them. She doesn't remember Arturio wearing this hat, but he attended the University of Georgia, as did his father, Randall. Eli and Sam never wore hats out here. Bud and Burle? Who knows? Taking the hat inside, she tosses it on the window seat where Arturio will find it on his next visit.

She rummages through the freezer, discovering one last casserole from Elsie. She can't make out what it is, but it's bound to be good. Placing it in the microwave to hasten its thawing, she tosses a salad and unearths some frozen bagels she can split and toast at the last minute. It won't be fancy, but Eli knows she's an indifferent cook.

Uncorking a bottle of dry rosé from Monday's reception, she pours a glass and walks onto the porch to await sunset. She eases into a rocking chair and is struck by how comfortable it feels, how right. *What has changed?* Eli's presence, certainly. Her mother's return, of course. The two gaping losses in her life have been recovered. Or semi-recovered. She's unsure if Eli will accept her apology for the blatant lie about her drive with Ryan on the night of Aunt Millicent's murder.

And her mother. How easily Sloane told her she would return on Sunday and settle her into this house. *Will I spend the summer here?* She realizes she wants to.

Losses are part of her change in perspective too. As much as she grieves Aunt Millicent's passing, Sloane wouldn't be here if she were alive. And while she's not grieving her father, his specter still prickles. Maybe her body will eventually stop cringing when she passes the side yard, the inland waterway, shrimp boats moored at a dock.

She leans her head against the rocker and sighs, envisioning June, July, and part of August—living here, taking care of her mom, reconnecting with Eli, completing Elle's story. And listening to Robroy's band. Driving to coastal venues with Eli, Margaret, Joel, Nadine, and Randall. They'll be obnoxious groupies.

The wine is loosening her mood, and her mind wanders to Elle's unfinished tale. Does she need to revise the scenes concerning Elle's mother? Did she mar the manuscript by planting crazy suspicions? Why would Elle's mom *not* want her to solve a murder case from the 1940s? Was there something similar in the mom's past that she didn't want unearthed?

Sloane's rocking slows as her mind flits among the scenes she wrote after her mother's return. They were dark and hinted at something she'd not intended for the book. That's why she messaged her editor and agent that she needed time to edit it properly.

But what was her subconscious trying to work out? Margaret clearly suspects their mother of... *what, exactly?* She said she didn't want their mother to hurt Sloane or Robroy. When Sloane asked how she could hurt them, Margaret responded, "By pretending to be someone she's not. Or at least, that she is no longer."

What did she mean by that?

Sloane's mind returns to the letter she found behind the painting of Millicent House. Apparently, their mother had tried to kill their father by drilling a hole in his boat. She was so frightened that he might find out that she fled—and stayed gone for twelve long years.

Her mother contacted Aunt Millicent this past December, and their dad drowned in May. *Was there a connection?* Her father had been drunk, according to Chief Hartwell, very drunk. But that's when he was most dangerous. Would her mother have dared confront him?

Sloane's mind roams over everything she's learned in the past week, the currents that run openly through her island community and the ones that churn hidden and deep beneath its surface. The drowning of her Aunt Chelsea as a teenager. Aunt Sierra's move to Columbia. Jesse's disdain for her and her mother. Octavia's anger. And most disturbing of all, Randall's revelation about her father abusing Robroy.

Wait a minute. If Sloane just found out about Robroy, maybe their mother did too. Who was she in touch with? Idelle, and then this spring, Aunt Millicent. The two women knew everything that took place on this island. Did Idelle or Aunt Millicent tell her mother about Robroy's injuries? *Could that have spurred her to finally take action against Robert Cheney?*

Sloane springs from her chair and rushes to her aunt's study. She doesn't know what she's looking for. A document, a diary, a letter, a note. Did Aunt Millicent know what her sister was planning? Would she have tried to stop her? Sloane's mind is spinning, and she's aware it's leaping way past logic. But so many things don't make sense.

Her eyes zip over Aunt Millicent's wall of bookshelves. Her beloved murder mysteries. Women's fiction. Biographies, possibly chosen by a book club.

Her gaze flits back to the mysteries. There's a gap on one shelf where a book is missing, and she remembers *The Smuggler's Daugh-*

ter that she'd nabbed from the desk, its cover reminding her of their father's boat on the inland waterway. *Why was it on the desk?* In the hospital, her aunt said to Octavia, thinking she was Annie: "I left the boat for you."

Sloane's eyes dart to the sofa where Burle found her aunt, delirious with an infection. Was she looking at the book before she fell ill?

Sloane runs out of the study and up the staircase to retrieve the novel from the bottom of her duffle, a place the detectives never inspected. Slowly she flips through it. Inside the rear cover is a stiff cardboard envelope, the kind libraries used in the days when physical cards tracked their lending. This one looks handmade.

A piece of paper is jammed into the envelope. She eases it out, hardly daring to breathe.

It is a handwritten letter, undated.

Dear Annie,

I'm not sure you will ever receive this letter. Indeed, I don't even have a way of mailing it to you. But do you know how unresolved conversations keep playing in your head until you resolve them? This is where I find myself. So I'll transfer the chatter in my head to paper in the hopes it will leave me – and perhaps answer a question you may someday have.

It concerns your children. After having your name on my will for the past seven years, we have declared you dead. What an awful and heavy day that was.

Raeford has advised me to designate another beneficiary so the state will have no reason to step into the family's probate matters. I have chosen Sloane. Are you ever to find out, I'm sure you'll want to know, Why Sloane? Why not Margaret or Robroy, or all three?

I love your Robroy, but he is not suitable. I'll instruct Sloane to look after him, but he's too young and too unstable.

The real question is, why not Margaret? It's because, dear Annie, I fear she will have you arrested if you ever return. She was so angry when you left Sloane and Robroy that she began questioning me about the rumors that swirled around the near sinking of Robert's boat. When I told her nothing, she went to Clive Barnstable. She believed his denial and worked out the timing to determine that you had tried to kill Robert and then fled.

I thought her anger would pass, but she got worse after Emma Sue was born. Maybe her hormones were raging. But her exact words to me, even years later, were: "What kind of mother leaves her children? There is no excuse for that. None."

I hope that with more time, Margaret's stance will soften. But for now, she is so very angry, Annie. With you, and by extension, with me. I fear what she may do, without fully grasping the consequences.

That's good to get off my chest.

Your loving sister,

Millicent

Sloane works out the math in her head. The letter was written three to five years ago because Aunt Millicent had already declared their mother dead, but Robroy was too young for her to make him a beneficiary. No mention of Aunt Millicent's disappointment with Margaret for not adopting Robroy. She ponders how distinct perspectives have loomed so differently in their minds: What Margaret saw as the roadblock in their relationship was totally different than what Aunt Millicent saw.

Was Aunt Millicent right about Margaret's rage? And did their father's drowning end her determination to report their mother for attempted murder? Or exacerbate it?

Sloane's head is spinning. *This is Margaret, for goodness' sake.* Girl Scout leader. Cookie baker. Mother of the Year. She pauses. That's exactly what Aunt Millicent is accusing her of—being so judgmental of their mother's parenting. But to the point of having her *arrested*? It's hard for Sloane to imagine her sister going that far.

But there is the drug that went missing from Kramer Drugs about the time that Margaret visited. Could her anger at their aunt and mother have reached such proportions?

The doorbell rings, and Sloane is yanked back to her surroundings. She stuffs the letter back into its hiding place and returns *The Smuggler's Daughter* to the bottom of her duffle.

She walks slowly down the stairs, trying to reorient herself, to remember that Eli is not just a former boyfriend, but a reporter. An astute one.

She opens the door, pasting on a smile. But it's not Eli.

Margaret, Joel, and Nadine stand on the front porch. "We wanted to give you one last chance to join us," Nadine squeals like a teen. "This listening room in Charleston is one of the best."

"Come and go with us," Joel says.

Sloane looks at the three of them, grinning happily, Joel in khakis and a tropical shirt, Margaret and Nadine in bare-shouldered sundresses. "You look like Parrotheads." She laughs. "Will Robroy let you in?"

"Actually, this place serves a decent frozen daiquiri," says Margaret. "Can we tempt you?"

"I'm very tempted," she says.

There's movement in Joel's black Escalade.

"Is Randall in there too?" Sloane asks.

Before anyone can answer, a crutch slides out a side window and waggles playfully.

"Wait a minute. You've got *Mom* in there?"

"And Randall. And Idelle," says Nadine.

"Then where in the world would I sit?"

"Seven seats," Joel says. "Plenty of room."

Sloane laughs again. "I'm sorry, but Eli's on his way for dinner. Next time?"

"Next time. That's a promise," says Nadine.

Sloane waves as the three of them jump into the giant Cadillac. No sooner do they rumble past the iron seabirds than Eli pulls into the driveway.

Sloane and Eli are enjoying a glass of wine on the porch as the casserole heats. She hopes the corals, peaches, and oranges of the sunset distract him from noting her flittering attention. He starts chatting about the next steps for the Millicent Island story. And with that, he's finally snagged her interest.

"Hold on. What?" Sloan says. "Doesn't Ryan Carbonier's suicide put the story to rest?"

"Hardly. Even if it solves your aunt's murder, the bigger story—no offense—is what will happen to this town. Development? Or no development?"

Her eyes roam the spacious porch. "I assume my mom will settle in here and take her time to decide. So development of Camp Resurrection can go forward, I suppose. But not Millicent House."

"Are you sure about that?"

Am I? Maybe she is projecting what she wants onto her mother. She hears Margaret in her head: *...pretending to be someone she's not. Or at least, that she is no longer.*

Sloane assumes her mother feels the same need to make up for their lost years as she does. But where's the evidence for that? After all, she was Ryan Carbonier's willing partner. Maybe she intends to sell and run. Again. But this time with millions of dollars.

Sloane's mind skitters to a tangential thought: In the hospital, Aunt Millicent thought Octavia was Annie. Perhaps her mother *was* at the hospital. Perhaps Arturio's Auntie June was right all along.

She shakes her head as if to rid it of these wild thoughts.

Eli glances over. "What's up?"

"It's just been a hard week, you know? A lot to process."

He places a hand over hers. "I know. Sorry to keep hammering at it. But it's quite a story."

She's eager to change the subject. "Are you ready to eat?"

"Absolutely."

Moments later, she transfers the casserole from the oven to the dining room table, which is set with Aunt Millicent's good china.

"Fan-cee," Eli says appreciatively as she adds water goblets.

"Well, until you see the toasted bagels."

"Still. This is wonderful, Sloane. Really nice." Elsie's dish turns out to be a delicious chicken and broccoli concoction. They make it halfway through the meal before Eli's cell phone rings.

"Sorry," he says. "A source from the sheriff's office. I need to get this."

Eli rises to pace the hallway, phone pressed to his ear. She strains to hear his responses, but he's lowered his voice. When he returns, his face is serious.

"I have to go," he says. "I'm so sorry about dinner."

"What is it?"

He hesitates. "An arrest. Chief Hartwell and the Beaufort County Sheriff's detectives are meeting up with the Charleston Police for an arrest." He doesn't say for what. He doesn't have to.

But Charleston? She pictures Margaret and Joel, Nadine and Randall, Mom and Idelle trundling up US 17. Robroy, Sean, and Derek, unsuspecting and playing their hearts out. Arturio, minus his red-and-black Bulldogs hat.

"I'm going with you."

Eli doesn't try to talk her out of it.

Chapter 51

Annie

This trip was not a good idea. Annie had downed her pain meds minutes before Idelle sashayed into her hospital room, chattering about how a night out would do wonders for her.

"You're checking out day after tomorrow anyway, Annie. J.C. is babysitting the girls, which, believe me, doesn't happen often. So let's go hear Robroy!"

Annie had to admit she'd love to hear Robroy's band in a concert setting.

"Joel's got this big-ass Cadillac SUV," Idelle continued. "I swear, he and Margaret must be planning to have five kids. It'll hold all of us. What do you say?"

"I don't have anything to wear," Annie claimed feebly.

"Ta da!" Idelle whipped a hanger from behind her back to reveal a swirling, floor-length skirt and a flowing aqua blouse. "Custom made to accommodate a leg cast," she announced.

The medication had taken effect, and Annie was feeling no pain. "Oh, why the heck not?" She tossed the covers off.

The nurses had her sign a disclaimer since she was leaving earlier than scheduled, but no one seemed concerned now that the cast was on. After a quick stop at Millicent House, they were on their way to Ziggy's, a listening room an hour and a half away in Charleston.

Margaret didn't have much to say during the ride, though the way Idelle and Nadine were carrying on, she'd have had a hard time of it even if she did.

Now they're settled into their seats at Ziggy's, Joel having thoughtfully placed her at the inside end of a row so no one has to crawl over her cast. They're all enjoying beers or frozen drinks. She's afraid to mix her pain medication with alcohol, but the pill is wearing off, and her leg is starting to throb.

Despite the pain—and the fear of more pain before she can fill a prescription in the morning—it is delightful to hear Robroy. And the other boys, of course. But she's having a hard time taking her eyes off the tall young man commanding the stage, alternately breaking into guitar solos and giving his players the nod for their spotlit turns. Under these lights, his blond hair has strawberry highlights. That comes from her, not Robert. But his slim, muscular build is reminiscent of the young Robert she fell in love with. She shoves the thought away. She's gotten so very good at that.

Robroy pauses after the band's fourth song and grins shyly. "I'd like to welcome my family hiding back there on the tenth row," he says, and the audience whistles and applauds. "They've come up to join us from Millicent. Great to have you guys." He looks directly at her. "This one's for you, Mom."

He swirls and looks for a beat from Arturio then launches into Elvis's "That's All Right." "That's all right, Mama. That's all right for you." Nadine yelps and punches her, and Annie tries to smile as she shifts her leg. But now her back is aching too. *Yes, this was a mistake.*

And then police officers stop at their row.

Chapter 52

Sloane huddles against the passenger door of Eli's Honda, her mind ricocheting, rivulets of nervous sweat dripping between her breasts. *Are the police seeking Mom? Or Margaret?*

Am I awful to hope it's Arturio? Despite what he said about his family opposing the development, Randall and Nadine would profit from increased business at the Seafood Shack.

Or Sean? Perhaps he's long held a vendetta against Robert Cheney's family. Exasperation grips her. They weren't the ones in bed with a developer. They weren't the ones outside Kramer Drugs.

Then, Idelle? Eli thinks that Idelle and J.C. oppose the island's development, but they stand to profit handsomely if more traffic is lured to their gas stations. As does Joel.

God, what is wrong with me? "Eli, talk to me," she pleads.

He is concentrating on the road, speeding up US 17 and keeping a lookout for a caravan from the Beaufort County Sheriff's Office. "What do you want to know?"

"Did your source say anything about who's going to be arrested? A 'he' or a 'she'?"

"No, only the name of the place."

"Ziggy's. Have you been there?"

"Once. Seats about one fifty. Drinks. Limited food."

"I'm not asking for the menu!" She hears the screech in her voice. "Sorry. Sorry. I'm not upset with you. Obviously."

He glances at her.

"They stopped and asked me to come with them," she says. "Before you got to the house."

"Who all was going?"

"Margaret and Joel. Nadine and Randall. Mom and Idelle."

"My God."

"Right? That's why I'm freaked out."

Dense, dark woods blur on the side of the road as they speed toward Charleston. Her foot presses the passenger side floorboard in a futile attempt to make the car go faster.

"One more thing I found today," she says, needing to talk, needing to do something. "I found a Georgia Bulldog hat right below where the balcony rail collapsed. I guess it could've blown there from the beach. But it could have blown off when someone was sawing up there."

"Who wears a Bulldog hat?"

"Randall and Arturio went to UGA." She hates herself for saying it but plunges on. "And I didn't see Arturio wearing his hat this week."

"What are you saying?"

"Could he have lost it earlier? When he was on the balcony?"

"Wow. Arturio. That's hard to picture."

Guilt swamps her, but she presses on. "You know as well as I do how he's been hanging around all week. Every time you were at the house. Every time Margaret and Robroy and I talked. He even went to Octavia's post office and the hospital with me and Margaret." She pauses. "And his Auntie June. How convenient that she was there to see me." Instantly, she realizes her mistake.

"See you where?"

She'd meant to confess earlier about her trip to the hospital with Ryan, but they'd been interrupted. "It's too complicated to get into now. While you're trying to concentrate on the road."

Eli is quiet for a few moments, and she begins to breathe again. Well, as much as possible given the disaster they may find at the end of this trip.

"We're on a straightaway," he says finally. "Go ahead. Arturio's Aunt June is a nurse, so she saw you at the hospital, I presume. When?"

Sloane closes her eyes, watching all her plans for this summer, this relationship, evaporate. "On the night of Aunt Millicent's murder."

Eli directs a barbed gaze at her. "So the trip to Bluestone Village with Ryan Carbonier—that was a lie? You went with him to Mercy Hospital instead."

"Yes." When he doesn't respond, she adds, "Eli, I am so sorry."

"Why did you lie to me, Sloane?"

"It wasn't just you. I was trying to keep it from Chief Hartwell. And Eli, you *are* a reporter."

His jaw is as rigid as a statue. "Have I ever betrayed your trust? What makes you think I would?"

She shakes her head. "No, no, it's not that." She inhales. "I was trying to keep a secret. An old secret I was ashamed of. Ryan Carbonier found out and threatened to tell the trustees at Warner. I would've been fired."

"So he coerced you into going to the hospital. But why?"

"To see how sick Aunt Millicent was. He claimed he'd need to change his plans if she was going to live another twenty years like I said. We visited her briefly. But when I returned to his car, he went back into Aunt Millicent's room and killed her." *Didn't he? But we are racing toward Charleston and another arrest.* "At least, that's what I thought."

"Yeah, me too." Eli is angry and trying not to speak to her again. But his curiosity gets the better of him. "So what was it? This secret that had you lying to everyone."

Her stomach spasms, and she feels sick. It's time to expel this final poison. "The year after we graduated, after we broke up, I went a little wild. You knew that." She closes her eyes, but it only makes the nausea worse. "One time in Columbia, I was in a bar and let this guy buy me drinks. He went to the bathroom and left his wallet on the table. I stole it and ran. I was charged with petit larceny."

Unlike Chief Hartwell, Eli doesn't laugh. He looks at her with disgust.

"Seriously?"

She sighs. "You see why I didn't want you to know."

"Yeah, I guess I do."

He exits US 17. "Ziggy's isn't far," he says abruptly then falls silent. Within minutes, they see the flashing blue lights of Beaufort County and Charleston Police vehicles blocking the parking lot of a low-slung cinderblock building. A lone Millicent Police Department SUV is pulled off to the side. Eli parks across the road and departs without speaking.

Sloane trails him as far as the police barricade, where a uniformed officer prevents them from going further. They crane to watch the front door where several officers wait. Nadine and Randall are the first to emerge, their expressions frozen in shock. Sloane looks for handcuffs and sees none. Then Joel emerges, head down, followed by her mother, grimacing on unaccustomed crutches, with Idelle fluttering on one side, Margaret soldier-stiff on the other. She's not touching their mother, and in fact, Sloane can't see her sister's arms at all. *Are they locked behind her?* She strains for a glimpse of metal.

Her sister raises her eyes and spies Sloane across the asphalt. Even from a distance, Sloane can see her contorted face, her tears. *Oh, Margaret. What did you do?* Her sister mouths something Sloane can't make out.

Then Chief Hartwell and a Beaufort County detective exit the building, a tall blond man between them, his wrists clearly cuffed. A beloved man. Now she understands what Margaret was trying to say.

Robroy.

Chapter 53

Annie

What would Annie give to be in her hospital bed, not to have heard "that's all right, Mama" squealing into discordant notes as first Sean, then Robroy, saw police officers mounting the stage?

What would she give not to have seen resignation, rather than confusion, cross her son's face? For then she knew. She understood.

He hadn't escaped Robert's violence at all. It was ingrained, etched into his soul. She wonders if he blamed his aunt for not rescuing him from his father's cruel grasp. Or if he blamed his sisters. *Or certainly, me.*

If she harbors any doubt, it is erased when she reaches Joel's Escalade.

Margaret, sobbing and gasping for air, turns to her with a ferocity that causes her to stumble backward. "This is on you," she shouts. "He's going to prison, but this is all on you."

Idelle catches Annie's arm to keep her from falling, but she doesn't speak. Her friend recognizes the truth in Margaret's accusation. As does Annie.

Chief Hartwell stands off to one side, letting Beaufort County's detectives take the lead. To his credit, he is taking no pleasure in this. Annie turns to him. He heard Margaret's accusation.

"May I speak to my son? One minute?" Her voice cracks.

He strides to the vehicle into which Robroy has disappeared and mumbles to the detective closing the car door. Annie limps over, her leg objecting with every step. The rear window slides down, revealing Robroy's handsome face, hollow cheeked, hollow eyed.

"Is it true?" is all she can manage, hoping he will contradict her, protest, proclaim his innocence.

He nods, refusing to look at her.

"You killed Millicent? But why, Robroy? She loved you."

There is no shifting to a monster before her eyes. No malice. No anger even. Only the resignation she saw on stage moments ago.

His voice is barely above a whisper. "You don't know, Mom. You weren't here. You don't know how it was to be poor for so long, to depend on other people's charity, to be the object of pity. When that multimillion-dollar house was sitting there with my name on it."

"So you did know she was leaving it to you."

"Yeah, I knew."

Annie thinks of her intelligent, savvy sister, suspicious of developers, of outsiders, of Robert, but trusting Annie, trusting her flesh-and-blood nephew, never suspecting that danger could come from within. It turns out that Annie's mistake was not in bringing Ryan into her sister's life but deserting Robroy in it.

She whispers an apology, what amounts to a prayer. "I'm so sorry, Millicent. How can you ever forgive me?"

Chapter 54

Sloane

By unspoken agreement, Sloane takes the last seat in Joel's SUV, leaving Eli to his reporting. The seven of them say little on the way home. Even with the roominess that accommodates her cast, her mother is in pain. Sloane squeezes her hand, and her mother gives her a look of purest gratitude. Sloane overheard Margaret's screamed indictment—as did every police officer in the parking lot. It will be a common sentiment on the island.

Joel drops Nadine and Randall at their place, but he and Idelle accompany them to Millicent House. Sloane and Joel help Annie, staggering with fatigue, up the front steps. Sloane will bring blankets and linens down later, but for now, they stumble onto the parlor sofas. Idelle ushers Joel into the kitchen, leaving Sloane, Margaret, and their mother to stare at each other.

"Robroy wanted the money?" Sloane asks dully. "So he *did* know that Aunt Millicent left him half the estate." Her mother nods, and Sloane turns to Margaret. "Did you know?"

"I suspected," she says. "He spent lots of time here, and Octavia hinted that Aunt Millicent was changing her will. I put two and two together."

"And the digoxin," Sloane says. "Did you get it for him?"

Margaret looks horrified. "No! Why would you think that?"

"It went missing from Kramer Drugs." She doesn't need to go further.

Margaret sighs. "That's when I knew. When you told me the digoxin had disappeared from Jayroe's pharmacy."

"But you didn't take it?"

"No, Sloane. The reason I was in Augusta was to see the band. They were opening at the James Brown Arena, which was a big deal. They filled in for an opening act that cancelled at the last minute." She pauses, squeezing her eyes shut. "Robroy was with me when I stopped at the pharmacy."

Sloane still can't quite picture it. "Okay."

"He said he went to get a burger at that McDonald's next door. But when I came out to my car, he wasn't crossing the parking lot. He was walking around from the back of the shopping center."

Sloane thinks about the layout of the center. "He passed the pharmacy's back door."

Margaret nods. "Which apparently was unlocked. He must have helped himself while I was talking to Jayroe."

"So he cut the balcony rail in late April, and nothing happened. He saw another chance when Aunt Millicent went into the hospital." Sloane's chest squeezes painfully. Sawing through the rail is the piece that is hardest to imagine for the brother she thought so mild mannered. *But then, in both of his plans, he wouldn't have had to witness the violent result, would he?*

Their mother speaks for the first time. "Margaret, did he need money that badly?"

She shrugs. "Musicians at his level barely break even. If that. They were always looking for free places to stay." She pauses, exhales shakily. "But it went deeper than that. He hated being poor when he was younger. Absolutely hated it. When Joel and I bought things for him or gave him money, it only seemed to make things worse."

Margaret casts a look at Sloane, which reminds her of Robroy's theft from the Espeys. Before either can mention it, a knock on the door makes them jump. Sloane rises, hoping it's Eli. But it's Chief Hartwell.

"I'm sorry to stop by so late." He drops heavily into a wing chair. "But I figured none of you would be sleeping."

"Where is Robroy?" her mother asks.

"Beaufort County Detention. He's being charged with the murder of Ryan Carbonier along with the murder of your sister."

Her mother's eyes zoom frantically among them. "He killed *Ryan*? But..."

"He missed one fingerprint," says the chief. "Under the sink countertop. We matched it to his fingerprint from an old shoplifting charge."

"So he was talking to Ryan about selling Millicent House?" Sloane asks.

"He didn't have to," the chief says. "You had taken care of that. But what he did have to cover up was the fact that Ryan Carbonier had *not* killed your aunt. If Carbonier was able to prove it, the investigation would reopen. But if Carbonier committed suicide out of guilt, the case would be closed." He pauses. "We searched the apartment at Ziggy's and found the last of the digoxin Robroy took from Kramer Drugs."

The three of them lean back on the stately sofas, revulsion and sadness equally mixed. Sloane looks around the beautiful, old-fashioned room and marvels that it has contributed to such madness. "How did he convince Aunt Millicent to put him in the will?"

"He told her he would persuade you not to sell," says the chief. "She didn't want to cut you out entirely because she'd given her word years ago. But she'd become increasingly unhappy with the developers who were circling. Robroy took advantage of that."

He pauses then adds, "One other thing bothered me. I thought it was serendipitous that you located Miss Roundtree's latest will in a children's book. The *Grinch*, wasn't it? That could easily have gone undiscovered."

"I guess so," Sloane says. "But it *was* my favorite book."

"Well, it turns out that Robroy found the new will in her top desk drawer on the evening you two arrived. But he heard you coming down the hall and crammed it into that book, intending to dispose of it later. You stumbled onto it before he could."

Sloane glances at her mother. That document alerted them to the possibility she was alive. Annie's face is white with pain—both physical and emotional, Sloane imagines—and she's beyond responding.

Idelle comes in with a tray of mugs holding hot tea. "I added lots of honey," she says. "I hear it helps with shock."

Joel is right behind her with the Georgia Bulldogs hat Sloane found earlier. "Whose is this?" he asks.

"Arturio's," Sloane answers, now aware of the truth. "He lost it while playing on the beach."

As silence descends on the room, Sloane returns once more to the act that most disturbs her, the act that undermines everything she thought she knew of her brother. "The balcony rail," she says. "I still can't picture Robroy doing that." She recalls Sam's heart-stopping loss of balance and envisions her aunt alone on the balcony. If a fall didn't kill her instantly, she could've lain for hours, days even, in the yard below. In excruciating pain.

"Well," the chief says, not unsympathetically, "he cried when he admitted that part."

She follows Robroy's confession to its logical conclusion. "But that means..." She can't continue. Her brother was willing to let her go onto the balcony as well.

The chief seems to read her mind. "Let me stop you there. Once you all were in the house, he claims he planned to trigger the rail collapse himself so none of you would get hurt. But as you know, your friend Sam got to it within minutes of arriving on your very first night." He looks at her and shrugs slightly. "That's what he says anyway."

She remembers Robroy's ashen face as he dragged her across the balcony and into the safety of Sam's room. She recalls his iron grip on her arm, the trembling of his body.

She chooses to believe her brother.

Chapter 55

The trees tell her she is home. It seems impossible that she made this same drive only six days ago. She whizzes past St. James' oak-guarded cemetery where Aunt Millicent lies. Then Octavia's little blue house.

Her graduation speech was a hit—according to the trustees, anyway. But what were they going to say? "What a terrible speech! What were you thinking?" At least the laughs came at all the right places, and the sections where she paused because her eyes were brimming seemed to pass unnoticed. Her creative-writing seniors and fellow faculty members were effusive. Except for Dr. Avery, who *harrumphed* past her to exit the stage. She's just glad it's over.

She packed two large suitcases this morning because she doesn't know what the summer will hold. With two murder charges, Robroy will not be granted bail. She and Margaret and their mother have lots of perilous territory to tread, lots of lost time to make up. Sloane's unsure how their relationships will untangle—if her sister can forgive their mother, if their mother can forgive herself. If the suspicions and doubts can be forgotten. If there will be any connection left among the Cheney women at the end.

But they are bound by a secret—a secret all of them are committed to keeping. Confronted by her daughters' knowledge of the failed attempt on Robert's life twelve years earlier and Sloane's suspicion of his recent drowning, Annie confessed to her daughters. The trio had experienced Robert Cheney in a way no one else had. The case had been closed as an accidental drowning; it was an easy decision for Sloane and Margaret to keep it that way. Well, easy for Sloane. A little more grudging for Margaret.

And Eli. He's been so caught up in reporting her family's sorry saga that Sloane hasn't seen him since Friday night. *Can he forgive my lies?* She doesn't know. If she's lucky, he doesn't know yet either. Which means there's a chance.

She doesn't know how she feels about Millicent. The town, that is. The island. Her despised father is gone, but so, too, are her beloved aunt and brother. Her mother is back. How the cast of characters has changed. One minute she is numb with grief. The next she is confused. The next she is hopeful.

She's had a lot of time on this drive, too, to think about her novel, about Elle's story. She's decided to choose hope. Elle's mother will shift into the background as a minor character, and her grandmother will be the beacon of courage and resilience that the young woman needs. Mother figures can be as defining as mothers: Sloane has to look no further than Aunt Millicent to confirm it.

A briny scent wafts through the vents, and she opens the SUV's windows to let the wind whip through her hair. On her right appears the entrance to Camp Resurrection. With Ryan's death, the company that owns it is in disarray. Now that it's in private hands, though, development there is inevitable.

Her mother, on the other hand, is not going to let anyone hurry her decision on Millicent House. She has promised to live there for a few years at least, give the town a chance to settle down. Without the house and its surrounding property, development will be held to a minimum. Not a bad compromise.

On her left appears the Seafood Shack, its parking lot half filled with locals on this Sunday afternoon. It occurs to Sloane what a shame it would be to have the Shack, Elsie's Diner—indeed, the entire island—overrun by strangers. Between them, perhaps she and Margaret can persuade their mother to hold onto the family property for the long term.

A half mile farther, their driveway snakes between brick columns topped by iron seabirds in flight. She's not surprised when a lump rises in her throat.

She is home.

Cast of Characters

Sloane Cheney – Inheritor of the family home in Millicent, SC, and creative writing instructor at Warner College in Atlanta

Annie Roundtree Cheney – Sloane's mother

Margaret Cheney Simpson – Sloane's older sister, businesswoman in her in-laws' Gas 'N' Such chain

Robroy Cheney – Sloane's younger brother, leader of a rock band

Robert Cheney – Sloane's father, a fisherman and a shrimper

Millicent Roundtree – Sloane's aunt and town matriarch

Joel Simpson – Margaret's husband

Idelle Simpson – Annie's best friend and Margaret's mother-in-law

J.C. Simpson – Idelle's husband and Margaret's father-in-law

Emma Sue and Sarah – Margaret and Joel's eight- and seven-year-old daughters

Burle and Jesse Jenkins – Owners of Seafood Shack, occasional workers at Millicent House

Mack Sanderson – Banker who favors development of the town

Kent Espey – Sloane's childhood friend, shrimper, part-time police officer in Millicent, older brother of Robroy's childhood friend Scott Espey

Randall Jenkins – Burle's nephew and co-owner of Seafood Shack

Nadine Jenkins – Randall's wife

Arturio Jenkins – Son of Randall and Nadine, drummer in Robroy's band

Auntie June – A nurse at the island's Mercy Hospital, Nadine's sister and Arturio's aunt

Sean Barnstable – Bass guitarist in Robroy's band

Derek – Keyboardist in Robroy's band

Raeford Carlisle – Family lawyer for Millicent Roundtree and the Cheneys

Octavia Hargrove – Millicent's best friend, island postmistress

Bud Randolph – Owner of boat repair shop

Elsie Dennehy – Owner of Elsie's Diner

Dan Hartwell – Police chief

Eileen Cheney – Robert's mother

Ian Cheney – Robert's older brother, a shrimper

Caroline Cheney – Ian's wife and a waitress at Elsie's Diner

Sierra Cheney – Robert's younger sister who lives in Columbia

Elliott Cheney – Robert's younger brother who lives off the island

Ryan Carbonier – Florida developer who wants to develop the town of Millicent

Dr. John Avery – Head of the English department at Warner College, Sloane's boss

Sam Kinnecky – Warner College grad student and intern in the English department

Travis Kildaire – Chairman of Warner College's Board of Trustees

Dr. Erin Rasmussen – Medical director of the island's Mercy Hospital

Jayroe Martin – Pharmacist in Augusta, GA; Dr. Rasmussen's sister; Margaret's high school friend

Leah – Sloane's friend who gave her the idea for her latest novel

Acknowledgments

A big thank you to Lynn McNamee and Red Adept Publishing for their help in getting this book and, previously, *Through Any Window* into the hands and Kindles of readers. Thanks, too, to editors Diane Byington and Meghan Portillo for their thoughtful improvements to this manuscript.

Thank you to my writers' group members Allison Green, Wanda Owings, and Susan Simmons and early reader Elaine Nocks for their insightful comments. And to Taylor Moore for Robroy's band names, all his at one time.

Thanks to Paulette and Jeff Alden for a stint in their Key West cottage, where much of this book was written. And to the Smokin' Tuna Saloon for providing dance music at the end of a long writing day.

I am most appreciative to my readers and their book clubs who so generously tell me of their eagerness for the next book, and the next, and the next. You truly are wonderful encouragers. I call you to mind on those days when my inner critic is most vociferous.

Thanks to all the family members who cheer me on and argue over which of them appears in a given manuscript—Rick, Candace, Maggie, Lori, Robert, Sam, Ryan, Bennie, Robin, and Tyler. I appreciate you guys for ignoring Susan Lay Smith's plea to "Hide that woman's laptop."

And to Vince, Dustin, Taylor, Madison, and Michael. Always.

Discussion Questions

1. What did you think of Annie Cheney? Could you understand her decision to abandon her children?

2. How did Sloane's novels play into the plot? Did they expand your understanding of her character?

3. This is the author's second novel in which the plot centers around development in her native South Carolina. Are there places such as the fictional barrier island of Millicent in danger of vanishing?

4. The author has spoken of planting "little bombs" in a manuscript so the reader is not waiting entirely for the murderer's reveal. What were some of the ones that exploded along the way in this story?

5. Have you spent time on South Carolina's barrier islands? Would you prefer to visit a "Mayberry by the Sea" or a more authentic coastal town?

6. Sloane ruminates that all families are tied to a home but that Aunt Millicent's life *was* Millicent House. Does your family have such a tie to a property? Is it a positive thing or not?

7. One of the hardest things for Sloane to contemplate was Robroy's sabotage of the balcony railing. She seems to accept his remorse when the police chief shares it. But would he have allowed her—or their mother—to fall to their deaths?

8. The author deliberately leaves open questions at the end about the future of Millicent House and the relationships among Annie, Margaret, and Sloane. Would you prefer that she answered them for you? Or were you content to imagine resolutions?

9. Do you think Sloane and Eli will get back together? Why or why not?

About the Author

Deb Richardson-Moore has worked as an award-winning newspaper journalist and as a pastor to homeless congregants. Her murder mysteries fall somewhere between cozies and gritty psychological thrillers and have twice been named finalists in Killer Nashville competitions.

Deb and her husband live in upstate South Carolina, where she enjoys gardening, volunteering, public speaking, and watching TV thrillers adapted from favorite books. She travels frequently to the beach.

Read more at debrichardsonmoore.com.

About the Publisher

Dear Reader,

We hope you enjoyed this book. Please consider leaving a review on your favorite book site.

Visit our site to find more quality books!

Read more at https://RedAdeptPublishing.com.